After the death of her abusive husband, Sarah Gregg is free to join her family along with thousands of others in the nation's westward march for gold. But in the middle of the hard journey, Sarah's younger sister, Florrie, disappears. Devastated by the family's failed attempts to find her missing sister, Sarah now wants only to settle into a quiet, uneventful life when she reaches California . . .

But Jack McCoy, a drifter and one-time gambler riding along their wagon train, sees so much more for Sarah. In the roaring mining town of Gold Creek his attentive persistence points Sarah toward new vistas. Then unexpected news of Florrie arrives—and it's worse than anyone expected. But driven by a new hopefulness, Sarah seeks help from Jack, despite his troubled past. The two have traveled a rough road together, and only their hearts can tell them where they are headed . . .

Visit us at www.kensingtonbooks.com

Books by Shirley Kennedy

Women of the West series
Wagon Train Cinderella
Wagon Train Sisters

Published by Kensington Publishing Corporation

Wagon Train Sisters

Women of the West series

Shirley Kennedy

LYRICAL PRESS
Kensington Publishing Corp.
www.kensingtonbooks.com

Lyrical Press books are published by
Kensington Publishing Corp. 119 West 40th Street New York, NY 10018

All Kensington titles, imprints, and distributed lines are available at special quantity discounts for bulk purchases for sales promotion, premiums, fund-raising, and educational or institutional use.

Special book excerpts or customized printings can also be created to fit specific needs. For details, write or phone the office of the Kensington Special Sales Manager:
Kensington Publishing Corp.
119 West 40th Street
New York, NY 10018
Attn. Special Sales Department. Phone: 1-800-221-2647.

Kensington and the K logo Reg. U.S. Pat. & TM Off.
Lyrical Press and the L logo are trademarks of Kensington Publishing Corp.

First Electronic Edition: July 2016
eISBN-13: 1978-1-60183-593-2
eISBN-10: -60183-593-0

First Print Edition: July 2016
ISBN-13: 978-1-60183-594-9
ISBN-10: 1-60183-594-9

Printed in the United States of America

As we go through life, friends come and go. Only a few last a lifetime. This book is dedicated to three lifetime friends dear to my heart: Julie Gettys, Carol Eversole, and Larry Wonderling.

Chapter 1

It was late afternoon before Sarah realized something was wrong. Earlier, the wagons had stopped for the noon meal beside a clear, gently flowing stream. The wagon master wanted to move on, but the women insisted they cut short the day's journey and spend the night. Who could blame them? After days of crossing the bare, dusty plains, each had more than her share of dirty laundry. Kneeling by the stream, Sarah enjoyed this ritual of chatting with her neighbors, despite scrubbing clothes until her knuckles were raw and red.

But where's Florrie? Sarah sat back on her heels and looked around. "Has anybody seen my sister?"

Lined along the bank, the ladies of the train dutifully halted their labors. "Haven't seen her since this morning."

"Haven't seen her all day."

"Maybe she ran away."

Everyone tittered at that last remark. After weeks living in the forced closeness of a wagon train, they knew each other well, and in some cases, better than they wished. Sarah was known to be the hard worker of the family. Her sister-in-law, Becky, was the one with the sharp tongue. Florrie was the quiet one, hadn't made many friends, and stayed close to their wagon. She'd be the last person in the world who'd run off. Besides, where would she go? Two days ago they'd left the last vestiges of civilization at Fort Hall and were now in a land where rivers raged, wild animals roamed, forests stretched to the horizon and beyond.

So where *was* Florrie? Come to think of it, Sarah hadn't seen her since right after they stopped for the day, and that was hours ago. It wasn't like her, but she must be visiting at one of the wagons. She'd surely appear in time for supper. Nothing to worry about.

When Sarah lugged her bagful of laundry back to her family's wagon, she half expected Florrie to be waiting, but she wasn't in sight. Ma was fixing supper, grunting with pain as she bent over the campfire. Sarah hastily set down the laundry and took the poker from her mother's hand. "Is your rheumatism acting up? Here, let me do that. You go rest. Have you seen Florrie?"

Luzena Bryan frowned with concern. "No I haven't. I was beginning to worry, but then I decided she must be with you."

"I haven't seen her for hours."

"Then she must have gone visiting one of the wagons."

"Of course. She'll be back any minute." As Sarah bent to stir the pot of beans hanging over the campfire, a faint quiver of worry coursed through her. Florrie never did anything out of the ordinary. She would never disappear like this. Twenty-three and still unmarried, she didn't have a whole lot of friends, nor did she seem to want any. Back home in Fort Wayne, she hardly went anywhere except church. Aside from helping with the housework, she spent her time producing bumpy needlepoint canvases and reading romantic, derring-do novels by the likes of Mrs. Southworth and Mrs. Wilson. No gentleman ever came calling, which Florrie said was fine with her, but Sarah knew otherwise. Florrie was no great beauty. In a rare moment of honesty, she once complained to Sarah, "God gave you the beautiful eyes and the nice little nose and the curvy figure, but me? God made me ugly, and don't tell me otherwise."

Sarah had hastened to reassure her younger sister with, "Beauty is only skin deep," and other useless platitudes. The truth was God had given Florrie a chin too weak, lips too thin, eyes too close together and a chest too flat. All of which wouldn't have mattered had she possessed the kind of bubbly charm that made men overlook such imperfections, but she didn't. Men never looked twice at Florrie Bryan. Her plodding gait, dumpy figure, and lack of sparkling conversation turned them away.

Her family cared deeply for her, though. No one could have a more generous heart or be more loyal than Florrie. Now, as the sun sank ever lower on the horizon, the Bryans finished their dinner while sitting around their campfire, discussing her disappearance with growing concern. "She's the last person on this train who'd do this," said Hiram, her brother. He looked toward the tall trees surrounding them and the mountain peaks beyond. "Where would she go? We're in the middle of nowhere."

Hiram's wife, Becky, spoke up. "Why the fuss? There's fifty-four wagons in this train. She could be visiting in any one of them."

Ma ignored her less-than-lovable daughter-in-law. "I'm worried. I think we should start looking." She looked at her husband. "Don't you think so, Frank?"

Pa gave an elaborate shrug. "I think we should wait. She's bound to turn up."

Sarah could tell her mild-mannered father was concerned and trying not to let it show. As if he didn't have enough problems. For years, he'd led a quiet life running his newspaper in Fort Wayne. When he wasn't working, he read books, wrote poetry, went fishing, and enjoyed his family. Sarah couldn't remember her parents ever arguing. Ma kept the household running and disciplined the children. Pa earned the money and gave wise advice. A perfect arrangement, but it didn't last. Ma's health had never been good, but this past year, she'd grown ever more frail. Pa's newspaper began to lose money. His worry over going bankrupt created constant anxiety in what had been a comfortably happy family.

How lucky Joseph died. The irreverent thought often popped into Sarah's head these days. At the age of twenty-two, she'd married Joseph Gregg and moved to his farm. At the age of twenty-eight, she became a widow. Childless, she moved back home, soon discovering how much she was needed, even more so now.

Since they left Indiana, her parents had changed, and not for the better. Pa, the respected newspaper owner, had always been elegantly dressed in frock coat and brocade vest, never without his walking stick, watch, and top hat. Now he was hard to recognize in his flannel shirt, baggy pants, and scraggly beard. Ma, too, had always dressed in the height of fashion. She wouldn't have been caught dead in the plain dress, sturdy boots, and white apron she was wearing now.

A look of sudden awareness crossed Ma's face. She slammed a hand to her heart. "It's almost dark. Where is that girl?" She leaped to her feet. "Florrie would never stay out this long. Something's wrong. We've got to find her."

Sarah put her plate aside, rose, and placed a comforting arm around her mother. "You're right. I'm worried, too, but I'm sure she's just gone visiting and isn't aware of the time."

Pa and Becky remained seated and unperturbed, but Hiram quickly got to his feet. "I'll start looking. We'll find her."

Becky sniffed with disdain. "She'll show up, Hiram. Sit down and finish your supper."

Why did he marry her? Sarah had long since grown accustomed to her sharp-tongued sister-in-law's selfish attitude, but there were times she'd like to give her a good shake. Ma and her brother were right to be concerned. "I'll come with you, Hiram. Let's each take half. We'll ask at every wagon."

Parked in a meadow by the stream, the wagons of the Morehead wagon train were positioned in a big circle. Starting with their own wagon, Hiram went one way around the circle and Sarah the other. "Have you seen Florrie?" she asked at every campfire. Always the answer was no. No one seemed concerned, and humorous suggestions abounded.

"Maybe she's playing hide-and-seek."

"Maybe the wolves got her." That was said with such an unfeeling giggle Sarah's temper flared. Couldn't they see how worried she was?

When Sarah asked when Florrie had last been seen, nobody seemed to know. No wonder. Who would notice her sister? Everything about her was unremarkable, from her plain looks to her dull conversation. Not until Sarah reached the wagon master's campfire did anyone take her seriously.

Dissension reigned in many of the wagon trains, but so far the Morehead train had traveled without major conflicts, thanks mainly to its leader. A tall, gray-haired man of about fifty, Albert Morehead always maintained a calm, reasonable attitude and was admired by all. When she asked if he'd seen Florrie, he replied, "No I haven't, Sarah. Have you asked around?"

"I've stopped at every wagon, Mr. Morehead. Nobody's seen her."

In the gathering darkness, the wagon master cast an apprehensive glance at the thick woods surrounding the meadow. "I'd hate to think she's lost in those woods, what with—" He clamped his lips. "If she doesn't turn up, say, in the next hour, we'll form a search party."

The wagon master's unsaid words increased her uneasiness. Since the train left the monotony of the plains and started toward the mountains, the eerie howling of wolves had kept her awake each night.

Hiram appeared, shaking his head. "I asked at every wagon, but nobody's seen her."

"That settles it." Morehead nodded decisively. "We'll start searching for that young lady right now. Come on, Hiram, let's gather the men. Sarah, get back to your mother. She's going to need you."

At her wagon, Sarah found her mother wringing her hands, pacing back and forth in front of the campfire. Both Pa and Becky were trying to calm her, but she wasn't listening. "It's dark," she cried. "Something's happened to Florrie! I know it has. Oh, Sarah, what are we going to do?"

Sarah told them about the search party. "Florrie must have been in the woods and lost her way, but surely they'll find her." After Pa went to join the search party, Sarah led her mother to a seat by the fire. "We'll wait right here. It shouldn't take long."

Becky busied herself making coffee. She slammed the pot down with obvious annoyance. "I'd wager Florrie's doing this on purpose, just to get some attention. You know how she is. She'll show up when she gets hungry enough."

Shut your mouth, Becky. Sarah's sister-in-law loved to give her so-called expert opinion on every subject. Usually she was wrong, and now was no exception.

"I don't think so, Becky. Florrie has always been afraid of the dark. There's no way in the world she'd hide in the woods at night by herself."

"No, she wouldn't." Ma spoke in a voice both fragile and shaking. "Florrie must be very frightened by now. Alone...in the woods.... Soon the wolves will start howling...." Tears filled her eyes. She could not go on.

The three sat waiting as twenty men or more fanned out from the meadow into the surrounding woods. Soon night fell. All they could see were lights from the searchers' lanterns eerily bobbing among the trees. "Florrrieee..." came hollers from all directions. "Florrrieee..." The sounds drifted farther away.

"How kind of them to search," Ma said. "They didn't have to."

Sarah agreed. A grueling day on the trail left everybody exhausted, yet these men had given up their evening of rest for a girl they hardly knew.

After an hour of anxious waiting, rain began to fall. In minutes, they were caught in a drenching downpour and had to run for cover. Becky ran to her and Hiram's wagon, parked next to theirs. Sarah led her mother to their own wagon, helped her inside, and pulled the canvas flap back so they could keep an eye on the campground. "They'll soon be back, Ma. No one can search in this."

Sure enough, Pa and Hiram appeared shortly after, accompanied by Albert Morehead, all three cold and drenched to the skin.

"Any sign of her?" Sarah called.

Grim-faced, Hiram shook his head. "Nothing."

"Oh, God, my baby's lost!" Ma let out a heart-wrenching wail and started to rock back and forth. "She's out there in the wet and cold. You must go back. You must find her."

Pa took her hand. "We're doing all we can, my dear. Surely she'll come home soon."

Home? In the middle of the wilderness? What irony. If they hadn't found Florrie by now, she could be gone forever. Sarah kept her bleak thoughts to herself. For her mother's sake, she must appear optimistic. Florrie might be twenty-three, but she was the youngest, the baby of the family, and Ma's favorite child. Sarah never minded. She was only six when Florrie was born, but from the beginning she'd done more than her share of caring for her baby sister, sometimes feeling more like a mother

than a sister to Florrie. Now she didn't know which was harder to bear—
her own distress that Florrie was gone or her mother's anguish.

Albert Morehead walked to their wagon, wiping the rain from his face.
"That's all we can do tonight. We'll search again in the morning."

"We must find her." Ma clasped her hands together imploringly. "You
won't leave until we do, will you, Mr. Morehead?"

The wagon master's long, hesitant pause spoke volumes. "We'll do our
best, Mrs. Bryan, but you've got to realize people on this train are hell-
bent on getting to California. We have a schedule to keep. You know if
we lag behind, we could get stuck in the snow. They're not going to like
it if we stay too long."

Ma gasped. "You mean you'd leave without Florrie?"

"Let's see what tomorrow brings." With a somber shake of his head,
Albert Morehead walked away.

Sarah watched after him with a sinking heart. One thing was certain.
Sympathetic though he might be, the wagon master would stick
to his schedule.

* * * *

In the morning, the rain had stopped, the sun came out, and most of
the men of the company, and some of the women, returned to the woods
to search for Florrie. Sarah wanted to search, too, but by now Ma was
in such a despondent state she couldn't be left alone. "Sarah, don't you
leave me," she had implored. "You're the one I count on. Don't leave me
here with Becky."

If she hadn't been so upset, Ma would have probably gone into her
usual rant about why Hiram, her adored son, had married Elizabeth
"Becky" Marshall, a pretty enough young woman with her rosebud
mouth and voluptuous figure, but known for her sharp tongue and
superior attitude. Sarah knew very well why he hadn't escaped Becky's
so-called charms. At twenty-two, her tall, affable brother held an ordinary
clerk's job in a lawyer's office, but he was also an artist with a dreamy
look in his blue, deep-set eyes. With his finely drawn features and blond,
rumpled hair, he'd been so popular with the ladies he could have had his
pick. Then Becky set her cap for him, and he resembled a helpless insect
caught in a spider's web. Flattered by her interest, he'd shown her some
attention. Sarah wasn't sure how much he loved her, if he loved her at
all, but apparently he'd given her enough "attention" that when Becky
announced she was in a family way, he married her without a murmur.
Two months later, when Becky "lost" the baby, Ma suspected Becky
had lied. Sarah was sure of it. Too late now. The family did their best to

make her feel welcome. At first, she was pleasant enough, but as time went by, she became difficult to deal with. It was easy to see why. Becky desperately wanted a child, but as months, then years, went by with no sign of a baby on the way, she grew sour-faced and always complained. Most annoying of all, Hiram wouldn't stand up to her. Sarah cringed whenever she heard Becky ordering her easy-going brother around and saw how eagerly he did her bidding. *Assert yourself*, she would silently call, but he never would.

By mid-morning, discouraged searchers began to straggle back to the camp.

"Not a trace of her. Sorry, Mrs. Bryan."

"We scoured the woods. There's just no place left to look."

A glazed look of despair covering her face, Ma could barely manage a reply. Despite Sarah's pleas, she refused to eat.

By noon, the disheartened members of the wagon train had all returned. Sarah's father and brother were the last ones back. Shoulders sagging in discouragement, Pa sat by the campfire beside his wife and took her hand. "Our girl is gone, dear. Lord knows what's become of her."

"No, no, no!" Ma stared at him wild-eyed. "Florrie's out there somewhere. You must keep looking."

Hiram knelt by his mother's side. "We've looked everywhere, couldn't find a trace."

"Then keep looking. I won't leave without my Florrie." Ma clenched her jaw and looked away.

Albert Morehead appeared at their campsite. Ma rose to greet him. "Tell me you've found her."

Morehead swept off his hat, regretfully shaking his head. "We can't find her, Mrs. Bryan. Scoured the woods. Looked everywhere. I can't think what happened to her unless she ran off by herself and—"

"Florrie would never run off!" Ma's eyes blazed with anger.

"Then...of course, she wouldn't." For once the confident leader of the wagon train appeared unsure of himself. "It's surely a mystery, and I don't know the answer, but the thing is we've got a schedule to keep. We can't—"

"But you must keep looking." Ma turned a shade paler than she already was. "We can't leave without her." She turned to her husband. "Tell him, Frank."

Pa bit his lip. "They can't find her, Luzena. They can't wait around forever."

Desperation flared in Sarah's chest. She stepped beside her mother and looked the wagon master square in the eye. "Florrie can't have gone very far. Surely someone will find her if we search long enough. You can't—"

"Sorry, Sarah." Morehead turned to Ma. "I have no choice, Mrs. Bryan. The others want to leave and there's no stopping them."

The desperate look on Ma's face changed to one of stubborn resolve as comprehension dawned. "Go ahead if you must, but I'm not leaving until we find Florrie."

The wagon master let loose a breath that was half sympathy, half frustration. "You must come with us. There's no point in staying. Besides, it's dangerous to be alone on the trail. Indians—wild animals—you would not do well by yourselves. What about your food supply? Don't forget winter is coming. God forbid you should get stuck in the snow."

"We're staying."

Morehead sighed in defeat. "I see I can't dissuade you." He looked at Pa. "Try to make her see reason, Mr. Bryan. I'll check back before we leave." He turned on his heel and hurried off.

A stirring began around the circle of wagons. Parents called for their children. Oxen bellowed as they were yoked. Ma looked around the campground, eyes wide with shock. "They're really leaving? Oh, they can't, they can't!" As if she'd lost all her strength, she fell to her knees and put her head in her hands.

Pa knelt beside her. "You'd best reconsider, Luzena. Morehead's right. There's nothing to be gained by staying."

"But there is." Ma talked through her sobs. "How will Florrie find us if we don't stay right here in this very spot? I can't bear to think how hurt and bewildered she'll be when she comes back and finds us gone."

Sarah knelt and faced her distraught mother. She reached out and took her hands. "I'm afraid Pa's right." She spoke as gently as she could. "You're not thinking clearly right now. We don't know what's happened to Florrie, but there's no reason to stay in this godforsaken spot. Look around you. The wilderness is a dangerous place. It's best we stay with the train. That way, we can inquire along the way and..." Why go on? Judging from the mad desperation in her mother's eyes, further words were worthless. Nothing could comfort her right now. Most certainly nothing was going to change her mind. Sarah looked at Pa. "Why don't we at least stay the night? We can search the rest of the day, and tomorrow we can search some more. Then it shouldn't be too hard to catch up with the train."

Hiram and Becky stood listening. "That's a good idea," Hiram said.

"No, it's not!" Becky jammed her fists to her waist and scowled. "I refuse to let myself be stranded in this awful place. There's wild animals and snakes out there, and Indians and God knows what else. I'm sorry Florrie's lost, but I refuse to stay. I want the protection of the company."

Becky's words caused Ma to set her chin in a stubborn line. "The rest of you can go if you want, but I'm staying right here to wait for my daughter."

One by one, the wagons took their assigned place in line. As they slowly rolled from the meadow, the family did its best to dissuade Luzena Bryan from remaining behind. She grew silent, jaw firmly clenched, oblivious to all arguments. Finally Frank Bryan shrugged in defeat and addressed his son and daughter. "I give up. Short of hog-tying your mother and tossing her in the wagon, there's nothing more I can do." He cast a sorrowful look at his wife. "You win, Luzena. We'll stay behind with our wagon. Hiram, you and Becky will take your wagon and move on. Sarah will go with you."

Sarah raised a protesting hand. "I will not leave my mother."

Hiram's blue eyes filled with pain. "That won't work. What kind of a son would I be if I left my parents alone in the wilderness?"

Becky glared daggers at her husband. "How dare you even think we'd stay behind? I won't hear of it. We're going with the company and that's that."

"She's right," said Pa. "Son, there's no use you staying. Go with the company."

Ma nodded in agreement. "Go, the three of you. Florrie will soon be back, and then we'll catch up."

"We're going!" Becky screeched.

Sarah wanted to cover her ears. The Bryans had always been a peaceful clan. Harmony and good manners ruled in their household. What small differences they had were settled quietly without bickering. This was horrible, seeing her family torn apart by this sudden, shocking tragedy. There was only one way to handle this, and they'd better listen. "Hiram, you and Becky go with the train. I'll stay behind because Ma needs me." She crossed her arms. "Save your breath and don't argue. I won't change my mind."

Becky gave her a satisfied smile. "Thanks, Sarah, that's the perfect solution."

I'm not doing this for you. Sarah looked toward her brother. "We *will* catch up. If we don't, we'll find you at Uncle William's house in Mokelumne City."

Biting his lip in thought, Hiram hesitated. Despite her plucky words, Sarah halfway wished her brother would stand up to his belligerent wife and declare they were staying. But no such luck. "All right, Becky, we'll go." Hiram turned to Sarah. "I hope you understand."

Oh, I understand all right. Sarah hid her disappointment and gave him a smile. "You've made the right decision. Don't worry, we'll be fine. Florrie will show up soon. Then we'll catch up with you before you know it." Brave words, but she must remain optimistic. Florrie had to come back. She couldn't bear the thought her beloved sister had disappeared forever.

As the last wagon left the meadow, Albert Morehead, riding horseback, returned for the last time. Looking down, he addressed Luzena. "You haven't changed your mind?"

Ma folded her arms firmly across her chest. "No, I have not, Mr. Morehead."

The wagon master sighed in defeat. "I'm sorry your daughter is lost and will pray that you find her." His sympathetic gaze took in the entire family. "The best of luck to you all." He turned his horse to leave but rounded back again. "By the way, there's a small company of gold seekers coming through, by tomorrow I should guess. Rascals, the lot of them. Whatever you do, stay away from them. There's one in particular you must avoid. Some of my men encountered him back in Independence. Lost all their money, thanks to that card shark."

"What's his name?" Pa asked.

"Goes by the name of Jack McCoy. A scoundrel and ne'er-do-well if ever there was one."

Chapter 2

After the last wagon departed, Sarah spent the rest of the day in the woods calling for Florrie, listening for an answering cry that never came. By evening, her appreciation of her brother had grown by leaps and bounds. She had never realized how much of the workload fell on Hiram's shoulders. Pa, who'd never done hard labor in his life, had little to no aptitude for the hard work involved in driving a wagon across the country. It was Hiram who yoked and unyoked the oxen on both wagons, greased the wheels, built the campfire, found feed for their eight oxen and two horses, pitched the tents at night, and so much more. During the day, Pa drove their wagon because he had to. Other than that, he'd been content to let his son attend to the chores while he sat around the campground with similar-minded neighbors, discussing such topics as "manifest destiny" and why the United States must extend across the entire continent. He frequently quoted his favorite poet, Henry David Thoreau, with phrases such as "Go confidently in the direction of your dreams. Live the life you've imagined."

Lately Ma greeted his remarks with a scornful sniff. "Right now the life I imagine is a soft bed and a roof over my head."

With Hiram gone, Sarah assumed Pa would take over the tasks that needed to be done. Instead, when they returned from their search, he wearily sank to a seat by the campfire and waited for his supper. That they might need firewood never occurred to him. He looked so tired and drawn she didn't have the heart to complain. Instead, she gathered sticks and branches herself, clumsily chopped them with an ax, and built the fire for their supper. Ma usually did the cooking, but tonight Sarah fixed biscuits, beans, and bacon while Ma sat silently by, occasionally throwing an angry glance at Pa. Not like her at all. Luzena loved her husband dearly, and he loved her. They never quarreled, but it was plain to see Ma was getting agitated. Each glance seemed angrier than the last until, while Pa was taking the last bite from his plate, Ma declared, "This is all your fault, Frank."

Startled, he asked, "What's my fault?"

Ma bristled. "All of this." Her sweeping gesture took in the camp and surrounding forest. "You're the one who insisted we come on this horrible journey. If it weren't for you, I'd be sitting in my beautiful home in Indiana, and Florrie...Florrie..." She choked and could not go on.

"But that's not so, my dear..."

Sarah shut out their voices. This whole disaster *was* her father's fault, yet Ma wasn't being fair. Never a good businessman, he couldn't recover when his newspaper went bankrupt. Deep in debt, he was forced to sell the family's home. Perhaps they could have stayed and somehow survived, but with unaccustomed firmness, Pa announced they were moving to California. Everyone assumed he, along with thousands of others, wanted to rush to the newly discovered goldfields, but his motive for moving was far less exciting. Mokelumne City was a small town in California, not far from Sacramento. When his brother offered a partnership in his general store there, Pa gratefully accepted. Others might get carried away by the prospect of picking huge gold nuggets off the ground, but he valued peace and security far more.

Like most of the women on the wagon train, Ma hadn't wanted to go. Sarah didn't either, although after her disastrous marriage, she would have been grateful to be back with her family, no matter where they went. No one suspected how awful her marriage had been. She'd never told. Even after Joseph died, she played the part of the grieving widow, fooling everyone. Well, not quite. Her perceptive brother guessed how miserable she'd been. Before they left Fort Wayne, Ma had wondered why she showed no interest in the suitors who'd begun to call. One of these days, she'd be honest and explain why.

Sarah slept fitfully during the night in the small tent pitched beside the wagon. Along with the eerie howling of the wolves, an unending swirl of unanswered questions kept her awake. Would they find Florrie? How much longer would Ma want to stay and search? Would they be able to catch up to the Morehead train? Loneliness gnawed at her. She missed her friends back home and the new friends she'd made on the train. She missed her brother, Hiram, the only member of her family who could even begin to understand her troubled heart. "Do you really miss Joseph?" he'd asked the day after the funeral.

"Why do you ask?"

Hiram got a quirky eyebrow-raised expression on his face. "They all think you're grieving, but I know you, and I'd wager you're not."

She and her younger brother had always been close. She gave him a vague answer but wasn't the least surprised he'd seen the truth. "I'll tell you all about it when I'm ready."

"That'll be soon, I hope." He eyed her with concern. "All you do is read and paint your little pictures. You need to get out more. Why throw the rest of your life away because of one bad experience?"

"I'm content as I am," she'd told him, and she was. What more in life could she want than her watercolors, her books—she loved the works of Jane Austen—and feeling safe and secure in her parents' home? This trip was simply an unpleasant interlude. When they reached Mokelumne City, she'd take up where she left off. Back home, she'd belonged to the Thursday Afternoon Ladies Literary Club. Maybe she'd start one in Mokelumne City. She would go to church on Sunday and do good works for the sick and poor. That was all she wanted out of life.

The next morning, she was up at dawn, had a fire going and coffee boiling by the time her parents emerged from the wagon. "What shall we do today, Ma? Shall we catch up with the train?" She held her breath, hoping her mother had decided to give up this hopeless search and get back to safety.

"We'll keep looking."

Sarah hid her disappointment. "All right, then. Maybe Florrie decided to go back the way we came. That's where I'll ride today."

Pa looked skeptical. "Don't know why she'd do that."

"Neither do I, but do you have any better idea?"

Of course he didn't. After breakfast, while Pa scoured woods they'd already searched, Sarah saddled Rosie, their chestnut mare, and set out on the barely discernable trail from which they'd come. If not for her worry over Florrie, she would have enjoyed her ride through the thick forest of pines, firs, and white-barked sycamores while the sun warmed her face and the pleasant scent of the evergreens wafted into her nostrils. Thank goodness, she didn't have to ride sidesaddle anymore. Pa had sold her sidesaddle before they left, and she hadn't been the least bit sorry to see it go. How nice to plant both feet firmly in the stirrups. One good thing about a wagon train journey was many of society's old, tedious rules were forgotten. Good. She was finding she liked it that way.

Every once in a while, she'd rein in her horse and call, "Florrie?" Nothing followed but silence, broken only by birds chirping and the gurgle of a nearby stream. *Where is my sister?* Anguish tore at her heart.

Oh, Florrie, what has become of you? Are you all right, or has something awful happened?

She rode for at least an hour. Far enough. Better turn back. She'd rest a while, drink some water from the stream, and then return. She tied Rosie to a tree and was sitting on a rock by the gurgling water when a group of men on horseback, followed by a single wagon, came into view. As they drew closer, she searched for a woman in the crowd, but no, this wasn't an ordinary wagon train. These were all men, moving at a fast clip. This must be the company of gold seekers Mr. Morehead had warned them about. Her first impulse was to run and hide, but one of horsemen had already caught sight of her. Her heart beat faster as he rode to where she sat by the stream and dismounted. She rose to greet him, immediately catching a whiff of whiskey mixed with stale sweat. How disgusting. His looks were disgusting, too. Unkempt black hair sticking out from beneath a battered hat, big red nose, scraggly, tobacco-stained beard, wrinkled, spotted clothes that could use a good wash.

"Well, look what I found!" the man called to his companions. His insolent gaze swept her up and down. "Hello, little lady. What are you doing here?"

She didn't like the way the man was looking at her with his bold, beady eyes. Anxiety shot through her. More than ever, she wanted to run, but she'd been raised to observe the social graces. She'd be polite if it killed her, and maybe it would. Good manners decreed she give him a polite answer. "Good morning. My name is Sarah Gregg. I'm with the Morehead Company. My sister disappeared two days ago, and that's why—"

"Your sister!" The man let out a raucous laugh and addressed the eight other horsemen who'd ridden up. "Do you hear that? There's more than one of 'em out here." He stepped closer. "Are you all by yourself?"

His rotten, whiskey-laden breath made her want to wretch, but she kept the smile on her face. "My wagon train is right up ahead."

With a smirk, the bearded man looked back at his friends again. "Do you believe that, boys? I say there ain't no wagon train up ahead. I say this pretty little lady's all by herself."

As the men on horseback replied with hoots and jeers, sick fear coiled in the pit of her stomach. They all looked as slovenly as this man, most with unkempt beards, not one friendly face among them. No more polite conversation. She was in trouble. She must get away. If she didn't…

"Give her a kiss, Josiah," one of the men shouted.

Oh, no! This loathsome man was going to hurt her. She bolted, began to run, but the bearded man ran after her and grabbed her arm. She tried to yank her arm back, but his grip was as strong as iron. "You let me go!"

His grip tightened. He pulled her toward him. Oh, God, she'd rather die than feel those slobbery lips on her mouth.

A deafening crack filled the air. The man let out a scream of pain and let go his grip. He uttered a cuss word and clutched his arm, now encircled several times by a whip's thin leather thong. "God almighty, Jack!" The man named Josiah glowered at a tall man in a wide-brimmed black hat who'd just ridden up. "Hell, I was just playin' around." He unwound the thin leather strip that had cut into his arm. "You didn't have to use that whip."

"Looks like I did." The man named Jack pulled back the thong and wrapped it around the handle. Whip in hand, he slid off his horse and addressed Sarah. "What are you doing out here by yourself?"

"I..." Her voice shook and her heart pounded in her chest. The man with the scraggly beard was bad enough, but with his hard, dark eyes and unfriendly voice, this man with the whip was just as frightening. But she mustn't show fear. She gulped and steadied herself. "I'm looking for my sister."

"Out here?" His gaze swept the tall pine trees. "In the middle of nowhere?"

She looked up at him. He was tall and lean, somewhere in his thirties, she'd guess, with brown hair hanging nearly to his shoulders. At least he didn't have an unkempt beard like the others. His deeply tanned face was all rugged angles, sharp planes, and high cheekbones. It would be a handsome face if he didn't look so grim. "My sister disappeared from our wagon train two days ago..."

She explained how her mother would not give up, how the rest of the train went ahead and left them behind to continue searching.

When she finished, he shook his head and said sternly, "This is dangerous territory. You should never have stayed behind."

Did he have to sound so hostile? "My sister is missing. What were we supposed to do?" She'd defend her mother against this stranger, even though she, too, thought Ma was wrong to stay behind. "I want to thank you for saving me from..." The image that presented itself to her mind was so horrifying she couldn't find words. "From these men," she ended lamely.

"Any time." Hastily he turned to address his fellow riders who were still gawking at the scene. "That's all there is to see. Get going. You've still got a lot of miles to travel yet today." He gestured at the bearded man who by now was back on his horse, holding his arm in pain. "That means you, Josiah."

The man sneered. "I don't take orders from you."

In a velvet soft voice, the man in the black hat replied, "No, you don't, but you'll take orders from this." He raised the whip he was carrying.

Hatred blazed in Josiah's eyes. Sarah held her breath while she waited to see what he'd do. After a long moment, he grasped the reins and turned his horse. "Let's go, boys."

Except for an older man with salt-and-pepper whiskers, the men turned their horses and headed up the trail. The older man watched them go, then looked down at his companion, his expression holding both amusement and amazement. "Jumpin' Jehoshaphat, Jack! What are you doin' tangling with the likes of Josiah Peterson? He's killed two men that I know of and probably more."

"He didn't kill me, did he?" The man with the whip looked at Sarah. "Get your horse. We'll take you back to your parents."

She commanded her voice to come out strong and pulled back her shoulders. "And you are?"

"I'm Jack McCoy."

Where had she heard that name before? She held out her hand. "I'm Sarah Gregg, and I'm pleased to—" Albert Morehead's words popped into her head. *Lost all their money thanks to that card shark. Goes by the name of Jack McCoy. A scoundrel and ne'er-do-well if ever there was one.* "Oh, it's you!" The words popped out before she could stop them.

He looked puzzled. "Do I know you from some place?"

She so wished she'd kept her mouth shut. "No, but I've heard of you."

"Good or bad?"

She disliked lying and wouldn't lie now. "Bad. I heard you were a card shark and a scoundrel."

The faintest glint of humor flickered through his eyes. "So what do you think?"

"I think where there's smoke there's fire." She didn't care for the way her words came out sounding prim and proper. She'd said them, though. Too late to take them back. "I don't need an escort, Mr. McCoy. You needn't bother."

"No bother, Miss Gregg. Get your horse."

"It's *Mrs.* Gregg. I don't like gamblers, Mr. McCoy."

"I'm not going to leave you in the wilderness, *Mrs.* Gregg. Get your horse."

The cold firmness in his voice told her he wouldn't accept no for an answer. Well, she'd ride back with him and his friend if that's what he wanted. Maybe she should. She didn't want to be alone while Josiah Peterson was still in the area. "All right, then."

After she untied Rosie and mounted, she watched as he got on his own horse. How graceful, the way he swung his lean, sinewy body into the saddle. He held a commanding air of self confidence about him, as if he would never hesitate and blunder around like Pa did sometimes. As if she could always count on his strength, and he'd never let her down. Her pulse quickened, ever so slightly, but what was she thinking? She didn't want a man, especially one like Jack McCoy. Once they got back to camp, she'd have nothing to do with such a scoundrel and he could be on his way.

* * * *

Jack got a fast glimpse of bare leg when the girl got on her horse and her skirt billowed. Women were crazy not to wear pants. At least she wasn't using one of those nonsensical sidesaddles the ladies doted on. When they started out, she rode ahead as though she didn't want to talk, and that was fine with him.

Riding beside him, Ben Longren chuckled. "Stuck up little thing, ain't she? She ought to be more friendly, considering you saved her from the likes of Josiah. That could have been bad, Jack."

He threw his friend a look of disgust. "You think I care if she talks or not?"

Ben stayed quiet for at least two seconds. "Did you notice how pretty she is?"

"I noticed how stupid she is to be out in the wilderness by herself."

Ben remained silent. Good. He knew how to keep his mouth shut. His friend was right, though. Yes, he'd noticed how pretty Mrs. Gregg was with her long, auburn hair and warm brown eyes. She was dressed like most women on the trail—faded homespun dress, white apron, and sturdy boots. Those plain clothes couldn't hide her tall, slim figure, though. Full breasts, tiny waist. Riding behind her, he had a fine view of the pleasant curve of her hips and the easy way she rode without bouncing or slouching, as if she'd spent a lot of time on a horse. If he was looking for a woman...

But, no, he wasn't looking for a woman. Furthest thing from his mind. He turned to Ben. "After we take her back, we'll catch up with the rest."

Ben didn't answer right away. When he did, a troubled expression rested on his weathered face. "Don't know as I want anything more to do with those jackasses. Why'd we join up with them in the first place?"

"Don't you remember? They were hell-bent for California with nothing to slow them down. Had a chuck wagon—"

"Yeah, the grub's been good, but I don't much care for that Josiah Peterson. All he wants is to get to California and get his share of the gold. He don't care who gets in his way."

"They're all the same." Never in his thirty-four years had Jack seen anything resembling the crazed rush for riches that had swept not only the country but the world. Thousands of men were headed for the goldfields to make their fortune, each a fool if he thought he'd get rich. He, too, was a fool, but an eyes-wide-open fool.

* * * *

Sarah's parents were sitting by their campfire when she and her two companions rode into the meadow. "Any luck?" Pa called.

She wearily shook her head as she dismounted. "No, nothing." She nodded toward Jack and Ben, who remained on their horses. They'd be riding on, so no need to introduce them. "These gentlemen were kind enough to escort me back. I…just happened to come across them." Nothing would be gained by telling her parents how that man had attacked her. They had enough to worry about.

Pa looked up at Jack. "Were those your friends who just rode through here?"

"We're riding with a group of gold seekers. Can't say we're friends."

"Is that so?" Pa eyed him suspiciously. "They were a rowdy bunch, had no manners. I suspect they're the ne'er-do-wells our wagon master was talking about."

Ma rose to her feet. Back in Fort Wayne, she was known for her gracious hospitality. Despite her grief, she hadn't changed. "Won't you gentlemen stay and have something to eat? In fact, you're welcome to spend the night by our campfire."

Oh, no. Sarah didn't want them to stay. "I'm afraid they're behind their schedule, Ma. They don't have time to—"

"Don't mind if we do!" The old man with the whiskers dismounted and addressed her parents. "The name's Ben Longren."

Pa stood and shook his hand. He looked toward the second rider. "And this is?"

"This here's my friend, Jack McCoy."

The fleeting raise of Pa's eyebrows told Sarah he recognized Jack's name and remembered the wagon master's warning. But being that Pa was first and foremost a gentleman, Sarah expected he'd be polite.

She was right. Pa managed a tight smile. "We're having simple fare today, just beans and cured bacon, but you're welcome to join us."

They said they would, and soon everyone had filled their plates and were sitting in a circle around the campfire. Sarah heartily wished they'd declined Pa's invitation and gone on their way, but despite her unease that a notorious gambler was in their midst, she soon became engrossed in the conversation. At first, Ben Longren did most of the talking—all about the Gold Rush and how he and his fellow group of gold seekers could hardly wait till they got to California and staked their claims. Jack McCoy sat silent until Ben flicked a glance at him and remarked, "But not my friend here. You won't find him with a pick in his hands. He's got higher ambitions."

"And what might those be, Mr. McCoy?" Pa asked.

The tall man in the black hat took his time answering. A thoughtful look came over his face. "My friend says I won't touch a pick. That's not so. I leave all options open. I have a lot of reasons for making this journey. One's called manifest destiny."

"You're absolutely right!" Pa practically leaped off his chair with delight. "I'm happy to find a person who sees that, Mr. McCoy."

"Of course I do. This country is bound to grow. Sounds crazy, but I want to be a part of it."

Soon Sarah sat fascinated as her father and Jack McCoy got into a lively discussion over manifest destiny and the reasons why the United States must spread across the continent to form one nation. From there, the conversation drifted to the reasons half the men in the country were rushing to California. "They want to get out of their dreary lives," said Pa. "Imagine if you were a low-paid clerk spending twelve hours a day, six days a week, with a quill pen in your hand, copying wills, mortgages, whatever else, in duplicate and triplicate."

Jack nodded in agreement. "They can only dream of riches and adventure, a change of scenery. Then one day they hear if they head for California, they can make their fortune. It's not just an empty dream."

Pa leveled a piercing gaze. "Aside from being a part of our manifest destiny, why are *you* headed west, Mr. McCoy? Why aren't you dead set on finding those gold nuggets they say are yours for the taking?"

Jack's answering laughter held a dry, cynical sound. "I'm a wanderer, Mr. Bryan. Left home when I was twelve and haven't put roots down since. I've run cattle in Texas, worked on steamboats on the Mississippi. I've already found gold, not in California but up in Wyoming Territory on the Sweetwater River. Found it, but couldn't keep it. The Shoshones drove us away."

"My, my, you've had an interesting life," Ma said. "Where did you grow up?"

"Back east." The abrupt manner of Jack's answer clearly signaled he'd prefer a change of subject.

Ma caught on fast. "Are you familiar with this area?"

"Been through a few times. For a while, I ran cattle up north of here."

"Can you tell me about the Indians?"

"The different tribes, you mean? You've got the Cherokees, Blackfoot, Chippewa, Shoshones—"

"Just hope you don't meet a Comanche," Ben chimed in. "They butcher babies and roast their enemies alive. Why, down in Texas I hear there was a woman kidnapped—"

"Ben!"

The older man looked sheepish after Jack's sharp warning. "Sorry, ma'am, hope I didn't upset you."

Ma gasped and clutched at her throat. Sarah said quickly, "The Comanches are far away in Texas, aren't they, Mr. McCoy? Not around here."

Jack looked at Ma. "Not within a thousand miles, Mrs. Bryan. I don't know what happened to your daughter, but she wasn't kidnapped by a Comanche."

Too late. Ma started to wheeze—that awful sound Sarah dreaded to hear. She went to her mother and clasped her shoulders. "Relax. Just breathe easy."

Ma stared at her with frantic eyes. She tried to speak but all that came out was, "Can't…breathe." Her face lost its color as she began fighting for breath. The wheezing got worse, gradually turning into a rasping, desperate struggle for air that sounded as if it was tearing her insides apart. Sarah called to her father, "It's another asthma attack. Did we bring the eucalyptus oil?"

Pa shrugged helplessly. "She hasn't had an attack for quite a while. We couldn't bring everything."

Jack McCoy sprang from his seat. He knelt by Ma's side and said softly, "You're going to be all right, Mrs. Bryan. Don't panic. That only makes it worse." He stood and gripped her arms. "You and I are going to walk, very slowly and very carefully, around the campfire. Moving should make your breathing easier. Have no fear. If that doesn't work, we'll try something else."

He pulled Luzena to her feet. She slumped against him, continuing the desperate, deep wheezing. Her skin gleamed with perspiration as Jack, his arm securely around her waist, began to walk her slowly, one step at a time. "Good, you're doing fine. No hurry…and we're not going to panic." After one circle of the campfire, her wheezing eased but didn't stop.

Sarah stood by, helplessly watching. One of her cousins had died of an asthma attack. It could happen again. Ma had these attacks before but none as bad as this one. "Is there something we can do?" she called to Jack. "Shouldn't she lie down?"

"No, that makes it worse. She's going to need something more. Do you have any ginger?"

"No."

"Mustard oil?"

"No." She hated saying no. Had they nothing that might help?

"Honey?"

"Yes!" *Thank God.* She hastened to the wagon and retrieved their jar of honey and a spoon. When she returned, Ma was still fighting for breath, and Jack was easing her back in her camp chair. He took the honey, poured a big spoonful and held it under her nose. "Breathe deep. This is going to help."

As her mother inhaled the fumes from the honey, Pa stood by, face strained with anxiety. "What does the honey do?"

Jack didn't look up. "It soothes the mucous membranes in her airways."

Minutes passed while Ma continued to inhale the vapor from the honey, Jack still holding the spoon directly under her nose. "Take your time," he kept repeating. After a while, she stopped struggling for breath. The wheezing lightened its intensity and finally ceased. Breathing normally again, she sat back in her chair and smiled. "I do believe I'm better now. Mercy, all that fuss. You can take that spoon away now, Mr. McCoy."

A cry of relief broke from Sarah's lips. "You had us worried, Ma. Don't do that again."

"I'd wager it's all that worry over Florrie," Pa said. "That's it, Luzena. We shouldn't be out here by ourselves. We should rejoin the train. We'll leave first thing tomorrow."

Ma folded her arms. "We're not going until Florrie gets back."

Pa threw up his hands. "You're not thinking clearly…"

When Sarah's parents started arguing, Jack McCoy turned away and headed for the nearby stream. She went after him. He had just saved her mother's life. He might be a notorious gambler, but she had to thank him. He was bending over the stream, washing his hands when she found him. His shirt was off. A gold ring hung on a chain around his neck, a ring so small she doubted it would fit his little finger. It had to be a woman's.

When he saw her, he said, "Hello," and leisurely pulled his shirt back on.
"It seems I must thank you again, Mr. McCoy."

"Don't bother. No trouble."

His clipped words told her she need say nothing further, but she couldn't let it go. "How do you know so much about asthma?"

He straightened, casually wiping his hands on his pants. "Someone I once knew had asthma." A glint of some undefinable sadness appeared in the dark depths of his eyes. "It was a long time ago." She started to answer, but he interrupted. "Let's get back. Got to get some sleep." One side of his mouth lifted in a slight smile. "Your notorious gambler will be leaving first thing in the morning."

She thought of the ring she'd just seen on the chain around his neck. Where did he get it? There must be a story there, but something told her this wasn't the right time to ask.

Chapter 3

Sarah spent a fitful night in her tent by the wagon. Her mind churned with images—Ma fighting for breath—Jack holding the honey under her nose—her vast relief when Ma could breathe again. Thank God, Jack McCoy had been there. Otherwise...

She mustn't even think it! Outside her tent, less than twenty feet away, Jack lay sleeping. Why was she so acutely aware of his presence? Thank goodness he was leaving in the morning. Jack McCoy was a gambler, and that was not an admirable occupation. Not only that, if he'd chosen to ride with that bunch of lowlifes, there could be but one reason. He, too, was a lowlife, as disreputable as that disgusting Josiah Peterson. So why, then, was she tossing and turning, thinking about a notorious card shark? After tomorrow, she would never see him again, and that would be none too soon.

And where was Florrie? A wild flash of grief ripped through her. She'd lost her sister, God knew how or where, and there was nothing she could do. Before they went to bed, she and Pa had again tried to talk Ma into leaving, but she wouldn't listen. How much longer must they stay in this desolate area conducting a useless search? Their only hope now was that Florrie had been kidnapped. They'd have a better chance of finding her if they rejoined the train and searched for her along the way.

When morning came, Luzena felt so much better she went out of her way to fix a hearty breakfast of fried bacon, corn meal mush, and soda biscuits, all to be washed down with a big pot of coffee. After they finished, Jack said, "Thanks for the breakfast, Mrs. Bryan. It's time for us to leave."

Luzena gazed at Jack with grateful eyes. "I shall be forever indebted, Mr. McCoy. How can I ever repay you?"

Jack took a final gulp of coffee before he spoke. "You can repay me by giving up this fool notion that you'll stay in this godforsaken place until your daughter comes back."

His abrupt reply caused Ma to sit back in surprise. "But…but…I can't do that. Florrie's coming back, and I shall be here when she does."

Jack shook his head. "You know that's not so. I doubt she got lost in the woods. I'd wager someone knows where she is. You'd have a better chance of finding her if you keep going and search as you travel along the trail."

Ma bit her lip. She examined her fingernails and looked into space. Obviously she held a deep respect for the man who'd helped her through the asthma attack. She could easily ignore all the fervent pleas from her family, but Jack McCoy's blunt opinion had made a profound impression. Finally she spoke. "I do believe you're right. Hitch the oxen, Frank. We're leaving. Sarah, let's pack the wagon."

After an astounded silence, Pa got to his feet and placed his battered hat on his head. "That was a wise decision, my dear." He set out for the spot where their four oxen were grazing.

Sarah breathed a sigh of relief. Out of Ma's hearing, she said, "I owe you another thanks, Mr. McCoy. You worked a miracle."

"Not a miracle, just common sense. Come on, Ben, let's pack up."

He was leaving. Part of her was glad, but another part of her wished he would stay. Just ridiculous. The man hardly looked at her, and anyway, why should she care? For the next few minutes, she busied herself helping Ma pack pots, pans, and dishes back in the wagon. Ordinarily, Hiram took down the small tent where she slept. Now Pa must do it all himself. But maybe that wouldn't be so easy. Every time she looked, he was struggling to herd the animals to the wagon, not making any progress at all. She was starting to take the tent down herself when Jack appeared behind her. "I'll do that." In no time, the tent was down and packed away.

Pa continued to struggle. He'd managed to drive the oxen to the wagon but couldn't position the animals in the right place. No sooner had he got one lined up, another would run off. Finally he slammed his hat to the ground. "These damn, stubborn animals won't do what I tell 'em!"

Poor Pa. How sad to see an old man of sixty so bungling and inept in this alien world. He ought to be home sitting in his library, cup of tea by his side, reading a volume of Shakespeare or his favorite, *The Vicar of Wakefield.*

Jack and Ben had mounted their horses and were about to leave, but upon hearing Pa, Jack dismounted. "Looks like you need help. Stand back, Mr. Bryan." He led the animals to the front of the wagon where he tied them about the same distance apart. "You've got to position them so their heads will go in the yoke." With practiced skill, he placed the yokes over the oxen's backs, slid in the oxbows, and fastened the ends with iron pins. "Nothing left but to hitch them to the wagon. See?"

Pa scratched his head, uncertainty written all over his face. "Yes, I see. Thank you, Mr. McCoy. It should be easy." His voice wavered with uncertainty.

"You're welcome." Jack returned to his horse, placed one foot in the stirrup, hesitated, and then took it out again. "Ben, you ride on if you want. I'm staying another day."

* * * *

Following the Bryan's wagon, Ben uttered a near inaudible, "Jumpin' Jehoshaphat."

Riding beside him, Jack slanted a sardonic glance. "I told you to ride ahead. You could have caught up with Josiah and the boys by now."

"I know why you did it."

"That old man needs help." Jack shook his head in disbelief. "Couldn't even yoke the oxen. He has no business in the wilderness."

"Most of us don't, but that don't stop us from going for the gold. You stayed because you've got a hankering for that girl."

"You mean Sarah? I hardly noticed her."

"I caught you watching her when you thought she wasn't looking."

"She's a fine looking woman."

"Why is it you never married?"

"Never thought about it."

"Maybe you haven't been around women very much, and you're woman shy."

"Woman shy?" Jack threw his back head and let out a great peal of laughter. He nudged his horse and moved forward. Ahead of the wagon, Sarah was riding Rosie, the chestnut mare. *Those hips.* The view of their luscious curve caused a stirring inside him, a stirring he would ignore. *Woman shy? Jenny, oh, Jenny.*

* * * *

That day they traveled a good twenty miles. Sarah had hoped they'd catch up with the Morehead Train, but there'd been no sign of them. Along the way, they'd encountered a family that had given up the hard journey and were returning home to Pennsylvania. "We run out of money and patience," the father said. And no, they hadn't seen a young woman of twenty-three with gray eyes and brown hair.

Shirley Kennedy

They stopped for the night by a pretty grass-filled meadow with a creek not far into the woods. Sarah unsaddled Rosie and led her to the water for a drink. It looked so inviting she removed her boots and stockings and thrust her feet into the stream. She leaned back on her hands, kicked, and splashed. Ah, that felt good.

Jack McCoy appeared, leading his big bay gelding. She pulled her feet from the creek and hastily reached for her boots. He broke into a leisurely smile. "Don't bother. I'm not filled with lust over the sight of your feet. You're safe. Put them back. Get some comfort while you can."

No man ever spoke to her so honestly before. In her family, *lust* was a forbidden word. The same with *sex.* She wouldn't let him know she was the least bit taken aback, though. She slid her feet into the creek and watched while his big bay drank its fill. "What's his name?" she called.

"Bandit."

When the horse finished drinking, Jack carefully went over him with a soft-bristled brush. Obviously, he loved his horse. She could tell from the gentle way he handled him. So he wasn't all bad. "Join me, Mr. McCoy." She waved to the grassy spot next to her.

As he sat beside her, she searched for something polite to say, but he spoke up first. "So where are you from?"

She was glad he asked and found herself eager to talk. "I was born and raised in Fort Wayne, Indiana. Until I got married, I lived in the same house all my life. When my husband died, I moved back. I would have never moved again except for this." Frowning, she waved her hand toward the creek, woods, and mountains beyond.

"So you wish you'd stayed home?"

"Of course. I had a well-ordered life before my father had some financial difficulties. He lost just about everything, including our house. So here we are, headed for California. Not for the gold, mind you. He'll work with his brother who owns a general store in a place called Mokelumne City. It's near Sacramento. I can hardly wait to get there. More than anything, I want to feel secure again, read my books, go to church, do good works for the sick and poor—just lead the quiet life."

Jack glanced at her, a twinkle in his eye. "It sounds quiet all right, and boring."

She raised her chin. "It's not exciting at all, and that's the way I like it."

"Tell me about your husband."

He was getting personal, but somehow she didn't mind. "We were married six years. Joseph owned a farm not far from Fort Wayne. One day he was cutting down a big sycamore tree. It didn't fall the way he thought and"—she shrugged—"that was the end of Joseph."

"You don't sound too heartbroken."

Never, except with her brother, had she given the slightest indication she was anything other than grief stricken over the death of her husband. But this strange man sitting next to her was different. She suspected nothing could shock him, no matter what she said. "I wasn't heartbroken. The truth is"—she couldn't believe she was saying this—"I'm glad he's gone, and I don't miss him at all."

She waited for his expression of shock, or at least surprise, but all he did was nod agreeably. "Care to tell me why?"

She had kept her miserable life with her husband a deep, dark secret, shared with no one, not even her mother. It would have always remained that way, or so she thought. She would certainly have never revealed her innermost thoughts to a man said to be waster. She should never have listened. Jack McCoy was anything but a waster, not with his sympathetic manner and the way he regarded her with those understanding eyes. Besides, she was tired of pretending to be grief stricken while her true feelings about her husband seethed within her. What a relief to finally get them out. "I met Joseph at a church social. He was tall, good-looking, and ever so charming. He had just inherited his family's farm not far from town and was quite well off. All the girls fell for him, me included. At the church picnic, you can imagine how flattered I was when the box lunches were auctioned off and he bought mine. After that, he came courting. By then I'd fallen deeply in love with him. He was everything I ever wanted in a man, kind and courteous, charming, and handsome besides. When he asked me to marry him, I was thrilled."

"Did your parents approve?"

"Not exactly." She wasn't being honest. Why hold back? "Actually, they were dismayed when I told them I wanted to marry Joseph. They didn't care for him. When I asked why, they couldn't say exactly, other than there was something they sensed about him that didn't seem genuine, as if his charm was all on the surface and he was hiding his true character underneath. I paid no attention. I was madly in love. If my parents hadn't caved in, I would have run off and married him anyway. We had a huge wedding, and I moved to his farm—he had a big farmhouse ten miles out of town."

"And then?"

"His charm disappeared in a hurry, from the day we were married." Every detail of that first awful night still burned in her memory. With her limited knowledge of married life, she'd dreamed of a romantic wedding night when he would gently hold her in his arms, shower her with tender kisses, stroke her hair, all the time whispering how much he loved her, and then, gradually... She hadn't been sure what would happen next except it would all be wonderful and she would soon be floating away on the wings of love. It hadn't happened that way. He'd thrown her on the bed, ripped off the lace-trimmed, chambray nightgown she'd made for her wedding night, and plunged himself inside her. The pain was excruciating. Afterward, she found blood on the bed.

No, Jack wouldn't hear that part of her story. "I soon discovered Joseph had a jealous side, and he was extremely possessive. If he gave me money for food, I had to explain how I spent every penny. As time went by, he would hardly let me out of the house, not even to visit my parents. If I did go into town, I had to account for every minute I was gone. I had to resort to sneaking so I could visit my family. I hated that."

"Did you tell your family?"

"How could I? Can you imagine how humiliated I felt, knowing my parents had been right and I was wrong? I had too much pride for that."

"Did he ever hit you?"

"No, but he threatened to. I think eventually he would have." She paused. She'd told this stranger too much. "That's all behind me now."

"So what do you want in life, aside from reading your books and... what was it? Oh, yes, going to church and doing good works for the sick and poor?"

She'd heard the slight thread of amusement in his voice but would give him an honest answer. "Needless to say, I shall never marry again. Aside from finding my sister, all I want is to get to California and settle into the same sort of life I had in Indiana. I want to live a life as ordinary and safe as I can. If I see any sign of danger, I shall run the other way."

An easy smile played at the corner of his mouth. "A noble goal if ever I heard one." He arose and took his horse's reins. "Time to get back."

Returning to the campfire with Rosie in tow, Sarah couldn't imagine why she'd revealed so much about herself to a stranger. He'd never tell, but that wasn't the point. She didn't care for the way he'd looked at her when she told him what she wanted in life. Not that his expression was in any way disapproving, but when he had said she had a noble goal, she got the impression she'd disappointed him. But why should she care? Hadn't she vowed never to depend on a man again, nor be influenced by his opinions? Well, she'd better try harder because every time she talked to Jack McCoy, she got all atwitter inside. Everything about him intrigued her: that faint light that twinkled in the depth of his dark eyes; his ruggedly handsome face, bronzed by wind and sun. She liked the way he dressed, not in the baggy, shapeless clothing the other men wore but in well-fitting dark pants that didn't conceal his slim hips and flat stomach, and a fringed, buckskin jacket that hung nicely over his broad shoulders.

She absolutely, positively must stay away from him.

"Sarah, I want to talk to you."

Her father was calling. He sat alone and frowning by the campfire. She walked to him and asked, "What is it, Pa?"

"What were you and Jack McCoy doing at the creek just now?"

At first, she bristled. She was twenty-nine years old. She'd been married, for heaven's sake. She didn't need a chaperone. But then Pa was only doing what he thought best, trying to protect her. He'd lost one daughter, so he worried, although needlessly, about losing the other. She gave him a reassuring pat on his arm. "It was nothing. We just happened to go to the creek at the same time. Mr. McCoy and I are barely on speaking terms."

Pa didn't look convinced. "Don't forget he's a gambler who cheats at cards."

"How do you know that? Just because Mr. Moorehead said so? Don't forget all the kind things he's done for this family."

"You're quick to defend him. Just watch yourself. I suspect there's something between you whether you realize it or not."

Pa stalked off, leaving Sarah in a fury over his unsolicited advice. The trouble was he was right, and that made her angrier still.

* * * *

Sarah's vow to stay away from Jack McCoy lasted until the middle of the next morning. She was riding Rosie a distance behind the wagon when he, on Bandit, dropped back and fell in step beside her. "You ride well," he said.

She gave him a simple thank you, concealing her delight at his compliment. Funny, he could have told her she was the most beautiful woman in the world and she wouldn't have cared because she'd long since grown tired of men's shallow compliments. Even so, she greatly prided herself on her riding skills, and he'd noticed the one thing that would make her glow inside and like him all the more. In return, she should find something nice to say about him, but what? A man as strong and independent as Jack would scorn any attempt at easy flattery. Ah! She'd thought of just the right thing. "I like your horse."

"You do?" He frowned in puzzlement. "And may I ask why?"

"Bandit gallops big and turns really fast. He has a huge step and moves very straight."

Jack broke into a pleased smile. "Not only that, he's gentle and quiet, never gives me any trouble."

She patted Rosie's withers. "If I didn't have Rosie, I'd be envious. Your horse is truly a fine animal."

"No woman ever complimented me on my horse before." Jack burst out laughing. "You have found the key to my heart, Widow Gregg."

She threw him a mischievous grin. "I wasn't looking for it, Mr. McCoy."

They continued riding in comfortable silence, Sarah pleased with her answer about the key. But of course he'd just been joking. She hadn't known him long but already knew Jack McCoy was a complicated man who kept his thoughts and feelings strictly to himself. No simple key would ever open the way to his heart.

Not that she cared.

* * * *

The next morning, Sarah and her parents were packing the wagon when Ma suddenly yelled, "Oh, dear Lord, Indians!" She looked to where Jack and Ben were saddling their horses. "Mr. McCoy, Mr. Longren! There's Indians coming. What shall we do?"

Five Indians were approaching on horseback. Wearing breechcloths and leggings, they were bedecked in an array of feathered headdresses and bright colored beads. Blue paint covered part of their faces. Odd-looking symbols decorated the flanks of their horses.

These were not the first Indians Sarah had seen along the trail. So far, the ones they'd met had all been friendly and didn't look the least bit menacing. Some wanted to trade. Some wanted to steal. Every night, Mr. Morehead had to post guards because Indians from various tribes would take the company's horses or anything else they could get their hands on.

Jack stepped forward. "Don't worry, Mrs. Bryan, they're not going to scalp us. Likely they've come to trade."

Ma clutched a nervous hand to her throat. "We have nothing to trade. Please, Mr. McCoy, tell them to go away."

Sarah shared her mother's panic but vowed not to let it show. "What kind of Indians are they?" Thanks goodness, she'd kept her voice steady.

"Shoshone. I won't say they're dangerous, but the calmer you are, the better."

The Indians rode into camp. They were not smiling. Jack raised a hand in a greeting so calm and easy-going he could have been hailing his best friend. He said what sounded like, "Buh-nuh."

The lead Indian sat tall and straight. Wide silver bands adorned the upper part of his muscular arms. His face remained expressionless as he raised his hand and returned the same greeting. "Buh-nuh." He was leading a horse with a stack of beaver skins piled on its back. Pointing at the beaver skins, he said something Sarah couldn't understand.

"What's he saying?" she asked.

Jack shook his head. "I only know a few words in Shoshone, but it's plain he wants to trade."

"For what?"

Jack pointed at the skins and held out his palm in a questioning gesture. The Indian brought his hand to his mouth, curved it around an imaginary bottle and tipped his head back as if he were drinking. "Oh, yeah," Jack said. "They want to trade those skins for whiskey."

Pa shook his head vigorously. "We're teetotalers, Mr. McCoy. We don't—"

"For the best. Not a good idea giving whiskey to Indians. What else have we got? Whether you want those skins or not, it would be wise to give them something, just to get rid of—"

Luzena's scream ripped through the air. It so startled Sarah that, for a moment, she could only gape at her mother in surprise. Luzena screamed again, brought up a shaking hand and pointed. "Look, look!"

"Ma, what is it?"

Wide-eyed and staring, Ma kept pointing a wavering finger at the Indian. She was stuttering, so unnerved she couldn't get words out. "There— there on his head mixed in with all those feathers. Don't you see it?"

Sarah took a closer look. *Oh, my God.* Why hadn't she noticed? The Indian's elaborate headdress consisted of rows of turquoise and black feathers attached to a beaded headband. A yellow gold pendant on a gold chain was entwined among the feathers. Shaped like a delicate basket, the pendant was adorned with rose cut diamonds and tiny gems of various colors. Two white enameled lovebirds sat on either side, facing one another.

Sarah recognized the pendant. She knew it well. It belonged to her sister, Florrie.

Chapter 4

When Sarah and Florrie's maternal grandmother passed away, she left each of her granddaughters a prized piece of jewelry. Sarah treasured her blue sapphire ring with its circle of seed pearls. Florrie adored her yellow gold pendant and wore it most of the time. Now Sarah gasped from the shock of seeing her sister's beloved necklace adorning the war bonnet of a Shoshone Indian.

"It's your daughter's?" Jack asked Luzena.

"There's only one like it. Of course it's Florrie's." Ma clasped her hand over her mouth. "They've killed her, haven't they? And scalped her and heaven knows what—"

"Stop it, Ma, you don't know that." Sarah spoke sharply. Her mother was on the verge of hysteria, not a good idea when talking to a strange bunch of Indians. She asked Jack, "Can you find out where he got it?"

Ben Longren spoke up. "Let me try. I know a few words of Shoshone." He began an incomprehensible conversation with the Indian, who remained on his horse, stoic and unsmiling. Ben threw up his hands. "There's no telling where that savage got ahold of your daughter's necklace. Even if I understood him, he wouldn't tell me. My guess is he traded for it, but there's no way of knowing for sure."

Luzena reached out and clutched Jack's arm. "I must have it back. Do you think he'll give it to me?"

"No, but he might trade." Jack looked toward their wagon. "What have you got?"

No one spoke. They had no whiskey. They certainly wouldn't trade Pa's one and only rifle. Their food supply had dwindled. Sarah couldn't come up with a suggestion, except... Only one possibility, her one precious possession. She hated to give it up, but if Ma wanted that necklace, then she should have it. Pulling the pearl and sapphire ring from her finger, she strode to where the Indian sat imperiously on his horse and held it up. She pointed to Florrie's necklace and made a give-and take gesture. "What shall I say?" she called over her shoulder.

"Don't say anything," Jack called back. "He understands."

After a long moment of deliberation, the Indian surprised her by holding up his palm in a *no* gesture. "You don't want it?" How silly to ask aloud since he couldn't understand what she was saying. She offered up the ring again, but the Indian shook his head and pointed. She turned to see where he gestured. It appeared to be Jack McCoy's horse, grazing nearby, saddled and ready to go.

Ben Longren emitted a long, low whistle. "Now, that ain't right. You can't give him your horse, Jack."

"He doesn't want my horse." Jack walked to the horse he had just saddled. On one side hung his rifle, on the other, wound in a circle, hung his whip. Jack untied the whip from the saddle. Without hesitation, he walked to where the Indian sat high and proud atop his horse and held it up. With his other hand, he made the same give-and-take gesture. The semblance of a smile flitted across the bronze face of the Shoshone. He nodded. With what sounded like a grunt, he detached the necklace from amid the feathers of his headdress, took the whip, and gave Jack the necklace in return. With a nod to the others, he wheeled his horse around. Next minute, amid a cloud of dust, the Indians disappeared down the trail.

"How can I thank you?" Luzena cried when Jack handed her the necklace.

"Happy to do it."

Luzena held the necklace lovingly to her cheek. "What do you think it means?"

Jack took his time before he answered. "I don't know, Mrs. Bryan. If I were to guess, I'd say it's a good sign. Today you found something that belonged to Florrie. Tomorrow, who knows?"

* * * *

Later, as Jack and Ben followed the wagon along the trail, Ben kept shaking his head, as though he couldn't believe what happened. "What's your problem?" Jack asked.

"Wasn't that whip one of your prized possessions? You gave it to that Indian like you didn't care, like it was just a piece of trash."

"I got the necklace back, didn't I?"

"Why should you care? You ain't beholden to the Bryans." Ben quirked an eyebrow at his friend. "Ain't it time we moved on? That gold won't be lying around the streets forever."

"I told you—"

"I know what you told me. You're not after the gold, but whatever you're after, if you stick with this slow-as-molasses wagon, it'll be the next century before we even get there."

Jack didn't answer. Maybe Ben would keep his mouth shut, but no such luck.

"It's that girl, that Sarah, ain't it, Jack?"

"You're crazy." Jack nudged his horse forward. He didn't want to hear anymore from Ben, especially since the old man got it right. The whip that now made up part of the Shoshone's fancy gear wasn't just any whip. He'd made it himself, leather-wrapped handle, nine-foot thong. After years of practice, he could cut a card at 10 paces, for what that was worth, and it wasn't much. He'd never struck an animal with the deadly metal tip. The sharp, cracking noise alone kept an animal in line. Well, it didn't matter. He wasn't herding cattle anymore. That life was behind him now. At least Luzena got the necklace, although what good it would do her, he couldn't say. As for Sarah...

Ben rode up beside him. "Did you see how the girl got her courage up? I surely admired the way she walked right up to that Injun and offered him her ring. Most girls wouldn't have the guts to do that."

Jack gave a non-committal grunt. He'd noticed, all right. She'd surprised him. After all that talk about how all she cared about was an ordinary life and never wanted to take chances, he never expected she'd be that bold. Maybe he was mistaken about Mrs. Sarah Gregg.

Maybe Mrs. Sarah Gregg was mistaken about herself.

* * * *

That night after supper, Sarah noticed her father had drawn Jack aside and had a chat. She wasn't sure why until she went to hobble her horse for the night. High in the trees, birds were chirping their goodnight songs when Jack, leading Bandit, came up beside her. "Ben and I will be moving on tomorrow."

Oh, no. Somehow she'd thought he'd stay. Since this morning when he'd retrieved Florrie's necklace from the Indian, he'd been on her mind. He'd done so much to help them, but that wasn't the reason she kept thinking about him. During the day, she'd caught herself looking at him more than she should have. She liked the way he walked, so light-footed and confident, as if he was stalking an animal through the woods. She admired the way he rode his horse, his body all lean, hard muscle, moving with fluid grace in the saddle. Now she looked into his sharp, assessing eyes and politely inquired, "Are you leaving because of something my father said? I noticed you were talking."

"It doesn't matter. It's time to move on."

He wasn't going to reveal his conversation with Pa. She could guess, though. "My father wants you to leave, doesn't he?"

A smile ruffled his mouth. "Your father thinks I'm a scoundrel."

"After all the help you've given us? Pa doesn't understand. I'll go speak to him."

"No, don't. Your father has been an honorable man all his life, a real pillar of the community. I'm the one with the bad reputation, the card shark who cheats. It's best I go. He's not going to change his mind, no matter how many good deeds I do."

The question hammered at her. She had to know. "And are you a card shark who cheats, Mr. McCoy?"

"Depends on how you look at it. Yes, there are times when I play cards. I gambled on the Mississippi for a while, but I'm not a professional gambler. And no, I don't cheat and never have because I don't need to. When I beat someone, it's fair and square."

She believed him. "I still think I should talk to Pa."

"It's his decision, and I won't argue." Still holding his horse's lead rope, he drew closer. "You'll do fine. I liked the way you stepped right up to that Indian today, bold as brass. You'd lost your fear. Do you realize that?"

"I wasn't thinking about being afraid. I just wanted my sister's necklace back."

He started to laugh. Admiration filled his eyes. "You're braver than you think, Widow Gregg." He dropped the lead rope, drew closer still, and clasped her upper arms.

What was he going to do? What did she want him to do? She looked him square in the eye. "I'll miss you."

"And I'll miss you." He dropped a feather-light kiss on her forehead and pulled away.

She didn't want him to pull away. She wanted him closer. She said the first thing that popped into her head. "Was that a fatherly kiss?"

As if her question had triggered some emotion deep inside him, he drew in a shaking breath. "No, it wasn't." Swiftly, his arms went around her. He pressed his palms against her back, pulling her close. His lips met hers in a hard, urgent kiss that set her pulse to pounding. The kiss went on and on. She didn't care and didn't want it to end. The feel of his whole body up against her caused a deep throb in the center of her being. His hands rested lightly on her back, then began to roam, first her hair—

His horse whinnied—a loud, harsh sound so close to their ears they both jumped. They broke apart and started laughing. Jack retrieved the lead rope. "Looks like Bandit wants my attention."

Her racing pulse began to slow. There was nothing more to say. The truth was, she'd just kissed a man who was leaving in the morning, and she'd never see him again. "I'd best be getting back. Will you stay for breakfast?"

"No. We'll get off to any early start."

"Then good-bye, Mr. McCoy. May your journey be a safe one."

"Yours, too." He touched the brim of his hat with two fingers and was gone.

* * * *

When Sarah came out of her tent in the morning, Jack and Ben were no longer there. She expected they'd be gone, but as she stood surveying the spot where they'd slept, a gloomy desolation enveloped her. Last night she'd been in a man's arms—something she'd never expected after her marriage to Joseph. She wanted nothing to do with men, and yet…Jack's kiss had stirred a passion within her she'd long thought dead. Now he was gone forever, leaving her with a life filled with…what? Her books? Helping the sick and poor? Vast, empty years stretched ahead.

"Good morning, Sarah." Already dressed for the day, Ma climbed down from the wagon. "We'll make a quick breakfast this morning. Your father wants to make a lot of miles today." She sighed. "He's going to have his hands full, having to do everything by himself."

"He should have thought of that before he told Mr. McCoy and Mr. Longren to leave." If her answer was sharp, she didn't care.

"You know your father."

"At least he's learned how to handle the animals." Sarah gave her mother a reassuring smile. "We're going to be fine. Maybe today we'll catch up with the train."

"Frank is hell-bent on catching up, but how can we when we go so slow?" Luzena cast a resentful glance to where her husband was yoking the oxen. "Look at him—all thumbs, stumbling around like an idiot. It'll be a miracle if we get there at all. And, no, I don't think we'll ever catch up with Mr. Morehead's train. Frank was a fool to send Jack McCoy away."

Sarah's gloom grew deeper, if that was possible. Ma never used to talk that way. Back in Indiana, she'd kept her husband on a pedestal, but not anymore. How sad to think their old life had disappeared forever, but it had, and there was no turning back. Even when they reached California, if they ever did, things would never be the same. With an effort, Sarah squared her shoulders. "It can't be much farther, and then it's all going to be fine. We're going to find the train. We'll keep looking for Florrie, and who knows? Yesterday we found a sign of her. I predict we'll find another today, or soon."

Ma smiled and patted her cheek. "You're such a good daughter. I know you're trying to keep my spirits up, but, Sarah, I don't know…" She glanced over at Pa who'd just finished hitching the oxen to the wagon and now stood exhausted and out of breath. "Look at him—tired already, and we've got the whole day ahead of us." Her face went grim. "So here we are, all alone with no one to help us if something goes wrong, and I know it will."

Sarah searched for something cheerful to say, but nothing came to mind.

* * * *

They started the day's trek under bright sunshine and a clear blue sky. By noon the temperature had dropped considerably. The fluffy white clouds that had gathered were soon replaced by the dark, low clouds that signaled an approaching storm. Late in the afternoon, they felt the first raindrops. Ma wanted to stop, but Pa was determined to keep going, rain or no rain. "We must catch up to the Morehead train." The rain grew heavier, but Pa urged the oxen on. Sarah was riding Rosie, but when her horse started slipping in the mud, she dismounted and led both Rosie and their other horse, Titan. Pa kept going, even though the oxen were straining for all they were worth to move the wagon along the muddy road. To lighten the load, Ma climbed from the wagon and walked with Sarah, both growing colder, wetter, and more miserable as they went along. "Frank, you've got to stop," Ma yelled.

"Just a little farther!" Oblivious to the rain, Pa sat hunched on the wagon seat over the reins. "Don't want to spend another night alone."

They stopped briefly to eat. The downpour made it impossible to build a fire, so they dined on beef jerky and hardtack, washed down with muddy water. To Sarah and Ma's dismay, Pa insisted they start again. As the rain poured harder, the trail got worse, and the oxen started slipping in deep mud. When they came to what resembled an impassable muddy mire, Pa halted the wagon and peered thoughtfully ahead. Ma called up to him, "We can't get through, Frank."

He called back, "Yes we can," and drove the wagon forward. Now the animals were slipping through a heavy, deep, sucking mud that tugged at their hooves and grabbed at the wagon wheels. Finally the wagon sank clear to the axle and sat immobile while the oxen flailed. Sarah grasped the lead ropes for Rosie and Titan. She was guiding them out of the mire onto a grassy spot by the side of the trail when they suddenly broke through the sod and were unable to pull their hooves out. Both animals whinnied and snorted in fright, and began heaving this way and that. Sarah held tight to the ropes. "Rosie, Titan, calm down," she called over the howl of the wind. Though their eyes were wide with fear, both animals heard her and settled down. Soon Titan broke free of the mud, but Rosie sank deeper.

The rain pounded. The wind howled harder. "Sarah, come get out of the rain," Luzena called.

Sarah looked to where her parents huddled in the wagon, trying to keep warm. So far, there'd been no leaks in the canvas, so at least they were dry. So tempting. How she'd love to join them. "I can't leave the horses! Rosie's stuck. I've got to keep her calm. If she panics and starts heaving around, she might break a leg." She would not desert her horses if she had to stand here until dawn.

Pa climbed from the wagon and unhitched the oxen. At least they weren't stuck like the horses, and he managed to lead them to a more sheltered spot under some trees by the roadside.

Ma braved the rain and mud to bring her a blanket. Tossing it over Sarah's shoulders, she said, "This is horrible. What have I done to you?"

"It's not your fault, Ma." Her lips were so numb from the cold it was hard to talk. "I don't blame Pa, either. He did what he thought was best for all of us."

"I feel so trapped." Luzena spoke in an anguished whisper that tore at Sarah's heart. "Every once in a while I think, I've had enough of this rain and cold and I'm going to get warm now. Then it hits me—there's no place to go, nothing I can do. I'm stuck and there's no escape."

Sarah looked for words of comfort, but they were hard to find. Nothing to do but somehow, some way, get through this long, horrible night. "We're going to make it, Ma. Get back in the wagon and try to keep warm." Such inadequate words but the best she could do.

Drenched and exhausted, Sarah stood between the horses for hours praying for dawn to come and the rain to stop. Without a doubt, this was the worst night of her life. Her feet were like chunks of ice, her clothing frozen stiff. She would never be warm again. At least the horses stayed quiet. Somehow she'd get them out of the mud when morning came. As dawn broke, she was resting her head, eyes closed, against Rosie's flank when she heard a voice.

"If it isn't the Widow Gregg. Need some help?"

She opened her eyes. Was it a dream or was Jack McCoy looking down at her from his horse, a little smile playing on his lips?

* * * *

The day before, after Jack and Ben left the Bryans, they had traveled for several hours when Ben held his hand out. "Uh-oh, just felt a raindrop. Judging from the looks of that sky, we're going to get a downpour."

Jack hoped Ben was wrong, not for his own sake—he'd ridden through many a storm—but for the sake of the Bryan family. He'd never seen a bunch so unprepared for the hardships of the trail. At least Frank now knew enough to yoke and unyoke the oxen. He'd better know enough to stop the wagon when the rain started. Otherwise...but wait, not his business.

By the time they made camp for the night, rain pelted from the sky and a chill wind caused them to don their warmest gear and cover themselves with the linseed-oil slickers that would at least keep them dry. "Wonder how them Bryans are doing," Ben called from beneath his poncho. "Like as not, they're bogged down somewhere."

"Like as not." Jack couldn't sleep. As each hour passed, the rain fell harder and the wind blew stronger. The Bryans had to be in trouble. No way could they survive the night in good shape, what with the ignorance of Frank Bryan. The rain was letting up, but only slightly when he rose and reached for Bandit's saddle.

Ben poked his head out of the poncho. "What the Sam Hill are you up to?"

"I'm going back."

"Jumpin' Jehoshaphat! You're going all the way back to help that crazy family?"

"You don't have to come."

"I knew it, I knew it." Muttering under his breath, Ben crawled from beneath his poncho. "You know I'll come with you, but don't tell me you're not interested in the welfare of a certain widow."

Jack stayed silent. What could he say when Ben had just nailed the truth dead-on?

Chapter 5

Jack peered down at the woman standing between the two horses, clutching the lead ropes in a death-like grip. Drenched to the skin, she was beyond shivering. Judging from the stark whiteness of her face and the bluish-white tinge of the skin around her mouth, she had the beginnings of frostbite. Quickly he swung off his horse. "You've been here all night?"

She opened her mouth to speak, but nothing came out. All she could do was nod. She resembled a drowned rat, her long hair plastered to her head and her clothes and blanket dripping wet. He pulled it from her shoulders, grabbed a dry blanket from his bedroll, and threw it around her. "Got to get you dry. Don't worry about the horses. I'll take care of them." He picked her up and carried her out of the muck and mire to the wagon where Frank and Luzena anxiously waited. "We need to get her dry and warm in a hurry."

Frank asked, "Will she be all right?"

"She'll be fine, but the next few hours will be tough. Have you ever thawed out from frostbite?"

* * * *

Ma helped Sarah out of her soaking wet clothes and boots and into another dress that had miraculously stayed dry. Clutching Jack's blanket around herself, she climbed from the wagon and huddled by the small fire Jack built with the last of the dry wood they kept in the wagon. Slowly the heat crept through her. So good to be warm again! She thrust her feet toward the fire. They were the worst, still numb with cold, especially her toes. Gradually they thawed, and then the pain began, a deep, throbbing agony that wouldn't stop for a moment. It kept getting worse until she was rocking back and forth, biting her lip to keep from crying out. She had never known such pain, yet she wouldn't make a fuss, especially with everyone so busy cleaning up after the storm.

Sometime during the night, the canvas had sprung a leak. Her parents had to haul sopping wet blankets and items of clothing from the wagon and spread them in the sun to dry. Jack and Ben got spades from the toolbox and dug out the wagon wheels. With Ma, Pa, and Ben leaning in with their shoulders from behind, and the animals pulling with all their might, Jack took over the driver's seat and urged the oxen forward. They all cheered when, with enough pushing and heaving, the wagon finally lurched free.

They cheered again when Jack dug Rosie and Titan from the mud.

At least Pa had the decency to apologize. "It seems I was mistaken, Mr. McCoy. You didn't have to come back, especially after I asked you to leave." For the first time in his life, a sheepish expression marked his face. "I'm beholden to you, sir. Don't know what I would have done—"

"Forget it." Obviously Jack wasn't interested in apologies. Despite how busy he was taking care of the animals, he kept the small campfire going, checking on Sarah often. Once, when she couldn't help moaning from the pain, he asked Luzena, "Do you have any laudanum?"

"I did, but Becky took it." Ma's look of disgust made it plain what she thought of her daughter-in-law.

"I'll get her something." Jack dug a small pouch from his saddlebag and was soon brewing some kind of tea. When he finished, he thrust a cup filled with steaming liquid into her shaking fingers. "Drink this."

She took a sip. Ah, that felt good, just to have something warm inside her. It had a bitter taste. "What is it?"

"It's a root called black cohosh. The Cherokees use it to make alcohol, but it's also good for pain. You're not pregnant, are you?"

What! If she'd been capable of blushing, she would have done so. At home, a gentleman never discussed such an intimate condition with a lady. But then, she wasn't home, this man was no gentleman and, at the moment, she wasn't much of a lady. "No, I'm not pregnant. Why do you ask?"

If he'd sensed her initial shock, he gave no sign. "Pregnant women shouldn't take black cohosh—for a lot of reasons."

A wave of pain hit her. She bit her lip to keep from crying out. Jack knelt in front of her, took her throbbing right foot in his hands, and massaged it vigorously. He kept on until the pain eased slightly and a touch of warmth returned. He did the same with her left foot—so competent, as if his skilled hands had done this sort of thing before. The pain lessened. She breathed a sigh of relief. "That was wonderful. I'm beginning to feel my feet again."

After he left, she stayed by the fire sipping her tea. The pain was all but gone. She suspected the black cohosh, which could also be responsible for the sense of well-being that enveloped her. After a while, when the animals had all been fed and the wagon dried out, Jack came to sit with her. By now, all work was done. Her parents were napping in the wagon, and Ben was asleep and snoring beneath his poncho.

Jack sat in that easy way he had, knees apart, hands loosely clasped in front of him, yet she sensed he was regarding her with keen, observant eyes. "So you're all right now?"

"The massage helped a lot."

"I've seen strong men cry when their frostbite thawed. You did well."

His praise meant a lot, more than she cared to admit. She gave a casual shrug and cocked her head. "I never heard of black cohosh."

"It's an Indian remedy. Tribes like the Delaware, Iroquois, and Cherokee use it for everything from arthritis and snakebite to easing the pain of childbirth."

"You know so much, like you must have been raised by Indians."

"No, I wasn't raised by Indians."

"Then where were you raised?"

"New York City."

"Really? My grandparents lived in New York, on the Upper East Side. I visited them once. They had a lovely home overlooking the East River. Where did you live?"

He took a long time to answer. "Five Points."

"Oh?" Five Points was the worst neighborhood in New York City, full of crime and slums that were unspeakably vile. To her knowledge, no respectable person would ever be seen in Five Points. She searched for something polite to say. "Does your family still reside there?"

He stared at her and burst into laughter. "Except for my mother, I never had a family. I grew up in a brothel, Sarah. My mother was a prostitute."

Now she was the one who was staring. "A...brothel?"

"Yes, a brothel, a bawdy house, where women sell their bodies." His lips twisted into a cynical smile. "And their souls."

"I...I..." Vainly she searched for something suitable to say.

"You don't have to say anything. I'm surprised I told you. Except for you, I've never told anyone." He smiled gently. "What have you done to me, Widow Gregg?"

Before she could answer, he got up and walked away.

* * * *

By the following day, Sarah had recovered from her frostbite. The road was passable again. After breakfast, accompanied by Jack and Ben, the Bryans got off to an early start. Ma was especially anxious and asked Jack, "Do you think we might catch up with the Morehead train today?"

"The storm might have held them up, too, so it's possible. Let's hope they had to stop for some other reason. Was anyone expecting a baby?"

Ma's face lit. "Mrs. Carpenter! She was due any day." She blushed, realizing she'd touched on a forbidden subject, yet the rest of the morning she had an eagerness about her, as if she expected to find the Morehead train around every bend of the trail. By the time they halted at noon, they'd come across a heap of garbage not yet rotted and fresh wagon tracks on the road—clear signs a wagon train had recently passed by. By now Ma was all eagerness. "I can hardly wait to see Hiram again. Who knows? Maybe he'll have some word of Florrie."

"Wouldn't that be wonderful?" With all her heart, Sarah hoped he would. She looked forward to seeing Hiram, too. She missed him. They'd always been close, even after he married Becky.

In the middle of the afternoon, when they rounded a bend, Ma gave a joyous cry. In a meadow ahead, parked in a big circle, lay the wagons of the Morehead wagon train.

The reunion was every bit as heartwarming as Sarah expected. Everyone was glad to see them. Sure enough, Mrs. Carpenter had just had her baby, and that's why they'd stopped an extra day. When Hiram saw them, he whooped with delight. Even Becky was smiling. That night after supper, Jack, Ben, and the Bryan family sat around the campfire catching up on all that had happened. How Florrie's necklace came to be part of a Shoshone Indian's war bonnet caused great speculation. Nobody knew. To Ma's deep disappointment, there'd been no news of Florrie. Hiram brought out his sketchpad. At one time or another, he'd drawn a sketch of every member of the family, including one of his younger sister. He tore it from the pad and handed it to his mother. "Here's her picture. I've been showing it to everyone we meet along the trail."

Ma took one look and had to hold back tears. She handed the picture to Sarah. "It looks just like her, doesn't it?"

Not really. Hiram, always kind, had softened the plain features of his sister's face and given her a slight smile so she looked almost pretty. Still, this was Florrie, and the sight of her image brought back all the anguish and heartache of her loss. Sarah swallowed the despair in her throat. "Yes, that's Florrie. We'll keep showing this picture to everyone we meet. Surely, someone must have seen her."

Becky had been fidgeting, as if she was anxious to change the subject. "You'd never guess what happened while you were gone." When she had everyone's attention, her eyes sparked with eagerness as she told her story. "It happened the day after we left you behind. When we camped that night, this band of men rode into our camp. Said they were gold seekers, just riding through, and could we put them up for the night? Well!" Becky had a habit of pursing her lips when she disapproved. "Such a rough bunch I never did see, loud and given to curses the likes of which I never heard before. There was one man in particular, had a scraggly beard, big red nose, and he'd been drinking."

"Had to be Josiah Peterson." Ben spat a wad of tobacco with contempt. "A bad actor if ever there was one."

Becky nodded in agreement. "I could tell. He had me scared, just the way he looked at me with those beady little eyes."

Hiram spoke up. "You shouldn't have worried. I was about to get my guns."

"You?" Becky laughed with scorn. "You couldn't hit the broadside of a barn. Just about then Mr. Morehead showed up, thank goodness. He told that awful man in no uncertain terms…"

As Becky went on talking, Sarah sent a glaring look of indignation to her brother who sat on the other side of the campfire. *Don't let her talk to you like that!* Poor, easy-going Hiram just sat there stony faced, as if he didn't care, but his wife's belittling words in front of everybody must have cut deep. Would he ever get the courage to stand up to her?

"…so they left," Becky continued on. "They won't be back. Mr. Morehead scared them off."

Jack had listened without comment, but at Becky's last remark his mouth curved into a thoughtful smile. "I wouldn't be too sure of that. Josiah Peterson is a dangerous man. Better hope you don't run into him again."

In her usual aggressive fashion, Becky jutted out her chin. "If that's so, Mr. McCoy, then why were you and Mr. Longren riding with that bunch of ne'er-do-wells?"

"Because Mr. Longren and I can take care of ourselves." Jack casually rose. "You have nothing to worry about, Mrs. Bryan, not with a fine husband like Hiram to watch out for you."

Becky had the decency to blush as he walked away.

* * * *

Sarah couldn't sleep. Jack McCoy was on her mind, and she couldn't get him off. So he was raised in a brothel? He'd said so little about himself, she was surprised he'd revealed as much as he did. Ever since then, she'd wanted to know more. The problem was, since their conversation the day she got frostbite, they'd had no chance to be alone and had barely spoken. She wished she could talk to him without half the wagon train within earshot. Among other things, she wanted to tell him how much she appreciated his standing up for Hiram and putting Becky in her place. Most of all, she wanted to know what his plans were now they'd caught up with the Morehead train. Would he and Ben leave the train behind or would they stay?

If she couldn't sleep, she'd go for a walk. All fires were out and the camp quiet when she threw a shawl over her long white nightgown and slipped from her tent. In the moonlight, she saw a figure walking, not too far away. *Jack.* What a coincidence—or was it fate? He stopped when he saw her. When she got close, he spoke in a low voice. "You couldn't sleep either?" Before she could answer, he took her arm. "Not here. Let's walk."

The moon shone bright as they strolled from the ring of wagons, far enough that they couldn't be heard. They stopped and faced each other. Sarah laughed and said, "I shouldn't be wandering around in my nightgown. Not ladylike at all."

"Are you really worried about being ladylike?"

She ignored his question. "I loved it when you put my sister-in-law in her place."

He shrugged. "I only said what needed to be said."

She wanted to ask if he planned to stay with the train, but the words stuck in her throat. Pride kept her from asking. If she did, he'd know she cared, that she wanted him to stay so much she'd be downright devastated if he left. No, she was not going to ask. Grateful though she was for all he'd done, she did not care to be beholden to any man. And most definitely, she didn't want thoughts of a man swirling around her head as they were doing now. But one thing she had to know. "Last time we talked, you said—"

"That I was raised in a brothel. I'll tell you more about it sometime. It's not a pretty story."

In the waning moonlight, she felt, rather than saw, the intensity of his dark eyes looking into hers—eyes that had seen more than she could ever imagine. She wanted to hear more, but he'd guessed wrong. Curious though was about his past, another question kept burning in her mind. If she asked it, she might be sorry, but she couldn't fight the urge any longer. "I have a question for you. The day you and Ben came back and found us stuck in the mud and me hanging onto the horses—"

"You're wondering why I came back?"

"Exactly, especially after Pa told you to leave."

He took a moment to collect his thoughts. "I could say I felt sorry for your family, and that would be true. When it started to rain, I knew you'd be in trouble, given that your father—"

"Doesn't know what he's doing."

"He's no different than thousands of others." He paused again. "But there's another reason I returned, and that reason is you. I tried, but I couldn't stop thinking about you. Ben thought I was crazy, but somehow I knew you were in trouble. Nothing, not even Frank Bryon's wishes, was going to keep me away."

He spoke softly but with an intensity that so surprised her she couldn't think what to say.

"I think about you a lot, Sarah Gregg, more than I want to. A corner of his mouth lifted in a wry smile. "Have I answered your question?"

No, he had not. Why had he stopped? She wanted to hear more, but before she could ask, Jack laid a gentle hand on her cheek. "Ben and I will be leaving in the morning. He's anxious to get to Gold Creek."

It was as if he'd yanked the ground out from under her. "And you?"

"And me."

Her heart ached with disappointment. She could hardly speak, but she must keep her voice steady, not overly concerned. "I understand completely. We're so grateful for all you've done, but we've held you up long enough."

"Glad I could help." He moved closer. Just as she thought he might wrap her in his arms, a dog barked. From the distance came a baby's wail. He took her elbow. "We'd better get back or the whole camp will know the wicked Widow Gregg is out here in her nightgown."

She forced a laugh. "I guess we'd better."

He walked her to her tent, said a quick goodnight, and left.

* * * *

Jack was crawling into his bedroll when, next to him, Ben woke up in mid-snore and asked, "So we're leaving in the morning?"

"Yes."

"Glad to hear it. We need to get to Gold Creek, Jack. Been dawdling around long enough. The Bryans will be fine now they've got Hiram to take care of things."

"I know." *Shut up, Ben. Get back to sleep.*

"You don't want to leave her, do you?"

Damn Ben. "What I want doesn't matter."

Ben raised up on one elbow and peered at his friend. "What *do* you want? I mean, not for tomorrow or next week, but for the rest of your life? Just wander around? Play cards? Maybe find a little gold? She's a great little gal, Jack. Lots of pluck and pretty besides. Seems to me—"

"You should know by now I'm not a marrying man."

"Just because you haven't had any luck with women in the past doesn't mean—"

"Good night, Ben." Conversation over. Jack turned his back. He touched the gold ring that hung from the chain around his neck. *Jenny.* He was only a boy when he knew her, only a boy when she died, but her death would haunt him forever.

Chapter 6

In the morning, Sarah wasn't surprised when her father claimed his back was sore and would Hiram please feed and yoke the oxen. They'd returned to their old routine: her good-natured brother doing all the work and Pa back to hobnobbing with his neighbors. Jack and Ben were still with the company when the wagons started to roll. As yet, they hadn't said goodbye. Surely they would, but why should she care? Time to put Jack McCoy out of her mind.

Pa couldn't get out of all the work. He drove one wagon while Sarah and Ma walked alongside. Directly behind, Hiram drove the other wagon. Becky sat next to Hiram, causing Ma to mutter, "That lazy woman! Why doesn't she walk like the rest of us?"

To lessen the oxen's burden, almost everyone walked, but not Becky. She didn't care how much the poor beasts had to haul and rode beside her husband most of the time. Sarah glanced back at her sister-in-law. "She'd better watch out," she whispered to Ma. "If she doesn't walk more, she'll get fat."

They both giggled softly. As they walked through a forest of beautiful fir and cedar trees, past a meadow full of wild flowers in full bloom, Ma remarked, "If not for Florrie, I could almost enjoy this day, what with the sun shining and all."

The beauty of the trail uplifted Sarah's spirits, too. "Do you realize we're more than half way there? Just think, we've only got one small desert to cross and a few mountains to get over and we'll be in California."

They passed a tangle of blueberry bushes loaded with plump, ripe berries. Sarah darted to the side of the trail to pick a few. As Hiram's wagon passed, she heard Becky say, "Hiram, look, blueberries! Climb down and get us some."

Hiram handed the reins to Becky. "Be right back." The wagon rolled at a steady pace as he rose from the seat and stepped onto the tongue.

Not a safe thing to do, but nothing to be concerned about. The young and agile made a common practice of leaping clear of the wagon without the oxen breaking stride. Hiram started to jump just as the wagon gave a lurch. Sarah froze in horror. Instead of landing safely, her brother fell to the ground beneath the wagon. Before he could move, two heavy wheels ran over his legs.

* * * *

It was the suddenness of it all that was so shocking. One minute, Sarah was walking with her mother, thinking what a beautiful day it was. The next, Hiram was lying on the ground writhing in pain. That night, when Sarah finally had a moment to herself, her brother's screams still rang in her ears. She had a blurry recollection of how she'd run and knelt by his side. His left leg was only bruised, but she'd gasped at the sight of his right leg, his pant leg torn away, blood gushing, a jagged, broken bone sticking through his skin. The train came to a jolting halt. Everyone came running. After Becky took one look, her hysterical screams blended with her husband's. Someone led her away. Thank goodness, a doctor and his family were part of the train. Dr. George Webster knelt by Hiram's side and shook his head at what he saw. "Bad break. Got to set it. Let's hope gangrene doesn't set in."

Now Sarah sat by the campfire with her father, both exhausted after the horrible day. She'd finally persuaded her distraught mother to go to bed. Becky, too, thank God. Her sister-in-law had proven totally worthless as far as helping her husband was concerned. Wrapped in her own turmoil at seeing her husband so badly injured, all she could do was wring her hands and wail. The worst part of the day occurred when Dr. Webster set Hiram's leg. Thank God, Jack hadn't left yet. He and three other men held Hiram down as the doctor set the bone in place and splinted it with two sticks and strips of cloth. Despite the strong dose of laudanum, Hiram didn't stop screaming. Jack and the others held fast, offering calm encouragement.

Pa sat with his head bowed, his body slumped in despair. "First Florrie, now Hiram. I wish to God we'd never come on this journey."

Sarah had to bite her tongue. *This was your idea, Pa. We didn't want to come.* "The doctor thinks Hiram will be all right."

"If he doesn't get gangrene. Even if he does get well, he'll never be the same. He'll walk with a bad limp."

How could life be so cruel? She'd never forget her last image of Hiram's final moment before he fell from the wagon—her golden-haired brother, so tall and lean, so very handsome. Now he'd be a cripple for the rest of his life—if he lived.

Her father threw up his hands. "What are we going to do? I can take care of the oxen, but I can't drive both wagons, and Hiram will be laid up for weeks, I suspect, completely helpless."

She'd driven the wagon occasionally, just for fun and only when the trail was flat and easy. She dreaded the thought of driving across the Humboldt Sink, the treacherous forty-mile desert that stretched ahead. Beyond that lay the mountains, but now wasn't the time to let her apprehension show. What choice did she have? "I can do it, Pa. I've driven the wagon before."

Pa shook his head. "No, daughter, it's too much for you. I won't have it."

"Then how about Becky?"

The vision of selfish, incompetent Becky driving the wagon to California brought about the only laugh of their grim day. It didn't last long. They were still discussing what to do when Jack appeared. In all the excitement, she'd forgotten he and Ben were supposed to leave today. "You're still here," she said.

"Yep, still here." Jack seated himself. "Mr. Bryan, you've got a problem. You're going to need a driver for Hiram's wagon. That'll be me. I volunteer."

* * * *

Next day, Hiram was in so much pain Albert Morehead declared another day of rest. The following day, the train moved on with Pa driving one wagon, Jack the other, Hiram lying in the back. The jouncing of the wagon caused him agonies of pain, even though Jack drove with as much care as he could. The train made good time the next day, traveling twenty-two miles on an easy trail. That night, after most everyone had gone to bed, Sarah and her mother sat by the glowing remains of the campfire. Luzena sighed with relief. "I'm so glad Mr. McCoy and Mr. Longren are staying with us." After Sarah nodded in agreement, she continued, "My goodness, we wouldn't have made it if it hadn't been for Mr. McCoy. He's done so much for us—saving you from that awful Josiah Peterson, curing my asthma, getting that Indian to give up Florrie's necklace."

"And coming back to dig us out of the mud when he didn't have to. Now this." Sarah didn't need to be reminded. "He's a remarkable man. He's done so much for us I don't know how we can ever repay him." She refrained from adding not only did she find Jack remarkable, she found him perplexing as well. Since their one kiss, all that time ago, he'd been friendly, polite, and that was all. Yet she sensed he was attracted to her. She wasn't sure of her own feelings except she couldn't get him off her mind. Even worse, despite her best efforts, she kept track of his whereabouts throughout the day. Utterly foolish. Why waste time on a man who had clearly stated he was leaving?

Ma looked at her thoughtfully. "It's been over a year since Joseph died. I know you're still grieving, but don't you think it's time to…well, you know…consider getting married again?"

Luzena's question came as no surprise. Like all mothers, she wanted the best for her daughter. Of course "the best" was another husband. Sarah took time to think before she replied. So far, she'd lied about her true feelings for her husband. Not only was she tired of lying, she had little desire to keep it up. She looked up to where the moon lit the tops of towering pine trees silhouetted against a sky full of stars, a sky so much bigger than she'd ever seen in Indiana. At another time, another place, she might have continued to hide her feelings. Not in this beautiful spot, though. It was as if God hovered close by, listening, and she'd better not let anything but the honest truth pass her lips. "I fell out of love with Joseph a long time ago. At the end, I almost hated him. Maybe I did hate him, and here's why…"

Ma sat quietly while she talked. Even when she finished, her mother remained silent for a time before she spoke. "I'm so sorry. It must have been awful for you. I'm not as surprised as you think. I don't want to say I told you so, but—"

"You don't have to. Both you and Pa warned me. I should have listened."

"But I hope you're not soured on marriage. There's lots of good men out there. Just look around you."

"Are you thinking of Jack McCoy?"

"Absolutely not."

Sarah sat back in surprise. "Why not?"

"Because marrying Jack McCoy would be a disaster. He's a wonderful man in so many ways, but he's a drifter. He'll never settle down. Remember what he said to your Pa? 'I'm a wanderer. Left home when I was twelve and haven't put roots down since.'" Ma sighed with regret. "He'll never put any roots down. It's a shame, but he's not for you, and you know it."

"I know." She mustn't let on how a sudden sense of loss had just twisted her heart. Ma was right. Loving a man like Jack McCoy was a waste of time. He would never want a wife and children. "I'm not thinking of any man right now. All I want to do is get to Mokelumne City and my nice quiet life."

Ma smiled with relief and stood. "I'm glad to hear you say that. Guess we'd better get to bed."

"Good night, Ma." Sarah hurried to her tent where she could be alone with her misery. Dammit, she did care, but Ma was right. Jack McCoy might be the most wonderful, caring man in the world, but he wasn't for her and never would be.

* * * *

Hiram suffered so much the next few days that there were times Sarah wanted to cover her ears to block his tortured groans. As often as she could, she visited her brother as he lay in the back of the wagon. At least his broken leg showed no signs of the dreaded gangrene, but even with generous doses of laudanum, he winced and gritted his teeth whenever the wagon hit a hole or bump. Thank goodness, Jack was driving. No one could have driven more carefully, but not even he could avoid all the rough spots on the trail.

A week after the accident, Hiram was still in great pain when the train stopped at the end of the day. As usual, Becky showed more interest in visiting with her neighbors than helping her husband, so it was Sarah who climbed into the wagon to bring him some water. What a pitiful sight: Hiram's splinted leg propped on a pillow, his face so pale and haggard she could hardly remember the handsome young brother with the bright eyes and charming smile. He raised his head to drink the water she offered, groaned, fell back on the pillow, and turned away.

She clasped his shoulder. "I'm so sorry it's still hurting, but you're getting better. And just think, no gangrene!"

"My life is over."

"It is not over. How can you say such a thing?"

Hiram turned to look at her with torment-filled eyes. "So I'll live, so what? You know this bone won't heal right. You know I'll be a cripple the rest of my life."

So hard to remain cheerful when he was probably right. "A little limp isn't all that bad."

He laughed bitterly. "I'm a failure, Sarah. Always have been, and now this."

"What do you mean?"

"I mean I'm a disappointment at everything I try. Even this accident was my fault. If I hadn't been so clumsy and stupid, I'd never have fallen off the wagon. Becky said so, and she was right."

How dare Becky say such a thing! At least a dozen answers rushed to Sarah's lips, but what was the use? Hiram would never listen, the mood he was in. When she left, she slipped from the back of the wagon so furious with her sister-in-law she could hardly wait to find her.

As she started away from Hiram's wagon, Jack appeared and took one look at her face. "You're upset."

Sarah looked to where Becky sat gossiping with neighbors. "It's my sister-in-law. You know how little she's done to help him. Now she's telling him the accident is all his fault. That's so...so outrageous!"

Jack nodded with sympathy. "She's not helping."

"I would love to wipe that smile off that smug face of hers."

"But you're not going to, are you?" The look he gave her was half amused, half admonishing.

She breathed a sigh and willed herself to calm down. "No, I'm not."

"Of course you're not." His eyes filled with admiration. "You remind me of a woman I once knew. She was brave and independent, just like you. She took whatever misfortunes came her way—there were plenty— and never let her emotions get out of hand."

She shouldn't ask, but his flattering words emboldened her. "That gold ring you wear on a chain around your neck, is that hers?"

He laughed and nodded. "I admired her and I admire you, very much, actually."

He'd caught her unaware, especially since he'd pretty much ignored her after that night they talked when she was in her nightgown. "And here I thought you'd forgotten I existed." She spoke in a casual voice, even though his praise made her feel all warm inside.

His mouth curved with tenderness. "I haven't forgotten you existed, Widow Gregg, even though..."

"Even though what?"

His gaze swept over her, his dark eyes smoldering with unspoken desire. "Don't you know I'm trying to stay away from you? Don't you know it gets harder every day?"

He turned and left abruptly, leaving her with a pounding heart. She wanted to go after him, but half the camp was watching, or so it seemed, and she wasn't about to set tongues to wagging.

Becky's shrill laughter came from a campfire two wagons away where she was visiting. Sarah clenched her fists and turned away. Jack was right. Much as she wanted to confront her sister-in-law, now was not the time. Someday, though. She wasn't sure when or how, but the time would come when Mrs. Becky Bryan would get her comeuppance.

Standing at the back of the wagon, Sarah's knees went so weak at the thought of her conversation with Jack, she had to clutch the backboard for support. Jack wanted her. Despite her mother's most practical and logical advice, she wanted him, not in the girlish way she'd wanted Joseph, dreaming of his kiss and she wasn't sure what else. She wanted to make love with Jack McCoy—to lie in his arms, hear his breath coming fast while his hands and lips explored every part of her body...

"Sarah, is that you?" Ma called. "You need to make the biscuits for dinner tonight."

"Yes, Ma." *Oh, my God.* She looked around the campground. Children playing, a couple of dogs barking, people building their campfires, others sitting around gossiping. What would they think if they knew at this moment the very proper Widow Gregg was so weak with desire for the very unavailable Mr. Jack McCoy she could hardly stand?

But where would they go to be alone? How could they escape prying eyes? She must pull herself together. Get practical. This was all just a fantasy, and she'd better get busy making the biscuits for dinner.

* * * *

Days later, the Morehead wagon train reached the beginning of the forty-mile stretch of desert that everyone dreaded. In preparation, they stuffed the wagons with what they hoped was enough hay and water to last until they reached the mountains. When they started out, Sarah had high hopes the crossing would be an easy one, but by noon the first day, she knew the horror stories she'd heard were true. As they trudged along in the blazing heat of the day, mirages from the heat shimmered ahead of them—pools of cool, inviting water taunting them because they seemed so very real. Whorls of dust tortured their eyes, causing constant irritation. The animals suffered greatly, the hooves of the horses and oxen swelling and festering as they plodded through deep alkaline dust.

Nearly everyone had packed too much. Loads had to be lightened no matter what the cost. Pots, pans, mattresses, chests of drawers, food, clothing, and everything imaginable had to be abandoned beside the trail. To her disgust, Sarah discovered much of what was left behind had been rendered unusable. *If I can't have it, nobody can have it.* Piles of sugar soaked in turpentine—heaps of flour purposely sprinkled with dirt—wagons chopped to pieces. Ma had a hard time believing what she saw. "How could people be so selfish? How sad we're seeing the worst of human nature."

Pa had to dump his leather-bound *Complete Works of William Shakespeare*, as well as his beloved copy of *The Vicar of Wakefield.* He left them in good condition, gallantly declaring, "Perhaps someone will have room for them." Sarah doubted it. Everyone was abandoning items they'd thought they couldn't do without. Ma cried when she discarded her treasured Tiffany sterling flatware and French Haviland china, both inherited from her mother. Sarah threw away all but one of her extra dresses. A gold-plated hand mirror her grandmother gave her also got tossed, along with shoes, hats, reticule, and nearly everything else she didn't need to survive. She, too, wanted to cry. So hard to bear—seeing all their lovely possessions, some of them heirlooms, lying deserted in the dust.

In the wagon behind, Becky was throwing away most of her clothing. She had a pair of scissors in her hand. Ma looked closer and gasped. "Becky, what are you doing?"

Her daughter-in-law jutted her chin. "What do you think I'm doing? I will not have some strange woman wearing my clothes."

Ma and Sarah could do nothing but exchange disapproving glances. Nothing they said would change Becky's selfish attitude. Besides, neither had the strength to upbraid her. Like everyone on the train, it was all they could do to keep going. The dust was ankle deep. Water was scarce. They resembled convicts in chains as they shuffled along, lips parched and swollen, their faces, hair, and clothing looking as if they'd been rolling in heaps of dry ashes.

At first, Sarah worried about how awful she must appear, especially in Jack's eyes, but by the end of the first day, she didn't care. Nobody cared. Nothing mattered except getting through this terrible stretch of desert. At least everyone else looked as bad as she did, sometimes worse. Her family suffered greatly, the oxen so exhausted Ma had to walk. Toward the end of the day, she could hardly put one foot in front of the other and cried, "I wish I could just lie down by the side of the road and go to sleep forever."

"But you can't do that," Sarah replied, even though she wanted to do the same thing. "It's only a little bit farther. By the end of tomorrow we'll be through the desert and into the nice, cool mountains."

She was right. Late the next afternoon, the oxen and horses started sniffing the air. Water ahead! At last, the Sierra Nevada Mountains! Just a few peaks and valleys to cross, and they'd be home.

Chapter 7

No bath ever felt so good as the one Sarah took in the icy cold waters of the Truckee River. How wonderful to be clean again—to feel her hair floating light as a cloud down her back after she washed the grit away. The train had camped by the side of the river. She, along with every woman on the train, spent a large part of the next day getting rid of the dust and grime that had accumulated on wagons, clothing, bedding, animals, and humans.

That night the members of the Morehead wagon train gathered around a big campfire to celebrate their successful arrival at the foot of the Sierra Nevadas. In her newly washed lavender gingham dress, Sarah's spirits reached a new high at the sights and sounds of a fiddler playing, people dancing and having a good time. So much to be thankful for. Hiram still suffered from his injury, but he'd left his sickbed to join the family. Both her parents looked more frail than ever, but at least they'd survived the cruel trek and would soon be settled in their new home. If only they could find Florrie. The mystery of her sister's disappearance was like an ongoing nightmare from which she couldn't awake. She wouldn't let it spoil her evening, though.

Jack. Where was he? People were dancing to the fiddler's lively rendition of "California Bloomer." Was he dancing? She hoped she wouldn't find him with another partner. It could happen, though. The young, unmarried girls on the train were always after him.

"Good evening, Widow Gregg. Care to dance?"

Her heart did a flip-flop. Jack stood beside her, offering his hand. How handsome he looked with those great wide shoulders, standing tall, straight, and so very sure of himself.

"I'd be delighted, Mr. McCoy."

He was an excellent dancer—something she would never have guessed—and graceful, too. They danced to fast-paced tunes such as

"Clementine" and "Sacramento Gal." When they stopped, both breathless, he seemed to be watching her intently, his eyes filled with...what? Curiosity? Desire? Expectation? She wasn't sure, only that she ached to be near him, no matter what her mother said. When the fiddler began playing the next tune, Jack took her arm. "Let's go for a walk, shall we?"

Oh, indeed she'd like to take a walk with Jack McCoy. People would notice, but she didn't care. He took her hand. They left the camp and strolled along the riverbank without speaking until the sounds of the fiddler nearly faded away. They found a grassy spot, sat down, and for a time were silent, listening to the soft ripple of the flowing river. At last Jack turned to her and spoke. "You don't know me at all."

What a strange thing for him to say. "How well am I supposed to know you?"

"I've done some things I'm not proud of."

"We've all done things we're not proud of."

He gave a cynical sniff. "You'd never understand."

"Does it have to do with that ring you wear?"

"The ring belonged to a woman named Jenny who I loved very much."

"You said I reminded you of her."

"In many ways, yes." He took her hand and gently cupped it to his chest. "There was only one Jenny, and there's only one you. You're like no woman I've ever known—beautiful, proud, and brave. I watched you crossing that desert—"

"I looked a mess, covered with grime and my lips all cracked."

"Looks don't matter. You're beautiful to me, always." His breath came fast. His arms slid around her and his mouth hungrily covered hers. Her heart pounded. She gave herself freely to his kiss, wrapping her arms around his neck and pulling him closer still. He lifted his lips and murmured, "Couldn't stay away from you."

"Why would you want to?"

Her words were a trigger. With a groan, he laid her back on the grass and covered her face with kisses. His hands roamed her body. Everywhere he touched caused a delicious shiver of wanting to run through her. All those years with Joseph—she'd never felt like this, never had any idea what she'd been missing. By the time he unfastened the top button of her dress, she could only moan with pleasure and arch toward him, wanting more.

It seemed so right, lying on the soft grass by the river under the brightest stars in the universe, breathing the pine-scented mountain air, making love with the man she'd longed for, who kept her from sleep at night imagining what this moment would be like. Now she knew how beyond wonderful it was to press close to the heat of him, to feel his hands caressing the most intimate parts of her body, to open up to him with heart throbbing in anticipation and hear herself moan with ecstasy as she tumbled over the last edge of pleasure. Hearing him cry out, too, she sensed a golden wave of passion and love flowing between them and knew no matter what lay ahead in their lives, she would never forget this moment.

Afterward, she lay in the crook of his arm. He lay propped on one elbow beside her, gently twisting a strand of her hair. "My, God, Sarah, that was—"

She reached to press a finger to his lips. "Beyond words, I'd say. We needed to do that, didn't we?"

In the moonlight she could see him grinning down at her. "Yes, we did."

When they returned to the campfire, no one seemed to notice they'd been gone, or so Sarah thought. At the end of the evening, when she and her mother strolled back to the wagon, Ma remarked, "I see you and Jack went off together."

"What an eagle eye you have."

Ma raised an eyebrow. "All mothers are eagle eyes when it comes to watching out for their daughters."

"So I spent some time with Jack McCoy, so what?" She hadn't meant to reveal her feelings, but the words burst out. "I think I've fallen in love with him."

They walked a few more steps in silence until her mother softly said, "Oh, dear."

"You don't have to worry. I know what I'm doing. Need I point out I'm twenty-nine years old?"

"I know how old you are. As I said before, Jack is a fine man, but he's not for you."

"I'm aware of that."

"I'm sure he's aware of it, too, Sarah. He'll never settle down." Ma slanted a warning glance. "Won't the train soon be splitting up? Some are headed for the goldfields, and that surely includes Jack and his friend. That most definitely doesn't include us. We'll be headed out of the mountains and straight to Mokelumne City where we'll have a roof over our heads, a warm bed and a bathtub, and we'll never have to ride in a covered wagon again."

During those blissful moments Sarah spent with Jack, they hadn't said a word about the future. She'd better face the truth. They had no future together, and she'd be a fool to think otherwise. "That's what I want, too,

Ma. Just the usual comforts of home and a secure, ordinary life. After this journey, I'd be content if nothing exciting ever happens to me again."

A shadow of a worry tugged at Sarah's heart. Was that really all she wanted, or was she mouthing those words for her mother's benefit? Either way, she'd be better off listening to her wise and perceptive mother who had a habit of always being right.

* * * *

Next morning, before the trek began, a group of men on horseback rode into camp. They had all been working claims at the mining town of Gold Creek on the other side of the mountains. Most were headed east with their bounty. Invited to stay for breakfast, the men described their successes at the goldfields.

"I found a nugget big as your fist," said one with great exuberance. "Just lying on the ground."

"I was boiling a salmon I caught in the Yuba River," said another. "When I dumped the water out, danged if there wasn't a bunch of gold specks on the bottom of the pot. I went back to the spot where I caught the salmon and found seventeen ounces of gold the first day. Ended up making over twelve thousand dollars in eleven days."

Another miner added, "Just a mile from his diggings, I found a nugget weighing fifteen pounds. Now I'm headed home, set for life."

Another thrust out his chest. "I panned for gold in Missouri Gulch. Earned at least a thousand a day the whole month of May."

Pa listened with rapt attention to the miners' tales of instant wealth. When they finished with their considerable bragging, he remarked, "Sounds like all a man has to do is put a pan in a stream and he's made a fortune."

A miner with a thin, haggard look about him remained silent while the others were bragging. Now, he laughed with scorn. "Don't you believe all you hear, sir. For every man who gets rich, there's dozens of failures, maybe more. They make finding gold sound easy. Let me tell you, it's back-breaking work standing hip-deep in freezing water for hours, sweating in the summer, shivering in the winter, getting poison oak all over yourself, smashing your fingers, wrecking your back, and God knows what. The insects drive you crazy. Swarms of mosquitos. Sand flea bites that cause a man's face and eyelids to swell. You can't get away from them. They fill the air like dust, stinging your ears, nose, eyes—everywhere. Then there's the diseases. Cholera, measles, diphtheria, scurvy because you don't eat right. Mostly you'll just plain starve. Many a time I lived for days with nothing to eat but flour mixed with water made into dough and baked in ashes." His mouth twisted wryly. "No, sir, they don't tell you that."

"Don't mind Virgil. He's going home broke," said the man who had bragged the most. "Sure, luck plays a part. Maybe you won't go home rich, but you sure as hell ought to try."

Sarah couldn't remember a time when her father listened to anyone so intently. He appeared to be pondering, his forehead furrowed in a deep frown. Finally he spoke. "I'm impressed by what you gentlemen have told me. So far, I've ignored this crazy rush for gold. I'd planned to join in partnership with my brother to run a general store in Mokelumne City."

"If I was you, I'd save that for later. Look at us!" The man made a sweeping gesture toward his friends. "Except for Virgil, we're rich, the lot of us. You could be rich, too, if you take a chance and try."

Pa said no more until the next morning while they were eating breakfast around the campfire. "I've been thinking about those miners we talked to, the ones who are going home rich."

Uh-oh. Sarah knew what was coming.

"They're not all rich!" Ma cried.

Pa ignored her. His eyes held a sheen of purpose. "If those men found all that gold, I can, too. I'd be a fool to miss this opportunity. We're heading for Gold Creek, Luzena. The store can wait."

* * * *

The two Bryan wagons weren't the only ones to change course. The miners' glowing tales of wealth caused four more families to change their plans. Now, more than half the wagons in the train were headed for the gold diggings. Ma surprised Sarah by accepting Pa's decision with little argument. "I know your father, and he won't last long. Besides, if we stay a while, maybe we'll come across someone who's seen Florrie."

Becky made no effort to hide her disapproval. Half the camp heard her screaming at Hiram. Still weak and disabled, he could at least drive the wagon now, but otherwise could hardly get around.

"I don't want to go to Cold Creek! There's lowlifes and thieves and God-knows-what there. I want to go to Mokelumne City like we planned."

In his quiet voice, Hiram tried to reason with her. "It's Pa's decision. Not much I can do."

"We don't have to stay with your parents. We could go to Mokelumne City on our own."

"Fine. If you can feed the animals and yoke the oxen by yourself, then I'm all for it."

Sarah and her mother exchanged smiles at the silence that followed. A reluctant Becky grumbled but said no more. "So what do you think?" Ma asked Sarah.

She returned an elaborate shrug. "If it's what Pa wants, how can I argue?" No need to mention her inner turmoil. The sensible part of her yearned for the peace and tranquility of a real home again. Another part of her, the crazy, unreasonable part over which she had no control, made her pulse leap at the thought she hadn't seen the last of Jack McCoy.

The following day, thirty-one wagons started on the trail that would take them over the highest peaks of the Sierra Nevadas and down into the gold country. Sarah was riding Rosie when Jack rode up beside her and touched the brim of his hat. "Good morning, Widow Gregg. I hear you're headed for Gold Creek."

"Fancy that!" She threw him an impudent smile. "You haven't seen the last of me."

"Nor do I want to." He nudged his horse and rode away, leaving her with a heart-welling uncertainty about what would happen when they reached the gold country.

* * * *

"Gold Creek dead ahead!"

Pa's excited yell caused the sagging spirits of the Bryan family to rise sky high. The trek over the mountains had been harder than Sarah could ever have imagined. In some places they traveled along sheer ledges that soared into the sky like dungeon walls and hemmed them in. In others, they crossed over passes so steep it seemed the oxen crept forward on their knees. There were times they encountered giant drops on both sides of the trail, making it necessary for several men to brace themselves against a wagon so it wouldn't tip over and plunge into a ravine far below. Sometimes the climb was so steep they had to take their wagons apart and drag them up over the ledges using ropes and a wench. Occasionally they had to pry and lever their wagons over huge boulders that blocked the way, all the time keeping an uneasy eye on more huge boulders hanging overhead. Deep ravines had to be navigated and mountains so steep Sarah couldn't count the number of times she had to get behind the wagon and push.

To make matters worse, during the five months they'd been on the trail, their food supply had dwindled to practically nothing. Their small store of "luxury" goods, such as tea, maple syrup, vinegar, and pickles was long gone. Eventually they used up their dried fruits, vegetables and potatoes. At lower levels, wild game had been plentiful, but the higher they got, the scarcer the animals. Toward the end, their diet consisted of hard biscuits, beans, and an occasional hunk of beef jerky. "If I never see another biscuit, it will be none too soon," Sarah complained over a cold supper one day.

Riding by, Jack overheard her. "When we get to Gold Creek, I'll buy you dinner at the finest hotel in town."

She'd laughed at his foolishness, so weary of trekking clear across the Sierra Nevada Mountains, she couldn't even imagine the delights of sitting at a real table, eating good-tasting food, actually enjoying her meal.

What a relief the day they crossed the highest summit of the Sierra Nevadas and started down the other side. Now, as they rolled into the busy main street of Gold Creek, Sarah stared with amazement. Buildings of all descriptions lined both sides of the street, some no more than tents. Others were rickety, thrown-together affairs built of wood. The only substantial buildings of any sort appeared to be two- and three-story hotel-saloons, all with tinny piano music blasting through their wide-open front doors.

All kinds of people swarmed the street, mainly men in their teens and twenties. Most wore bright flannel shirts—red was the prominent color—slouch hats and pants with suspenders. Many had let their beards grow long and looked as if they hadn't bathed for a while. The main street was laid out directly beside a river where, between the buildings, Sarah saw men wading hip deep in the stream, gold pans in their hands. A woman in a shortened skirt and rolled-up bloomers scooped her gold pan alongside the men.

"Lord have mercy, look at this mess." Ma pointed toward the endless assortment of litter strewn alongside the road. People stepped over or through it, no one seeming to mind.

A babble of voices filled the air—some in foreign tongues Sarah didn't understand. They passed by one of the largest buildings in town, a three-story building with a sign that read, The Alhambra Hotel & Saloon. From inside came the raucous sound of a poorly tuned piano playing "Sweet Betsy from Pike." As she watched, a woman in a fancy dress and feathered hat strolled out the front door and down the wooden steps. Ma gasped and whispered, "Look there, she's got rouge on her face!"

Pa threw her a stern glance. "She's a woman of ill repute, Luzena. Turn your eyes away."

Jack came riding up. "What do you think of Gold Creek, Sarah?"

"It's not what I expected."

Jack nodded agreeably. "You'll get used to it. If you keep going straight, there's a good place to camp right outside of town." He addressed

Pa. "If you like, tomorrow I can show you what you're going to need for the diggings."

"Why, yes!" Pa looked greatly relieved. "That'll be just fine."

Sarah could scarcely conceal her delight. Since that night she and Jack made love by the river, they'd hardly had a chance to talk. She had no idea what his plans were. "So you're staying in Gold Creek, Mr. McCoy?"

He grinned at her. "For a while."

"I thought you hadn't planned to look for gold."

His grin faded. "Maybe I don't know what I want. Maybe...let's leave it at that, shall we?" He looked at Ma. "I just talked to Hiram. He'll be coming, too."

Ma wagged her head. "He can't do that. His leg hasn't healed yet, and he's got that terrible limp."

With an amused twitch of his mouth, Jack replied, "That's what your daughter-in-law just said. He's going, though. She couldn't stop him."

Hooray! Hiram had defied Becky. Actually, she was probably right and Hiram shouldn't go because of his injury. Still, Sarah loved to see her brother defy his domineering wife.

At the end of the main street they found a campground filled with all manner of tents, lean-tos and wagons. Exhausted from the journey, Sarah went to bed early, but the boisterous sounds of revelers in town kept her awake. Past midnight, when she was finally drifting off to sleep, men's sharp outcries awoke her, followed by the sounds of someone running and three or four pistol shots. Peeking outside her tent, she saw Becky peering wide-eyed from her wagon. "What was that?" she called.

"I don't know," Sarah replied in a loud whisper, "but it sounded like guns going off."

From one of the nearby lean-tos, a gruff male voice declared, "Ladies, a few shots ain't nothing around here. Jest shut up and get back to sleep."

Chapter 8

Pa, Hiram, Jack, and Ben got off to an early start the next morning with Jack knowing exactly what to do. "First we go into town and buy what we need—gold pans, hammers, pick axes, something for lunch. All the nearby claims are taken, so we'll be going some distance. These mountains are too steep for horses, so we'll walk." He looked at Hiram. "You're sure?"

"Positive." The stubborn set of Hiram's jaw invited no argument.

Sarah watched the four men head for town. Would Hiram make it? The sight of his lopsided walk filled her with concern, yet she enjoyed the satisfying spectacle of Becky's disapproving face.

After breakfast, Ma and Sarah decided to walk into town to replenish their meager food supply. At first, Becky refused to go. "I will not set foot in that sinful place! There's drinking and gambling and God knows what going on there." Only after Sarah and Luzena convinced her they couldn't carry the supplies back by themselves did she reluctantly agree to come along.

Sarah put on a clean dress and combed her hair with extra care. How strange to be going to an actual destination instead of facing just another long day on the trail. Outside her tent, she heard her mother call, "Where is it? I can't find it!"

"Can't find what, Ma?"

"My reticule! The beaded one with the tassels."

"Don't you remember? You threw it away in the middle of the desert."

Becky appeared. "Mine's gone, too."

"Mine, too." Sarah sighed at the thought of her lovely blue satin reticule with the white tassels rotting in the sands of the Humboldt Sink.

Ma frowned. "How can I go into town without it?" She realized what she was saying and began to laugh. "After all I've gone through and I'm worried about my reticule?"

Even Becky joined in the laughter. Afterward, they knotted the four corners of white dishtowels into improvised handbags and headed for town.

The main street bustled with activity even at that early hour. Stores and saloons were open. Had they ever closed? Slouch-hatted miners carrying shovels and pickaxes hustled in all directions. Starting from camp, they had to pick their way around the mud holes until they reached a board sidewalk. Soon they found a tarp-roofed general store with goods priced shockingly high. "Well, I never!" Ma shook her head in disbelief. "Thirty dollars for a pound of coffee? Twenty for a pound of beans? I shall starve first."

"No you won't, Ma. We've got to eat."

They bought what they needed. Pa would be horrified at the cost, but they'd deal with him later. They hauled their purchases home and headed back, this time to take a look at the town. Strolling along the wooden sidewalk, they passed a boarding house, another general store, a blacksmith shop, brewery, meat market, and the stagecoach depot. Toward the end of the sidewalk, they saw a long row of decrepit, one-story shacks just ahead. As they approached, Ma asked, "What are those?"

Sarah gazed at the rickety buildings. "I don't know. Maybe rooms for rent? If so, they must be awfully cheap." As they approached the first shack, a slight young woman with long black hair appeared in the doorway. How strangely she was dressed with wide-legged black satin pants and a long tunic top. The young woman caught sight of them and stared.

In a loud whisper, Becky said, "Look there, she's wearing pants! I think she's one of those Chinese girls. See how her eyes are different? What's she doing here?"

Sarah paid no attention to her sister-in-law. The woman remained in the doorway. Something in her eyes stabbed at Sarah's heart. Grief? Desperation? Sorrow?

"Look at her scar," Becky hissed. "How ugly."

How sad. A scar ran from directly below the woman's eye down her cheek to her chin, a jagged, uneven scar that turned her face into a tragic ruin. Suddenly the girl disappeared, almost as if someone had yanked her back inside.

"Ladies, you'd best not go any farther," a male voice called. They turned to see a white-haired man, beard neatly trimmed, dressed in miner's clothing. He respectfully removed his hat and pointed toward the shacks. "There's nothing there for you to see. Better turn around."

Becky went into her huffy mode. "Whyever not, sir?"

The man gave a patient sigh. "Because those are cribs run by the Chinamen. They're not meant for the eyes of ladies."

"Cribs? Are there babies down there?"

"Becky!" Sarah rolled her eyes skyward. Even she knew what a crib was. She grabbed Ma's arm with one hand and Becky's with the other. "We're turning around right now." She gave a grateful nod to the man with the white beard as she hustled her mother and sister-in-law back up the sidewalk. When Becky asked what was wrong, Sarah said she'd tell her later and hoped she'd forget to ask.

On the way back, they passed a tent with a sign that read Fatt Cheng's Laundry. Inside, a Chinese man with a pigtail stood before a huge steaming pot, stirring a batch of clothes with a stick. The tent was full of steaming kettles and wood stoves with hot irons heating on top. Next to the laundry, they came to a tented, open-sided restaurant furnished with a dozen or so crude wooden tables. The sign outside announced, The Miner's Heaven Restaurant. It was empty except for a plump, cheery-faced woman clearing breakfast dishes away. "Hello there," she called. "It's not often I see ladies passing by. Do come visit. My customers have all left for the diggings."

Soon they were seated at one of the tables, sipping tea and chatting with Mrs. Beatrice Amelia Butler of Boston, owner and proprietor. "I never intended to open such a place," said the talkative Mrs. Butler. "I came here to be with Patrick, my dear husband. We had a lovely life in Boston, but he got the gold fever so here we are. One day, after he'd gone off to work his claim, I baked some biscuits over an outdoor fire where we were camped. A passerby took one sniff and offered me five dollars for the batch. Naturally, I accepted. That's when I realized I could make some money if I opened a restaurant. I'm not much of a cook, but that doesn't matter. My tables are always full. These poor, starved miners will just about sell their souls for a home-cooked meal."

Sarah asked, "Has your husband found any gold?"

"Oh, indeed, yes! It's all a matter of luck, of course. Patrick got here early before the placers were all worn out." Seeing they didn't understand, Mrs. Butler continued, "Placer gold is the gold that's easy to reach—lying in the stream beds in plain sight or close to it. It's going fast now, and that's sad. People come here from all over the world thinking they can just pick those nuggets off the ground, but that's not so anymore. Now you need all kinds of equipment—sluice boxes that they call Long Toms—hoses to blast the mountainside. Patrick's done well until lately. Now a lot of the gold that's easy to find is gone."

"Oh, dear." Ma shook her head. "My husband and son went to look for gold today. From what you've told me, they won't have much luck."

"Not at all! Why, just the other day, two miners dug out nine thousand dollars' worth of gold in two days." Mrs. Butler related several more success stories. She ended by saying, "You can't always measure success by how much gold you've found. I can't tell you how much I, a mere woman, have enjoyed starting a business, especially since I never did anything remotely similar to this before. Back in Boston, my main concern was how I could be the perfect hostess and impress my lady friends with the most elegant tea and *petit fours*. I'd never have dreamed of running my own restaurant, but in a place like this, anyone who wants can make money."

Becky sniffed her displeasure. "How can you stand working in such an uncivilized place with all those rough, uncouth men?"

"They're not all that way. True, some don't know their manners, but they'd better behave around me or out they go." Mrs. Butler lowered her voice to just above a whisper. "Naturally, there are some elements I don't allow in here, like those Chinamen who work in the laundry next door. I would never allow them as customers. Of course, hiring them to work for me is a different matter. You have no idea how hard it is to keep the help around here. Sooner or later every white man I've hired runs off to the goldfields. I ended up hiring Fatt Cheng's son, Fatt Li. Isn't that crazy? In China, the first name is the family name, which only goes to show how backward those people are. Still, Li's a hard worker, I must say. The Chinese are fine as servants, doing laundry and such, but it's best to have as little to do with them as possible."

Becky didn't surprise Sarah in the least when she asked, "What are those cribs down the street? They're run by Chinamen?"

Mrs. Butler pursed her lips with disapproval. "Those dreadful Chinese from the San Francisco tongs own the cribs. It's just terrible what they do to those poor girls."

All eagerness, Becky leaned forward. "Girls? What do they do?"

"Well, my dear..." The restaurant owner obviously relished a bit of gossip. "A man by the name of Au Fung is the one they fear. He belongs to a powerful tong and has the meanest face I ever saw. They call him a"— she lowered her voice—"*pimp*. From what I hear, he buys girls who've been brought over from China to serve as prostitutes. He treats them like slaves. Well, I guess they *are* slaves. The ones down the street are what they call end-of-the-line girls. That's because they've gotten older or they have some disease or they've been treated so badly they're scarred or disfigured in some way."

Becky was speechless. Ma put her hand to heart. "I never heard of such a thing."

"It's true. You should see what goes on down at those cribs every night. Long lines of cursing, drunken men waiting to pay their twenty-five cents and take their turn. I can only imagine what goes on inside and how those girls are treated. You never see them. I guess they're never allowed outdoors."

Sarah recalled the Chinese girl she'd seen that brief moment in the doorway, the one with the ugly scar on her face. "What happens to them, Mrs. Butler?"

"I'm told they don't last long. Then they're thrown away as if they were garbage. Many commit suicide." Mrs. Butler's expression brightened. "But let's forget all that. It has nothing to do with us, now does it?

They returned to more pleasant subjects. Before they left, Ma reached into her makeshift purse and pulled out Florrie's picture as she'd done many times on the trail. She laid it on the table before Mrs. Butler. "This is Florrie, my daughter. She's missing. Have you seen her?" She couldn't conceal the heartbreak in her voice, although, as always, she was making a valiant effort to carry on.

Sarah expected the restaurant owner to make the usual response—a quick glance and then *no, sorry.* Not this time. Beatrice picked up the picture and gazed at it closely. Sarah could have sworn that, for the briefest of moments, a gleam of recognition flared in her eyes. It vanished quickly, if indeed it had been there in the first place. The restaurant owner pursed her lips with regret. "I'm sorry, but I've never seen her. Such a shame. I do hope you find her."

As they prepared to leave, Mrs. Butler remarked, "If any of you ladies would care to have a job, just come by and I'll put you to work."

Sarah was so startled she took a moment to answer. "What would we be doing?"

"Helping with the cooking, waiting tables, washing dishes, that sort of thing.

"I've never had a job before."

Mrs. Butler cocked an eyebrow. "Since you left home, I'd wager you've done lots of things you've never done before."

Sarah had to smile. "Thank you, Mrs. Butler. We'll think about it."

On the way home, Becky tossed her head indignantly. "Think about it, indeed! Does that woman think I'd work as a lowly servant?"

She wouldn't if she knew you. Sarah bit her tongue. "It might not be such a bad idea. Let's keep it in mind."

Sarah had a hard time getting to sleep that night, what with all she had to think about. Was Jack avoiding her? They'd hardly spoken since that night by the river. Would Pa and Hiram find gold? Poor Pa, was he really up to the rigors of the diggings? Hiram, the same. Why did the image of that poor Chinese girl keep creeping into her mind? She kept seeing that ruined face, that hauntingly sad expression in her eyes, like the poor girl desperately needed help. *Nothing I can do about it, though. Get to sleep.*

* * * *

The next few days, Pa and Hiram returned from the diggings so exhausted they ate their supper and went straight to bed. Along with Jack and Ben, they'd staked claims on the branch of a creek high above the town. They'd built a sluice box that could process the gravel more quickly but still had turned up nothing.

Sarah saw little of Jack until one evening he rode up after dinner when everyone else had gone to bed. He swung off his horse with such agility she'd never have guessed he'd been shoveling gravel into a sluice box all day. She invited him to sit by the fire and poured him a cup of coffee. Seating herself, she asked, "So do you think you'll find gold?"

He shrugged. "No telling, but chances are we won't."

"How discouraging. Finding gold is so important to Pa, and Hiram, too."

"We'll keep trying."

"How important is it to you?"

He took his time answering, staring into his cup, then into space. "Men have come from many countries to search for gold. It's all they want—find enough gold to make them rich or die in the attempt. I'm not one of them."

"I suspected your heart's not in it. You're doing this to help my father and Hiram."

"Maybe." His mouth twitched with amusement. "But I didn't stop by to discuss my goals in life. I came to invite you to dinner."

"You want to cook me some beans at your campfire?"

"Don't you remember? I said when we got to Gold Creek I'd take you to the finest restaurant in town—that would be the Alhambra Hotel—and I'm a man of my word."

She sat speechless. Since that night by the river, they had exchanged nothing but the politest of conversations. He'd hardly looked at her. In return, she'd made it a point to ignore him. Even though her pulse spiked whenever he came in sight, she had her pride and would never chase after him. "Everyone knows the Alhambra. I've heard that it's—"

"Sinfully expensive? You let me worry about that."

"I've nothing to wear."

"That dress with the purple flowers will be fine. In case you're wondering, the dining room at the Alhambra is separate from the saloon. A lady can dine there without ruining her reputation."

Dinner at the Alhambra? Among the ladies of the camp, the hottest topic of conversation concerned the scandalous doings in the hotels of Gold Creek. The Alhambra had a reputation as bad, if not worse, than the rest. Because it stood closest to their camp, sounds of drunken revelry from the saloon disturbed their sleep. Gunshots were common. Through the front doors, painted women could be seen dancing and drinking with the customers. God only knew what wickedness occurred in those rooms on the third floor. Still, according to Jack, the dining room was respectable. Even if it weren't, she'd go because she wanted to talk to him again, discover what he was feeling. She tipped her head and tried to look casual. "What time?"

* * * *

As Jack walked away from Sarah, he blew out a frustrated breath. Ever since they'd made love by the river, he'd done his best to ignore her. She was not for him, never would be, and it wasn't fair to lead her on. Since he was twelve, he'd known he'd never marry. Up to now, he'd never questioned the life he'd chosen for himself, but now…what the hell was he doing? He'd half convinced himself he was inviting her to dinner out of companionship and good will. Because he'd be leaving soon, he would give her a pleasant, friendship-filled evening. At the end, they'd say goodbye and shake hands. But how could he manage when just the sight of her made him want her so bad he could hardly see straight?

But he had no choice. The demons that plagued him would never go away. Tonight he'd remain polite, courteous, and slightly distant, and would take care not to lay a hand on the achingly desirable Widow Gregg.

* * * *

After all those months of eating in the open by a campfire, Sarah could hardly imagine what it would be like to dine in a real restaurant again. To her surprise, both her mother and Becky not only approved of her going but helped her get ready. Ma laundered her dress with the purple flowers and mended a small tear in the hem. Becky, who had a knack for fixing hair, piled Sarah's long, auburn tresses atop her head and pinned them with a jeweled comb which had mercifully survived the Humboldt Sink.

Ma even went to town and bought her a new, white-beaded reticule so she wouldn't have to carry one made of a dishtowel. Now, as she sat in the carpeted dining room of the Alhambra Hotel, she tried not to stare like some starving urchin who'd never seen the inside of a restaurant before. How splendid this was, and so unexpected!

From the moment Jack came to get her, he'd been charming and attentive. She'd been hard put to conceal her excitement, and how her pulse raced at the sight of him, but she'd done her best. They'd had to walk through the saloon to get to the dining room, located beyond the lobby behind double oak doors with finely etched glass panels. At one end of the room, amidst potted palms, four musicians in tuxedos played string quartet selections from the works of Haydn and Mozart. She tried not to gawk at the white damask cloth covering the table, the place settings with their gleaming crystal glasses, delicate china, and sterling silverware. "How very elegant this all is."

Sitting across, Jack looked pleased. "Glad you like it."

She'd never seen him look as stylish as he did tonight. He wore the same buckskin jacket but with a white shirt and a wide silk tie horizontally folded into a flat half-bow. Other men in the room were dressed in the height of fashion—long frock coats, four-in-hand neckties, yet none looked more at ease than her dinner companion. "Jack, do you know these men? They don't look as if they've been standing in a stream filling sluice boxes all day."

"Not all millionaires get that way by finding gold," Jack replied. "You've seen the cost of things. There's a fortune to be made selling supplies to all these mining towns. It's a lot easier than breaking your back with a pick and shovel all day."

A waiter with a white cloth over his arm brought them gold-engraved menus. *Epigrams of Lamb—Escalloped Oysters—Fricassee of Chicken—Galentine of Turkey, en Bellavue—Apple Fritters.* No bacon and beans tonight! When she placed an order that included Mock Turtle Soup, the waiter asked, "And what would madam like to drink?"

"Water, I guess."

Jack raised an eyebrow at her. "God forbid you should lose your membership in the Lady's Temperance Society, but how about a little champagne? It's a special night."

What did he mean? What was he planning? She didn't know, and it didn't matter. She only knew this was indeed a special night and she would not spoil it by acting the prude. "I'd love a glass of champagne."

The waiter gave Jack a little bow. "I recommend the *Reims Brut Elite*, House of Benet."

"Then the *Brut Elite* it is."

* * * *

"That was the best meal I ever ate in my life." Sarah gazed fondly at the scant remains of a Charlotte Russe so delicious she had to refrain from scraping her plate. During the meal, they'd engaged in nothing but frivolous conversation. She was dying to know what he meant by "special night" but had refrained from asking. She picked up her champagne glass, now half gone, took another sip, and wrinkled her nose. "It tickles."

Jack grinned back. "You don't like it?"

"I love it." She raised her glass again. "To a perfect evening. If only the ladies of the Temperance Society could see me now."

"You deserve it." Jack's grin vanished. He drew in a deep breath, as if he was about to perform some disagreeable task. "Ben's leaving in the morning. He thinks he'll have better luck in Hangtown. Your father and brother still need me, but soon as I can, I'm leaving, too."

She went numb inside and had to fight for breath, as if someone had just punched her in the stomach. With more than necessary care, she placed her glass back on the table. When she thought she could speak past the lump in her throat, she said casually, "Hangtown, what an awful name."

"Yes, isn't it? It was called Dry Diggins until three men on horseback rode into town with guns blazing. They were hung for their trouble, so the town got a new name." Jack offered an apologetic smile. "I'll miss you."

"You're going to Hangtown, too?" Amazing she sounded so calm, considering her whole world had just fallen apart.

"Yes, to be with Ben. He's got some business ideas, so I thought—" He made a wry grimace. "I won't lie to you. I'm leaving because of you, Sarah."

The waiter appeared and began to clear the table. Grateful for the extra moments, she tried to put her chaotic thoughts in some kind of order. Above all, she must remember she had her pride and wasn't going to grovel and beg, no matter what. When the waiter left, she forced her lips into a smile. "You're leaving because of me? My, my, what bad thing did I do?"

"You know better than that. That night we sat by the river—"

"Oh, really, you remember? I thought it must have slipped your mind."

He looked away, as if to calm himself and not get angry. "You made me realize a lot of things that night. I've had women before, but none like you. I wanted you the moment I met you. Holding you in my arms was—" He bit his lip, as if he was having a hard getting the words out. "I knew I...had feelings for you. Since that night, it's been torment staying away from you. I've wanted you so much, I..." He shook his head, eyes hauntingly dark with some unspoken emotion she couldn't understand.

This was the first time she'd ever seen him less than utterly sure of himself. She wanted to scream, "If you care for me, why must you leave?" But no, she mustn't lose her fragile grip on her dignity. "I'm not sure I understand." Good, she'd sounded reasonable, not desperate.

"You made it clear you don't want a man in your life."

Oh, God. Why did I ever say that? "Anything else?"

"You told me you wanted to get to Mokelumne City so you could feel secure again. All you wanted was to read your books, go to church and—how did you put it?—do good works for the sick and the poor. Admirable, and God knows you wouldn't get that with me." The expression in his eyes seemed to plead for understanding. "There's a lot about me you don't know."

"You were raised in a brothel. That's awful. I can't imagine—"

"Of course you can't imagine. A brothel is not a home. I know nothing about homes and don't want to know. I've wandered this earth since I was twelve years old, and I'll keep wandering until the day I die. That's why I'm leaving, Sarah." He reached across the table and took her hand. "You're too fine a woman for me to—"

"Take advantage of, the way you did that night at the river?"

"That's not fair, and you know it. "

He was right. She wasn't being fair, but she couldn't help it. Time to leave before she burst into tears and disgraced herself. She jerked her hand back and rose from the table. "That was a lovely dinner, Mr. McCoy. I'm leaving. No need to escort me home."

She shoved her chair back, grabbed her reticule, and marched toward the heavy oak doors. A waiter held one open, and she swept through into the lobby. The noise from the saloon immediately assaulted her eardrums. She quickened her pace. All she wanted was to get to the street and back to her tent where she could let loose a torrent of tears. She walked through the lobby and into the deafening noise of the saloon. Keeping to the side as much as she could, she passed faro and monte tables surrounded by clusters of boisterous gamblers. She passed the long, mahogany bar crowded with men in working clothes whooping, hollering, and drinking whiskey. Across the room on a tiny stage, a company of dancing girls in scandalous, calf-length skirts kicked up their heels to a tinny piano tune. The doors to the street lay just ahead. *Almost there.*

Loud sounds of an argument came from one of the tables where men were playing poker. She stopped and looked. A bearded man in a dirty slouch hat rose from one of the tables, eyes blazing with anger. He reached for the holster hanging from his belt and pulled out a gun. *Josiah Peterson, the man who attacked me.* He aimed his gun at a man across the table. The man leaped up, gun in hand, aimed at Josiah. A shot rang out. Josiah fell to the floor, blood spurting from his head.

The whole room erupted into chaos. One man punched his fist into the face of another. Women screamed. Men shouted, shoved, and swung their fists. A dark, foreign-looking man yelling in some unknown language leaped on a table brandishing a knife. Sarah's breath caught in her lungs. *Must get out of here.* She tried to fight her way to the doors, but before she could, someone's fist struck her on the forehead and sent her flying against one of the tables. Suddenly she found herself flat on the floor, surrounded by groups of shouting, brawling men who didn't know she was there and wouldn't care if they did know. If she stayed there, she'd surely get trampled. She pulled herself to her hands and knees and tried to crawl, but got nowhere. Panic swept through her. She curled into a ball, hands protecting her head, and waited to get shot, trampled, or stabbed.

Two firm hands circled her waist, lifted her up, and placed her on her feet. *Jack.* Amid the jostling crowd, he swooped her into his arms. Holding her close, he shouldered his way through flying fists and falling bodies to the wide-open doors and down the steps. When they reached the wooden sidewalk, he set her down. "Are you all right?"

Between shallow, quick gasps she managed, "I'm not sure." She didn't know if she was all right or not, only that she'd never been so frightened in her life.

He stepped back to take a look. "Anything hurt?"

She pressed her hand to her forehead and brought it back. *Blood.* Not a whole lot, but blood, nonetheless. "I got thrown against a table. It hurts a little, but not bad." A strand of hair hung over her face. She reached for the jeweled comb. It had come loose. The tresses Becky had so carefully piled atop her head hung in a tangle down her back. "I'm a mess."

He took her arm. Gruffly he said, "Let's get out of here."

"Did you see Josiah Peterson?"

"He's dead."

He said nothing more as they started walking back to camp. Was he angry? She had no idea what he was thinking. Her best guess was her temper tantrum in the dining room had so disgusted him he could hardly wait to get her home and off his hands. The camp lay in darkness when they arrived, all silent except for an occasional dog bark. They reached her tent. She started to turn in, but his firm grasp of her arm prevented her. "What are you—?"

"Don't talk."

They kept on. He was leading her toward the river—toward the isolated area where he'd pitched his tent. When they reached it, he stopped at the entrance. "Go in. I'm going to fix that cut."

His voice was so commanding she wouldn't dream of arguing. Inside, a bed, small chest of drawers, and table made up the tent's furnishings. He took a match from the table and lit the kerosene lamp that hung overhead. "Sit on the bed." She dutifully sat and watched while he took a piece of cloth and dipped it in a pail of water. He bent to dab the cut on her forehead. "Hurt?"

"A little. Not much." Her heart pounded, not from the excitement of the brawl but because he was so close she could feel his body heat. So close, yet so very remote. Judging from his unreadable expression, he could be tending the wound of a stranger. He must be very angry.

"It looks all right now. It doesn't need a bandage. You'll be fine." He disposed of the cloth, sat beside her on the bed and turned to face her. "Do you want to leave?"

His question caught her so by surprise she had to gather her thoughts before she asked, "Do you want me to leave?"

"No." His expression softened. His steady gaze bore into her in silent expectation. Suddenly he shook his head. "I don't have any right to do this. What was I thinking? It's just that you're so... I'll take you home."

If she had any sense, she'd leave, get home and to bed. A quiver surged through her veins. *I want him.* Pride be damned. Dignity be damned. Consequences be damned. Her heartbeat throbbed in her ears. With a ferocity that astounded her, she yearned for the touch of his hands, the warmth of his flesh. "No, I don't want to leave."

With a quick intake of breath, he pulled her roughly, almost violently to him. "Ah, Widow Gregg," he whispered in her hair with a voice that shook with passion. Next she knew, she was on her back on the bed and he was settling kisses on her forehead, cheek, the hollow at the base of her throat. He groaned beneath his breath when his strong, hard lips took possession of her mouth. She threw her arms around him and pulled his hot, hard body close to hers, reveling in the taste, the scent and feel of him. His mouth never left hers as his hand stroked a slow, increasingly delightful path from her waist to the curve of her breast where it rested, sending a wave of warmth pulsing through her. Breathless, her heart racing, she yearned for more. *You fool*, she told herself before a throbbing began, deep in the center of her being, and she surrendered to the unrelenting demands of her hot, fierce desire.

Chapter 9

By the time Sarah got up in the morning, Pa and Hiram had already left for the diggings and Ma and Becky were cleaning up after breakfast. Since Sarah was usually the first one up, she wasn't surprised when Becky jammed her fist to her waist and declared, "Well, well, our little princess is finally awake."

Ma greeted her with a smile. "Good morning, how was dinner at the Alhambra last night? Did you have fun?"

Oh, indeed I had fun. Sarah helped herself to a cup of coffee. "It was a lovely evening." The less said the better.

Becky peered at her closely. "What's that bump on your forehead? Did you hurt yourself?"

"I fell. It's nothing."

"When did you get home last night? It must have been awfully late."

Shut up, Becky.

Ma spoke to her daughter-in-law. "Let's get these dishes put away, shall we?" She sent Sarah a knowing glance. "I'm sure your sister-in-law could do without all the questions."

Thank you, Ma.

As the morning went by, images of her passionate night with Jack swirled in her head. Her knees kept going weak. She had a hard time concentrating on the simplest of tasks. This was ridiculous. She must get him off her mind, but how? On the trail, she was laboring all day just to survive and never had time to daydream, but now they were settled in camp, she didn't have much to distract her. And it didn't help that her annoying sister-in-law was always around, always watching every move she made. By noon she had the answer.

* * * *

Mrs. Beatrice Amelia Butler was scrubbing tables when Sarah walked
into The Miners' Heaven Restaurant. "My, stars, it's Sarah! Do sit down.
Did you come for that job?"

"Yes, I did, Mrs. Butler."

"Call me Beatrice. When can you start?"

"How about today?"

Sarah loved her new job. Dressed in a fresh white apron over one
or the other of her two dresses, she and young Li served breakfast and
supper to a crowd of famished customers. In between meals, she helped
with the cleaning and cooking and usually had time to slip home for an
hour or two. The restaurant didn't provide such luxuries as a menu, so
there was no taking of orders. Her job couldn't have been more simple. In
the morning, she carried platters piled high with scrambled eggs, bacon,
sausage, and pancakes to the tables, along with plates of sourdough bread
and bowls of canned fruit, usually peaches. At night, she carried platters
of hash, stew, fried pork chops, whatever Beatrice Butler chose to prepare
in her makeshift kitchen, along with bowls of boiled potatoes, cabbage,
or some other vegetable, and more sourdough bread. Dessert depended
on Beatrice's whim, maybe apple pie, plum pudding, or spice cake. For a
beverage, the men drank tea or coffee in the morning but at night indulged
in mammoth glasses of beer.

Her customers were far from being all rowdy troublemakers. They
came from many walks of life: physicians, lawyers, merchants, teachers,
farmers, even a priest or two. When news had spread of the amazing
discovery of gold at Sutter's Fort, they all dropped whatever they were
doing and rushed to California to make their fortune. At night they came
in the restaurant exhausted. Just to reach the gold-bearing streams, they
climbed through unfamiliar wilderness, up steep hills, down sheer vertical
canyon walls, crossed over huge boulders while pushing aside tangled
brush, bushes, and the occasional poison oak or ivy. When they reached
their claim, they stood for hours in icy cold water panning for gold or
shoveling gravel into the sluice boxes. "Gold is heavier than water so it
sinks to the bottom," a physician from Illinois explained to Sarah. "So
you scoop gravel and sand into the pan nearly to the top, fill it with water
and swirl the pan with both hands. You keep swirling and swirling while
all the water gradually splashes over the side. If you're lucky, a nugget
of gold awaits you at the bottom. If not a nugget, you might find gold
dust or flakes."

Not all miners were professional men with good manners. Beatrice
claimed she knew how to handle them, but at the beginning, Sarah

feared she wouldn't be able to cope with the rough, rowdy ones similar to Josiah Peterson and his friends. She needn't have worried. She was always treated with respect. There were plenty of "please ma'ams," and "thank you, ma'ams." When she heard the occasional cuss word, a sharp reprimand was sure to follow. "Shut your mouth. There's a lady present!"

Li didn't fare as well. Even the more kindhearted men made fun of his pigtail, funny clothes, and pidgin English.

"Hey, Li, chop, chop! You want come scratchee my backee?"

He never seemed to mind and never lost his poker face, no matter how bad the insults.

* * * *

One evening, after she'd worked at the restaurant a week, Beatrice drew Sarah aside. "You've been wonderful. I don't know what I would have done without you." She held out her hand. "It's time I paid you."

Sarah knew she'd be paid, but they hadn't discussed it, and she hadn't given any thought to what she might be earning. She gazed in surprise at the five twenty-dollar gold pieces that lay on the palm of her hand. "I don't know what to say."

"Did you think I wasn't going to pay you?" Beatrice laughed and returned to her kitchen. Sarah sat at one of the tables to contemplate her newly found wealth. She lined up the five gold pieces on the table and gazed at them incredulously. She had earned these herself, these beautiful, gleaming coins, engraved with the profile of Lady Liberty surrounded by a ring of stars. In her whole life, she'd never possessed any money she herself had earned. When she was growing up, her father provided whatever she needed. When she married, she depended upon her husband for support. Stingy Joseph, always so cheap, made her account for every penny. When he died, he left her penniless. The farm he'd inherited went to his younger brother, leaving her no choice but to move back home. Now, for the first time, she had money of her own, not by way of a man's generosity but what she'd earned herself. Her own money! With loving care, she scooped up the coins and dropped them in her apron pocket. She wasn't sure how she'd spend them. It didn't matter.

What did matter? She wasn't the same person anymore. Lots of things had changed her: that long, God-awful journey, meeting Jack McCoy, losing her sister in that tragic, heartbreaking way. But those five gold coins in her pocket had changed her the most, giving her a new, exhilarating sense of independence she'd never dreamed possible. What she would become, she didn't know, but one thing was for sure—

that naïve, dependent woman who'd left Indiana only months ago had disappeared forever.

That afternoon, Beatrice took advantage of the long break between meals to go shopping. Sarah stayed in the restaurant to finish cleaning the kitchen. When she stepped out back to empty some garbage, she had a strange feeling someone was watching her. She looked toward the river that flowed only yards away. Nothing but tall trees and a few miners standing in the water with their gold pans. A cluster of old whiskey barrels used for the garbage sat a few feet from the building beneath some pine trees. She looked closer. Was that someone hiding? She walked to the barrels and peered behind. Two dark, almond-shaped eyes peered back at her. Dear God, the Chinese girl with the awful scar on her face. The poor creature crouched low, arms wrapped around herself. She trembled all over. Tears stained her cheeks. She looked at Sarah with pleading eyes and whispered, "Please, please, go away."

Sarah bent closer. "Why are you hiding?"

"Please! He'll find me. He'll kill me."

Beatrice had mentioned that fearful Chinaman who ran the cribs. "Do you mean Au Fung?"

Upon hearing his name, the girl cringed and shook even harder. "*Please.*"

Sarah took a quick glance around. Still no one in sight except the miners in the river. "How long have you been here?"

"Don't know," the girl whispered, "since last night."

"What's your name?"

"Call me Anming."

"But you must be hungry, and thirsty, too. Come inside and I'll—"

"No!" Terror filled her eyes. "I must hide."

"All right, you stay there, and I'll bring you something to eat."

Sarah hurried inside. She'd already thrown away the leftovers from breakfast, but she could scramble some eggs, throw in some bacon, and there was plenty of bread. She would fix the girl a plate and then...

Three Chinamen walked through the wide-open entrance, all dressed in embroidered tunics and wide-legged pants. Long queues hung down their backs. Not a smile among them. They carried no weapons, but the savage glint in their eyes sent a chill down her spine. It was a good thing she didn't have a plate in her hand, or she surely would have dropped it. She gulped to steady her voice. "We're closed right now. We won't open until—"

One man stepped forward. "No come to eat. We lookee for girl." He was hard to understand, the way he spoke in a heavy accent with that sing-songy voice.

"May I ask her name?"

His mouth got an ugly twist. "Anming."

Judging from the way he spat out the name, the girl must be in terrible trouble. Sarah could easily point to the whisky barrels outside and reveal where Anming was hiding. That way, she'd rid herself of any further inconvenience. Somehow, she couldn't do it. That desperate expression on the poor creature's face, those pleading eyes... No, she wouldn't give her away. "She's Chinese?"

Au Fung nodded.

"Then she certainly hasn't been in here. Mrs. Butler wouldn't allow it." She gestured toward the rear of the restaurant and gave an elaborate shrug. "She's not in the back, either. I was just out there."

Had her lies worked? She held her breath. Au Fung's eyes filled with suspicion. He peered into every corner of the large tented room. He turned to his companions and spoke a few words. She didn't understand them, but the harshness of his tone, the tightness of his jaw, revealed his seething anger. At least he no longer seemed interested in her. The three turned and left the restaurant without another word. She let out her breath and sank to a chair for a moment to recover. Never had she seen such hatred on a man's face. Anming feared for her life with good reason. After she'd calmed down, she finished fixing the plate and took it out back.

"Thank you, thank you." Anming regarded Sarah with eyes full of gratitude.

The two sat crossed-legged on the ground, away from the whiskey barrels, in a secluded clump of pine trees and thick bushes. Sarah waited patiently while the girl, who'd obviously been starving, gobbled down her food. When she finished, Sarah asked, "Are you running away from that man, Au Fung?"

"I can never go back."

"Why did you run away?"

Anming closed her eyes as if to shut out a flood of ugly memories. When she opened them, she sighed. "You don't want to hear my story. You'd be shocked, a nice lady such as you."

Sarah peered through the clump of trees. The Chinamen were gone, at least for now. Beatrice wouldn't be back for a while, and no one else was around. There wasn't much more she could do for Anming. Still, she couldn't help wondering how the girl had ended up in such a desperate situation. "Go ahead. I want to hear it all."

"All right, if you must, I'll tell you." The girl spoke with a Chinese accent, but unlike Au Fung, she spoke English with a pronunciation easy to understand. "I was born in Changsha, Hunan Province, China. Being a female child, I was practically worthless—just another mouth to feed. I stayed with my family until I was fourteen. Then a famine came, and the family nearly starved. I was the youngest daughter, so I was the one they chose for the slave traders. They sold me for fifty dollars."

Sarah gasped. "How could your family do such a thing?"

Anming shrugged as if it was nothing at all. "They needed the money. In China it happens all the time."

"But isn't it against the law?"

"Of course not. There are slave traders all over China who buy girls from poor families. Mostly they send them to America. That's what they did with me—put me on a ship to San Francisco, me and at least a hundred other girls. They jammed us deep in the hold. The food was awful. So was the smell. They wouldn't let us up on the top deck. I'd have died for a little fresh air, but it never happened."

"That's terrible."

"It gets worse. When we got to San Francisco, the customs officials stripped and searched us like we weren't even human. Then the slave dealers took us to what they called a barracoon. That's a large holding pen where they treat you like cattle. I'll never forget the old women who looked after us—sallow old hags in black dresses with bunches of keys."

"You were kept prisoner?" Sarah could hardly believe what she was hearing. "But surely that's against the law."

"You wouldn't understand. The Chinese tongs in San Francisco are very powerful, very"—Anming sought the proper word—"frightening. The authorities don't want to deal with them. If they do, it's to take their bribes and look the other way."

"So what happened to you?"

"They have auctions where men come to look and to buy. When my auction began, I was stripped, led in, and made to stand naked on a platform. They pinched and prodded me, all the time laughing, making insulting remarks about my body." Anming clenched her fists, revealing an old anger buried deep within her. "If I live to be hundred—and I know I won't—I will never forget the shame and humiliation of that day."

"So you were sold?"

"The pretty girls went first. I was pretty then, so there were lots of bids for me. That was before..." Anming's eyes clouded with pain as she touched the awful scar on her face. "Some of the highest bids came either from wealthy merchants who wanted another concubine or the high-class brothels where life wasn't so bad. The ugly girls, like the ones who were crippled or scarred by smallpox, went straight to the cribs. That's the lowest of the low. I was lucky. A rug merchant by the name of Lee Chuen bought me and kept me as a mistress for nearly six years. It wasn't so bad there. He had a nice home, and he was kind to me. One of his wives was especially kind. She's the one who taught me how to read and speak English." Her expression saddened. "She died in childbirth. Lee Chuen hardly waited a day to replace her. His new wife's name was Wong Ah Sing. From the start, she couldn't stand me. Jealous, I suppose. Everything I did annoyed her, no matter how hard I tried." A rueful expression crossed her face. "Sometimes I didn't try so hard. I talked back. Not a good idea when you're nothing but a lowly slave."

"So then what happened?"

"Wong Ah Sing hired two men from the tong. *Boo how doy*—hatchet men." Anming paused for an ironic little laugh. "Nice lady that she was, she hired them not to kill me but just to mutilate me a little." She touched her scar again. "They took a hatchet to my face. I was lucky they didn't chop off my fingers like they do sometimes. After that, I was worthless. Lee Chuen was a kind man, but even he could no longer stand to look at me."

"But that's so unfair." The horror of Anming's story shocked Sarah to her soul. She wouldn't have believed it except every stomach-turning word held the ring of truth. "How could such terrible things go on in this world? I never knew."

"Most people don't. How could they? The tongs are secret societies. Nobody knows all that goes on. A month ago, Lee Chuen sold me to Au Fung. He works for the tong and runs cribs in a lot of the mining towns. He brought me to Gold Creek in a wagon with some other girls—ugly ones like me, end-of-the-line girls. We got here two days ago. I refused to work. Au Fung gave me a day to decide if I wanted to live or die."

"He would have killed you?"

"Easily, but what choice did I have? Girls who work in the cribs aren't treated like human beings. They're forced to take on one man after another—excuse me, ma'am, but that's the truth of it. They're forced to do all sorts of unnatural things a lady like you has never heard of. They get roughed up by brutes, punched and kicked and tortured, and nobody cares. Then they get too old, or they get sick from the disease you get from that kind of work. They're bound to get it, and when they do and can't work anymore, they're either thrown out on the street or told to commit suicide."

Sarah slapped her hand over her mouth. "That's so hard to believe, but it must be true. You couldn't make up such a horrible story."

Anming nodded with understanding. "Do you see why I ran away? I refused to work even one night in the cribs even though I knew Au Fung would come after me."

"So where will you go? You must have a plan."

"I don't." With a matter-of-fact shrug, the girl continued, "There's no escape for me. I have no money. Even if I did, do you think a lowly Chinese slave girl would be allowed in the shops to buy food? Do you think they'd let me ride in a stagecoach so I could leave town? I'm trapped. All I can do is hide during the day and sneak out at night to search through somebody's garbage for food. With any luck, Au Fung won't catch me." She lifted her chin. "The trouble is my luck ran out a long time ago."

For a time they sat in a silence broken only by the soft ripple of the flowing river and the occasional bird's caw. Sarah sat frozen, deeply affected by Anming's story. She herself had seen the evil in Au Fung's face. She wished she could help in some way, but fear knotted inside her just thinking about the San Francisco tong that mutilated faces and cut off fingers. Au Fung would show no mercy to anyone who tried to help an escaped Chinese slave. But on the other hand...

How could she not try? Anming might be frightened and destitute, yet she'd shown the strength to fight back rather than meekly accept her fate. But helping the girl would not be easy. Sarah couldn't do it alone, but who could she turn to? Jack, Hiram, and Pa were working their claims and wouldn't be back for days. Beatrice was a kind, generous woman in many ways, but she'd made clear her low opinion of anything Chinese. Ma? Out of the question. Becky? Sarah could laugh. Fat chance her stoned-hearted sister-in-law would go to the aid of a Chinese slave girl. *That leaves just me.*

"Anming, I..." The words caught in her throat. With a determined breath, she forced them out. "I'm going to help you." What was she getting into? *Look at me now, Thursday Afternoon Ladies Literary Club.* She reached to take Anming's small hand in her own. "We must get you out of Gold Creek. Meanwhile, I want you to stay right here, and for heaven's sake, stay hidden. Tonight I'll bring you food and a blanket."

Anming's jaw quivered. She blinked back tears. "What will you do?"

"I'm forming a plan." A lie. As of this moment, her mind was blank. All she knew was if Anming stayed in Gold Creek, sooner or later Au Fung would find her. Somehow, some way, the girl must be smuggled out of town, and soon, but to where? When? How? All Sarah's life, someone was always there to solve her problems. This time she'd have to figure it out for herself.

By the time Sarah went to bed that night, she'd considered and discarded countless ideas that went nowhere. *Disguise Anming in white woman's clothing, put a sunbonnet on her head, buy her a ticket on the stagecoach.* No! The tiny Chinese girl would never pass as a white woman.

Find a small boat. Send Anming down the river to safety. No! The river turned into rapids below.

In the middle of the night, when she was half asleep, out of nowhere a plan that might very well work popped into her head. That was it! It would be dangerous, but then, what plan wouldn't be? The more she thought, the more she decided it was worth a try.

* * * *

The next morning, when she had a spare moment, Sarah slipped from the restaurant with a plate of food. She half expected Anming would be gone, but she was still hiding in back of the whiskey barrels. Sarah gave her a confident smile. "I have the perfect plan. It won't be long before you'll be gone from Gold Creek and in a place where you'll be safe." If only she could be as positive as she sounded.

She had grown to like Li, the eighteen-year-old son of the laundry owner next door. The young man never seemed to rest. When he wasn't serving tables in the restaurant, he was working long hours helping his father in the laundry. He never complained, although he once said he wished his father could find more help, not only for his Gold Creek laundry but for the laundry he owned in Hangtown. With his pidgin English, Li wasn't easy to talk to, but Sarah had made it a point to learn a bit of pidgin herself, just so she could understand him.

After breakfast, when the dishes were cleared, she drew him aside. "My wanchee help, Li." She minded each word carefully.

The young man squinted in concentration. "You wanchee help?"

As best she could, she explained about Anming. Not everything, only that she knew of a young Chinese girl who needed to leave town and who very much wanted to work. If his father, Fatt Cheng, could take her to Hangtown, she'd be happy to work in his laundry there. Sarah reached in her pocket, pulled out a five-dollar gold piece and displayed it in the palm of her hand. "My pay five dolla."

Li nodded as if he understood. "You wait." He left for next door to talk to his father and soon returned. "He say ten."

Fatt Cheng would do it! A vast relief swept through her. No matter that he asked for more money. Anything to make Anming safe again.

"My father ask where is girl."

Li's question caused a twist in her stomach. She could be making a terrible mistake. Far as she knew, Fatt Cheng and Au Fung didn't know each other, but she could be wrong. Maybe the Chinese in this town all stuck together, in which case, Au Fung could be getting an earful right now. She had no choice, though. In the well-ordered life she used to know, she would never think of taking such a risk. But that was the old Sarah, the never-take-chances Sarah.

She told Li all he needed to know.

* * * *

Even at midnight, miners seeking a good time crowded the main street of Gold Creek. Sounds of music, shouts, and rowdy laughter poured through the open doors of the saloons. The bars were crowded, the gambling tables full. Miners milling about, some staggering from too much drink, took no notice of a laundry wagon driven by a Chinaman rolling slowly up the street, stopping in front of The Miners' Heaven Restaurant. Sarah, Anming by her side, crouched in the shadows. "Let's go," Sarah whispered. They ran to the wagon. Fatt Chen, who held the reins, threw them a quick glance. "You makee hide quick."

With Sarah's assistance, Anming crawled in the back. Before she hid herself beneath a pile of laundry, she whispered, "How can I ever thank you?"

"I don't need to be thanked." Sarah pulled one of her three remaining gold pieces from her pocket. "Here, take this."

Anming took the coin. "I owe you so much. Some day I'll repay you."

"Thank you, but I doubt we'll ever see each other again."

"Yes, we will. I will repay you. That's a promise."

"Take care, Anming. Good luck." Sarah watched as the wagon rolled away. If all went well, they would reach Hangtown by dawn. Anming would be all right. She'd have a job in Fatt Cheng's laundry. It wasn't much of a job, working over steaming kettles and hot irons all day, but anything would be better than working the cribs.

Sarah headed home. Funny how Anming said someday she'd repay her. She seemed so sure. Nice of her to say it, but that would never happen. They would never meet again.

Chapter 10

Serving breakfast to the miners next morning, Sarah listened for any mention of a Chinese slave girl who'd escaped the cribs and how Au Fung was searching for the doomed person who'd helped her. Nothing. Just the usual talk about the newest gold find and what lucky fellow had just made his fortune. Li remained his usual silent self. Only once did he speak to her. It sounded like "Gel orait" which maybe meant "Girl all right," but she wasn't sure.

After last night's astonishing deed, she was bursting to tell, but so far had managed to stifle herself. Ma would be horrified at the chance she took. Becky would think she was crazy. Only Jack would understand. He'd soon be leaving, though, and she shouldn't be thinking about him anymore. Even so, she missed him and heartily wished he was here for her to confide in, tell him of the remarkable feat she'd accomplished, brag a little so she could see the admiration in his eyes.

When she went home at noon, she discovered her wish had been granted. The three gold seekers had returned. Jack had gone to his tent. Pa and Hiram, both with scroungy beards, looking exhausted, sat by the campfire. Hiram had something to show them. While Sarah, Ma, and Becky looked on, he took a small bag from his pocket and pulled out a nugget the size of a walnut. "See what I found?" His eye held a triumphant gleam.

Becky clapped her hands in delight. "How much is it worth?" Sarah had never seen her so animated.

"Not sure, maybe about two thousand dollars." A smile spread over Hiram's face. "And there's more where it came from."

Becky frowned. "There's enough to buy a farm, isn't there? We don't need more. It's time we left for Mokelumne City."

"We'll talk about it later." Hiram walked away. No surprise. He'd do anything rather than have a confrontation with his wife.

Sarah felt sorry for Pa. She had almost asked if he, too, had been lucky, but wisely did not. Only Hiram had made a fabulous find. Her downcast father produced a small bag of gold dust from his pocket worth practically nothing.

Despite the excitement of Hiram's find, Sarah couldn't keep her thoughts off Jack. As soon as she could, she excused herself, said she was going for a walk. Except for the one visit to Jack's tent late that night, she'd stayed away. A lady didn't visit a man's home unaccompanied, be it tent or mansion, or what might people think? Today she didn't care what they thought. A sense of urgency drove her as she headed for Jack's secluded tent, forcing herself to walk, not run. When she arrived, she found him outside, bending over a basin, lather on his face, razor in hand, stripped to the waist. She ached for his touch at sight of his wide shoulders, the ripple of muscles on his chest where the gold ring and chain nestled amidst a triangle of crisp black hairs. She stopped to catch her breath, forced herself to sound normal. "Good afternoon, Mr. McCoy. I see you're back."

He looked up from the basin. "*Sarah.*" He grabbed a towel and strode toward her, wiping the lather away. When he reached her, he flung aside the towel and swept her into his arms. "I missed you," he whispered into her hair.

Her heart lurched madly as she pressed against his naked chest. His body heat flowed through her, stirring the hunger. "I missed you, too." She raised her lips to be kissed. He groaned beneath his breath, settled his mouth on hers. After a burning kiss, he left a trail of kisses down her cheek to the hollow in her neck. She moaned and tilted her neck back, drowning in the taste, feel, scent of him.

He pulled away and said in a ragged breath, "We'd better go inside."

"I guess we'd better." Her voice sounded strange to her own ears. Not her ordinary voice at all, but a voice quivering with desire. This wasn't just passion. Until this moment, she never realized how much she wanted this man—loved this man.

He led her into his tent and let down the flap.

* * * *

Afterward, lying naked in Jack's arms, Sarah sighed in pleasant exhaustion. This time there'd been no gentle interlude. A hot tide of passion had raged through them both. They'd gone after each other with such unrestrained hunger they now lay drained but completely satisfied. She raised up on one elbow and peered down at him. "That was...very nice."

He raised a hand to her cheek and gave her his devastating grin. "Only nice?"

"You know what I mean." She waited for him to speak. Now was the time for him to announce how much he loved her, how much he wanted them to be together for the rest of their lives. Maybe she should speak first, pour her heart out, let him know she was his forever, and there would never be another man in her life, only Jack McCoy. But no. A warning voice within her kept her from speaking. That night in the restaurant, he had said he had feelings for her, that he wanted her, but tonight, passionate and loving though he'd been, he never mentioned the word love, never said a word about their future.

The remains of their passion ebbed away. They lay talking, but of ordinary things. He told her about the hardships he, Pa, and Hiram endured while they worked their claims. He was happy for Hiram, and, no, he himself hadn't been that lucky. When she told him how she'd outwitted Au Fung and helped the Chinese slave girl escape, he sat up and stared at her in amazement. "You did it all yourself?"

"You're surprised?"

The look he gave her brimmed with approval, admiration, and—she couldn't be mistaken—love shining warm and tender in his eyes. Jack loved her, she was sure of it, but until he spoke up and said so, she'd go to her grave before she revealed her feelings for him.

Tension filled the air when Sarah returned to her campsite. Her parents were unusually silent. Becky's face was a thundercloud. Hiram wasn't around. He'd taken refuge in their wagon, his usual behavior when they had an argument. Her heart sank when Pa asked Sarah to sit down, he had something to tell her. Whatever it was, it couldn't be good.

Pa began with a rambling description of how hard he'd worked at the claim and all the hardships he'd gone through. His right hip hurt. He'd twisted his left knee and could hardly walk. He was covered with sand flea bites. "So I'm done here, Sarah. I've had enough of this searching for gold. It's a young man's game, and I'm too old. In the morning we leave for Mokelumne City."

Becky nodded in agreement. "It's time we left. Hiram has discovered enough gold that we can buy our own farm. That's all I want. Why he wants to stay is beyond me."

From the wagon, Hiram overheard. His expression troubled, he climbed down and painfully limped to where they were sitting. "Don't you see, Becky, this is just the beginning. There's got to be more in that ravine where I found the nugget. I want to go back up there—"

"I've had enough of this sinful town!" Becky's eyes sparked. "You're a cripple. You have no business climbing around mountains in the state you're in. How you found that nugget, I'll never know, but I doubt you'll ever find another."

Hiram opened his mouth to speak, and then shut it again. Heaving a dispirited sigh, he walked away, leaving Sarah to stifle her anger once again. Why couldn't he ever get his way? Crippled though he was, he'd found that nugget. Of course he wanted to look for more, and Becky should be keeping her mouth shut. *And I don't want to go to Mokelumne City either.* She looked at Pa. "Are you sure? What about my job?"

Pa shrugged. "You'll give it up. I never approved of a daughter of mine working in a restaurant as if she were some servant girl. Or working anywhere, for that matter."

Ma said gently, "We know you enjoyed it, but it wasn't very ladylike. Just think, when we get to Mokelumne City, we can live in a real house again with real beds to sleep in, a real table to eat on, and our very own privy in the yard. We'll attend a real church on Sunday. You'll have your books and watercolors. If there isn't a Thursday Afternoon Ladies' Club, we'll form one ourselves."

Dear God, that sounds horrible. She didn't want to hurt her parents' feelings, but she must be truthful. "I don't want to leave. I like it here. I could even open my own restaurant."

"What?" Both Ma and Pa gazed at her wide-eyed.

"It isn't that I don't want to be with you. It's just…" How to explain? "I love living in a mining town. Fort Wayne, Indiana seems so dull now, and Mokelumne City would be the same."

Ma and Pa were staring at her like she was speaking Greek.

In frustration, Sarah threw up her hands. "Don't you see? It's all so exciting. Seeing a miner make a fortune overnight, meeting people from all over the world. I love the constant excitement on the streets. Even the fights breaking out are thrilling. Haven't you caught the reckless atmosphere? In Gold Creek, people don't live by ordinary rules. They don't care. It's like…live today for tomorrow you may die. Each day is different. You never know what's going to happen. Maybe somebody will get shot or find a gold nugget the size of a melon. It's all so…so…" Her parents kept looking at her in disbelief. "Don't you see what I mean? I won't find any of this in Mokelumne City."

They did not see what she meant. After a long, heavy silence, Pa remarked, "That's all very well and good, Sarah, but do you really want to abandon your family?"

Of course she didn't want to leave her family. She, the dutiful daughter who always did as she was told. "I'll think about it."

"Give it some careful thought." Pa's lips pressed together in disapproval. "I strongly suggest you forget this…this fantasy and come to your senses."

She fled to her tent. She wasn't lying. She loved working in the restaurant, loved the excitement of Gold Creek. What she hadn't said was that she loved Jack McCoy and didn't want to leave him. Maybe she was being stupid and foolish. He had just made love to her in the most passionate way she'd ever known, yet he hadn't said he loved her. She was positive he did, but why hadn't he said so?

It was almost time to leave for the restaurant. She would talk to Jack when she got home. But what could she say? Never would she throw herself at his feet and beg him to marry her. What on earth was wrong with the man? She ought to forget the whole thing, go to Mokelumne City like a good daughter should, but no, she would talk to him one more time.

* * * *

Occupants of the camp were settling in for the night and paid no attention to Sarah as she passed on her way to Jack's tent. He was sitting by his campfire, coffee cup in hand, doing nothing but staring into the darkness.

"Hello," she said.

"I've been expecting you." He spoke in an odd yet gentle tone. "Come sit down. Want some coffee?"

"No, thank you." She sat across and took her time before she spoke. "I suppose you've heard?"

He inclined his head slightly. "Your Pa has had enough of the goldfields. Well, I don't blame him. Men far younger have given up the struggle. He'll be much happier in…where are you going? Oh, yes, Mokelumne City. I suppose you're going, too." His voice held an undertone of resignation, as if he was sorry she was going but would do nothing to stop her.

"I might go. I haven't decided." Good. She sounded perfectly casual, as if she didn't care one way or the other.

He sat in silence until a faint smile ruffled his mouth. "You know I don't want you to go."

"Really?" She raised an inquiring eyebrow. "How am I supposed to know that? You've never said so and you say you're leaving."

He spent more time in silence before he drew a deep breath. "With one exception, in my whole life, I've never met a woman remotely similar to you. I fell in love with you the first time I saw you."

Her heart jumped. He'd said the words she longed to hear. Before she could respond, he continued, "How could I not love you? You're pretty. You're smart. You've got spunk. You're generous and kind. You're everything a woman ought to be. Since I met you, you've ruined my sleep at night. I'm a man possessed. I can't stop thinking about you."

She had to restrain herself, be a casual listener when all she wanted was to fling herself into his arms and declare her love. "Why have you never told me?"

"I've never told you because I don't want to hurt you. I'm not like other men. I could never give you what you need."

"So what is it you think I need?" Keeping the ache and longing from her voice wasn't easy, but she managed.

"You need what every woman needs—a home, children, security. I can never give you those things. What would I do if I came with you to Mokelumne City? Become a farmer? Can you picture me behind a plow?"

She had to smile at the image of tough, independent Jack McCoy plodding behind a horse up and down the furrows. "You could open a business."

It was his turn to smile. "And do what? Spend my time being nice to the customers? Get my excitement from counting the daily receipts?" He shook his head ruefully. "I can never settle down. I was meant to be a wanderer, and wanderers don't make good husbands. I can't do that to you, much as I—" His voice broke. "God, I'm going to miss you." He strode to where she was sitting, knelt before her and grasped her hands. "It'll kill me to lose you, but you'd never be happy with me. Can you understand?"

That settled it. She would not go to Mokelumne City. She would stay here on her own. Up to this moment, she'd toyed with the idea, never quite serious, but now she was. And why couldn't it happen? She didn't have to stay with her parents. She was an adult, capable of making her own living. She bent toward Jack, gazing deep into his dark, pleading eyes. "What if I decided to stay in Gold Creek? I'm making my own money now. I wouldn't be dependent on you or anyone else." The more she thought, the more she liked the idea. "I might even start a business of my own like Beatrice did." She laughed and tossed her head. "And you, Jack McCoy, wouldn't have a word to say about it."

He didn't join in her laughter. His face clouded with doubt. "You have every right to do what you please, but I might not always be here—"

"You let me worry about that." A weight lifted from her heart. She'd found the perfect solution. More than once, she'd thought about starting her own restaurant like Beatrice had done. In booming Gold Creek, no business was a failure, so she'd be sure to succeed. More important, she now knew Jack loved her. Something in his past held him back, but with enough time, she'd find out what it was. When she did, she would fix it, and Jack would be hers. *What a childish idea.* She laughed to herself. What folly to think she, a mere woman, could change a man's life, and yet…why not? She could do it. She *would* do it. She'd lived her life with somebody else telling her what to do. Not anymore. Her entire future had just changed. From now on, she'd make her own way in the world. Nothing was impossible.

With a buoyant step, Sarah returned to her campsite hoping her parents would still be up. The sooner she told them her decision, the better. Perhaps when they saw how truly happy she was, they would understand and wish her well.

She drew close to the wagons. *Uh-oh, something wrong.* Heaving and wheezing, Ma sat by the fire, hand pressed against her chest. Pa and Hiram hovered over her, not doing much except uselessly clapping her on the back while Becky frantically rummaged through the box on the side of the wagon. When she saw Sarah, she cried, "Where's the eucalyptus oil?"

Dear Lord. Sarah hurried to the wagon. "We don't have any eucalyptus oil, remember?" She shoved Becky aside and scrambled through their food supply until she found the jar of honey and a spoon. She rushed to where Ma sat deathly pale, frantic-eyed, gasping for every desperate breath, and knelt by her side. With a steady hand, she poured honey into the spoon and held it under Ma's nose. "Breathe, Ma, breathe. You're going to be fine, but you've got to stay calm."

Sarah lost track of time as she urged her mother to relax and breathe the fumes from the honey. The family looked on in tension-filled silence. This asthma attack was the worst Luzena had ever had.

Slowly the wheezing eased and finally stopped. With everyone hovering around, Ma leaned back in her chair exhausted, speaking in a weak, fairly audible whisper. "I'll be all right."

Sarah gave her a smile. "Thank goodness. You really scared us."

"This is my fault," Pa declared." I don't know why you get these attacks, but I'd wager it wouldn't be so bad once we get to our new home."

Ma gave him a grateful nod. "I'll be so glad to get to Mokelumne City. You don't know how grateful I'll be to have a home again, but…" Tears glistened in her eyes. "Things will never be the same, not without Florrie."

Sarah clasped her shoulder. "We'll never stop looking."

"Someday we'll find her," Hiram chimed in.

Shirley Kennedy

Sarah had forgotten Becky—didn't care where she was, but here she came, fist jammed on her hip, aiming a venomous gaze directly at her. "Ma's asthma attack is all your fault."

After a stunned moment, Sarah asked. "In what way?"

"How do you think Ma feels about you staying behind? You're going to open a restaurant in this sinful place? Have you lost your mind? Ma needs you more than ever, but you only think of yourself and what you want."

Hiram made a shushing noise, but Becky's scathing voice grew louder. "Ma hasn't lost one daughter. She's lost two."

"That's enough." Hiram grasped his wife's arm. In a voice that invited no argument, he continued, "We're going to bed now. Come along."

Sarah watched as her brother gently but firmly led Becky away. "Good for him," she murmured.

Pa looked Sarah square in the eye. "Is she right? Are you not coming with us?"

Sarah blew out a breath of resignation and stood to face her father. How old he looked—she hadn't noticed before—new lines of strain in his face, shoulders slumped more than ever. Ma looked older, too, and even more fragile. With his terrible limp, poor Hiram would never be the same. Only Becky had survived the journey healthy as ever. Selfish, self-centered Becky with a heart the size of a pea. Ma and Pa needed help. Lord knew what might happen if they didn't have someone strong and tough around to take care of them.

And that's me.

Sarah swallowed the despair in her throat. "Of course I'm coming with you. That other… I was just talking." She forced her lips into a smile. "I can hardly wait to see Mokelumne City."

Chapter 11

In the morning, Sarah served the customers at the Miners' Heaven Restaurant for the last time. When she told Beatrice Butler she was leaving, the restaurant owner gave her a hug. "I'm so sorry to see you go, but I do understand. I was a bit worried, you know."

"About what?"

Beatrice's eyebrows raised in amusement. "Did you think I didn't know about Anming? In case you're wondering, Fatt Cheng got her to Hangtown safe and sound."

"How did you—?"

Beatrice broke into a merry laugh. "Nothing much escapes me in this town." She grew serious. "You were very brave to tangle with Au Fung. All sorts of bad things could have happened. Don't ever, ever do that again."

"I don't plan to." That was the easiest promise she ever made.

She returned home with leaden feet. When she left, her family had been packing the wagons. She hadn't had a chance to talk to Jack yet, and by now they would be ready to go. Somehow she'd find him and say goodbye. This was the last time she'd ever see him. She'd be fooling herself if she thought their paths would ever cross again.

When she got back to camp, Jack was there, standing in earnest conversation with Pa. Her heart hurt just looking at his sharp, confident profile, at those strong, capable hands that just last night had caressed her in the most intimate places. He stood so self assured, as if he always knew exactly what he was doing and was completely in charge of his life. Not quite. Last night she'd seen a side of him she'd never seen before. *God, I'm going to miss you,* he'd cried, letting her see the hidden part of himself that craved love and an escape from loneliness. Only for a moment, though. Men were like that, their pride preventing them from letting their real feelings show.

Pa caught sight of her. He clapped a hand on Jack's shoulder. "Looks like our friend is leaving, too."

She stiffened, sucking in a shallow breath. If he said he was going to Mokelumne City, she'd faint on the spot. She put a smile on her face. "Where are you going, Mr. McCoy?"

Jack's gaze met hers. She couldn't mistake the unspoken pain smoldering in the depths of his eyes. "I'm leaving for Hangtown today. Ben's looking to go into business, maybe open a general store."

Pa gave a hearty laugh. "That's a smart move, Jack. The claims around here are overworked. Hangtown's the place to be."

She would keep smiling if it killed her to conceal her sinking anguish. "Good for you, Mr. McCoy. May you find one of those huge nuggets that will make you rich for life."

Pa guffawed. Jack struggled to smile. "Thank you, Mrs. Gregg. I'm not sure I'll head for the goldfields. Maybe I'll go into business with Ben. I've enjoyed knowing you and all your family."

Pa didn't hear the sadness in his voice, but she did. Not that it mattered. Much as Jack might love her, he wasn't about to change his mind. "I must finish packing. It's been nice knowing you, Mr. McCoy." She took one last look at the man she loved and walked away.

Chapter 12

Mokelumne City

Sarah and her mother sat on a bench and gazed at the two-masted schooner pulling to the dock. Not for the first time, Ma shook her head in wonderment. "I still can't believe there's a ship practically in my back yard."

"But it's true." Sarah could hardly believe it either. She'd assumed Mokelumne City was just another farm town. What else could it have been if it was located ninety miles inland from San Francisco? Not until she arrived did she realize the small town sitting at the forks of the Mokelumne and Cosumnes rivers had a port. Several times a week, schooners from San Francisco Bay, loaded with food, hardware, and lumber unloaded at the city dock. From there, the goods were transported by mule train to the goldfields where they brought a huge profit.

Uncle William had given them a warm welcome. Ten years older than Frank, and ailing, he was more than happy to share his home and give his younger brother the responsibility of running the store. In return, Pa was pleased at finding Bryan's General Store profitable and well run. "It's the Gold Rush," Uncle William explained. "Lots of miners come through here and buy supplies to take to the goldfields."

The town itself was smaller than Sarah expected with only three stores, two hotels, a blacksmith shop, one saloon, a church, warehouse, and a hundred or so houses. Uncle William's two-story home was one of the largest and, by not-very-high Mokelumne City standards, most luxurious. Walking through the first time, Ma couldn't contain her delight. Her own kitchen, a pump in the yard, bedrooms for everyone, and her very own parlor with a real fireplace.

Sarah didn't share her mother's enthusiasm. She'd arrived in Mokelumne City with a heavy heart. During the month they'd been here, nothing had changed. The pain of losing Jack remained as strong as ever. On the many nights she couldn't sleep, she'd hungered for the memory of his lips on hers, pictured every single detail of his face. To make matters worse, she soon found life in this strange, new town dull and monotonous. In Fort Wayne, she'd been content with helping her mother run the household, going to church, meeting with her lady friends for an afternoon of chatter. But no longer. She just wasn't interested. How could she be after the endless excitement of Gold Creek? The days dragged by, but she kept her feelings to herself. Only Hiram guessed how miserable she was. "You're not happy here, are you?" he'd asked one day.

She could never lie to her brother. "I miss Gold Creek, working in the restaurant, joking with the miners. Remember the thrill when somebody made a big gold find? Just walking down the street was exciting."

"I know exactly what you mean." Hiram gave her a small, sad smile. "I miss it, too. God knows, I didn't want to leave."

Poor Hiram. Since they'd arrived at Mokelumne City, he'd been as miserable as she was. Becky nagged him constantly to use the gold nugget money to buy a farm and grow sugar beets. He didn't want to buy a farm. All he wanted was to get back to the goldfields, but sooner or later he'd undoubtedly give in to her constant badgering. Meanwhile, he spent long hours working for Uncle William and Pa in Bryan's General Store. He never complained, but Sarah knew he hated it.

"You miss Jack, too, don't you?" Hiram asked.

She nodded, not trusting herself to speak without a quiver in her voice. Hiram put his arms around her. "I'm so sorry, Sis. I really liked Jack. I could tell he loved you, just the way he looked at you sometimes. I don't understand why he let you go."

"Neither do I," she answered in a small whisper. She didn't tell anyone how she often dropped by the post office to see if Jack possibly had written her a letter. How foolish. He'd never said he'd write, so she shouldn't be surprised he never did.

Every day, ever since she arrived, she walked the one block from their house to the river where she could sit and watch the arrivals and departures of the schooners and whatever excitement was going on at the dock. It usually wasn't much. Ma sometimes came with her. Now, as they sat by the river, Sarah pulled her thoughts together. Her mother was talking and she'd better listen. "I'm inviting a guest for dinner tomorrow night. That nice Theodore Goetzmann. He's the one who owns the beet farm outside of town."

Oh no. Just as she'd done in Indiana, Ma was matchmaking again. Theodore Goetzmann was a very nice man. A widower with four children as she recalled. "I'm not interested. You know what I said."

Ma rolled her eyes skyward. "I know you're never marrying again, but it won't hurt to get better acquainted, will it? He's such a fine man. Who knows? You might find he suits you just fine."

You don't understand, Ma. I don't want a man who suits me just fine. I want a man like Jack who can make me melt inside just at the sight of him, and that's not Theodore Goetzmann. "Don't get your hopes up. I meant what I said, and I'm not changing my mind."

Ma's face fell, filling Sarah with instant regret. Florrie's disappearance still weighed heavily on everyone's mind but especially her mother. Not a day went by she didn't talk about Florrie. Sometimes her eyes teared and her voice broke from the grief of losing her younger daughter in such a cruel, unexpected way. Hiram's sketch of his missing sister now hung on the wall behind the counter in Bryan's General Store with a *have you seen this girl?* sign tacked underneath. Tattered though it was by now, Ma had insisted. "Miners come through here all the time. Maybe somebody's seen her. You never know."

Sarah touched her mother's shoulder. "I've been dying to cook my Beef Wellington. On second thought, it would be nice to have a guest for dinner."

* * * *

"Sturdy" would best describe Theodore Goetzmann. Sturdy arms, legs, torso. As the dictionary said: *substantially made or built; able to withstand stress or rough use.* A large man with massive shoulders, Theodore made a more than acceptable guest at dinner, bringing flowers to the ladies, making the proper small talk at the table. Becky especially liked him. "He's a catch if ever there was one, Sarah. If you don't grab him quick, someone else will."

Sarah could hardly keep from laughing. Theodore might be a wealthy farmer, kind and dependable, but he bored her to tears with his plodding humor and endless discourse concerning the history and growing of sugar beets. When Ma said she planned to invite him for dinner again, Sarah simply shrugged. "Do what you want. I really don't care."

During the month that followed, Sarah fell into the same routine she'd had in Indiana. Ma was as fragile as ever, but with Becky in the house, the two performed the household chores with time to spare. Sarah joined the one and only ladies' club in town, but whereas she used to enjoy an afternoon of gossip and giggles, she found herself bored beyond belief, wishing the afternoon would end so she could leave. Theodore Goetzmann became a frequent visitor at the Bryans' home. She became accustomed to his visits, even flattered by his attention. There were times when he wasn't so boring.

One evening after Theodore had joined them for dinner, he and Sarah strolled the block to the river and sat watching the sunset. He'd acted nervous all evening. When he took her hand, she already knew what he was going to say. "I've grown fond of you, Sarah, and would like you to be my wife. I promise you'll never want for anything. I offer you a good, secure life."

Marry another farmer? Oh, my God. If she married Theodore Goetzmann, she'd face a lifetime of boredom on a beet farm. She cringed at the thought, and yet, would it be any worse than the tedious life she led now? Jack was gone forever, nothing but a disturbing memory in more ways than one. She'd not heard one word from him, nor did she expect she ever would. She would never love again, so why not settle for a man who offered comfort and security? She looked into the beet farmer's kindly grey eyes. "I'll think about it, Theodore. I'll give you my answer soon."

The next day, Sarah was washing the breakfast dishes when Hiram, eyes bright with excitement, came rushing in. "I've got news. You must come to the store. Is Ma upstairs?"

Sarah nodded.

"Good. She doesn't need to know yet."

"Know what, Hiram?"

"Come to the store. You'll see."

Despite his bad limp, Hiram moved at a fast pace as they headed for Bryan's General Store. She had a hard time keeping up with him. Once there, he led her to a bearded, white-haired man standing next to the counter. Judging from the scruffy condition of his clothes, he'd been working a claim not so very long ago. His bloodshot eyes and bulbous red nose hinted at a fondness for alcohol. Hiram performed the introductions. The man's name was Ethan Cartwright, and he'd just arrived from Hangtown. Sarah couldn't imagine why her brother wanted her to meet this unkempt man until Hiram pointed to the sketch of Florrie still tacked on the wall behind the counter. "Tell my sister what you told me, Mr. Cartwright."

The miner blinked his rheumy old eyes and spoke to Sarah. "Yep, I'm sure that's your sister. If that ain't her, then she's a dead ringer."

Sarah stood amazed and shaken, using all her willpower to keep her jaw from dropping open. "You—you saw my sister? You're sure, Mr. Cartwright?"

"Like I said, a dead ringer."

Hiram asked, "You said you saw her in Hangtown?"

"Yep, Hangtown." The miner scratched his head. "The young lady was waiting tables at one of the saloons. T'was the Gold Star Saloon, best I can recall. That's smack dab in the middle of Hangtown. Nice girl. Name was Florrie. She served me a beer or two."

They asked more questions, but Ethan Cartwright could tell them nothing more. After he left, Sarah and Hiram looked at each other in stunned disbelief. "We've got to decide what to do," said Hiram.

Sarah placed her hand on her chest. "My heart's beating like crazy. Do you believe him?"

"I don't know what to believe. The old man seems sincere, but he's a boozer. Maybe he's making the whole thing up, some kind of alcoholic delusion."

"Maybe so, but what if he's not? What if he really did see Florrie?" A bubbly laugh escaped her lips. "What if we found her? Wouldn't that be wonderful?"

A worried expression crossed Hiram's face. "Let's not get too excited. I tend to believe him, but think about it. What would our sister be doing in Hangtown serving beer in a saloon? Does that make sense to you?"

Her spirits fell as quickly as they'd soared. "I guess not. You're right. He's just a crazy old man who's seeing things."

"So should we tell Ma and Pa?"

Her mind raced. She hated to get their hopes up, especially Ma. With her delicate health, how could she stand another disappointment? But what if, for some unimaginable reason, Florrie really was serving beer in a Hangtown saloon? Maybe this would be their only chance to find her. "We should tell them. Let them decide."

That evening, with the whole family gathered in the parlor, Hiram revealed the news about Florrie. Ma gasped and sank into the nearest chair.

Sarah hastened to say, "It's just a rumor."

Hiram added, "Ethan Cartwright is a drunk. He could very well have been seeing things, and he probably was."

Ma bent forward as if the weight of the world sat on her shoulders. She started slowly swinging her head back and forth, as if in complete denial of their words. She finally spoke in a strangled voice barely above a whisper. "Ethan Cartwright is God's gift to me. In my heart, I've always known Florrie wasn't dead. For whatever reason, I know she's there in Hangtown."

Pa looked dubious. "I'm not so sure, Luzena. Can we believe a rumor told by a drunkard?"

Ma clenched her fists. "She's there, Frank. I know it. I want my daughter back. You've got to go get her."

"Of course, if you feel that strongly." He drew a resigned breath. "All right, I'll go."

Sarah heard the hesitation in her father's voice, and no wonder. His health had deteriorated to where it wasn't much better than her mother's. There were days when he came home early from the store because he got dizzy and had to lie down.

"I don't think you should go, Pa."

Hiram's firm young jaw clenched with resolve. "I agree with Sarah. I'm the one to go."

Becky, who had been sitting on the sofa, shot up like a canon. "You will do no such thing, Hiram Bryan. Your place is here with me."

Sarah waited for what was sure to come. Yet again, her spineless brother would give in to his bossy wife.

Hiram took his time answering. A strange expression came over his face, one Sarah had never seen before. It contained a combination of grit, resolve, and annoyance. "That's enough, Becky. I'm going to Hangtown. Is that understood?"

Amid gasps of surprise, Hiram limped from the room.

Becky stared after him. "Well, did you ever!"

About time. Sarah followed after her brother and found him sitting on the porch steps. Without a word, she sat beside him.

Hiram cast a warning look in her direction. "You don't have to say it. It was about time I stood up to my wife." His expression softened. "And, yes, you had something to do with it."

Sarah would have liked to discuss her part in his bold decision, but she had something more important to say. "I've thought it over. I'm coming with you."

Her brother's eyebrows raised high. "Really? That's fine with me, but neither Ma nor Pa is going to like it. You may be twenty-nine, but Pa still thinks of you as his precious little girl who's got to be sheltered from the big, bad world."

"Even after all I've been through?"

"Yeah, even after all you've been through." A small smile touched his lips. "That includes your little escapade helping the Chinese girl."

"You know about that?"

"Did you think you could keep a secret in a town like Gold Creek? Of course, I knew. Everyone knew except Ma and Pa. And that crazy Au Fung, I hope." He grew serious. "Ma won't want you to go."

"If I can help find Florrie, she'll understand." She grinned at her brother. "She'll do anything to find her favorite daughter."

Hiram ignored her attempt at humor. "Didn't Jack McCoy say he was going to Hangtown?" He slanted an inquisitive glance. "Do you want to see him again?"

Leave it to her perceptive brother to ask a soul-wrenching question. She'd give him an honest answer. "Jack McCoy is out of my life forever. If I met him on the street, I'd pass him by without a word."

"Really?"

"Absolutely. We are done forever."

Chapter 13

"Almost there." Hiram flicked the reins over the oxen and glanced at Sarah, sitting beside him. "Hangtown, dead ahead."

She could hardly sit still. "Just think, Hiram, we might soon be seeing Florrie."

"Let's hope this journey hasn't been for nothing."

It hadn't been easy. Pa hadn't yet sold the oxen and wagon, so they were able to travel in relative comfort. Still, they'd left Mokelumne City nearly a week ago. The road leading into the Sierra Nevada Mountains became rougher as they traveled through huge groves of pines and evergreens, past streams full of icy water that had recently been snow. As they approached the main street of town, she grew ever more anxious. "What if she's really here? What will we say?"

A flash of humor crossed Hiram's face. "We might want to ask what she was doing in Hangtown serving beer."

"Be serious." She gave her brother a friendly nudge. "If what Mr. Cartwright said is true, then she must have been kidnapped or forced in some way."

"We'll know soon enough, won't we?"

Night was falling as they came to the main street of town. "Look how big it is, at least twice the size of Gold Creek," Sarah remarked. Hiram drove the wagon slowly past stores of all descriptions lining both sides. A blacksmith's shop, stable, butcher shop, two general stores, three banks, and countless hotels and saloons. As in Gold Creek, the street teemed with activity. Horses, buggies, and wagons jammed both lanes. Miners on foot crowded the wooden sidewalks. Men were everywhere, but like Gold Creek, women were scarce. As they drove, Sarah impatiently examined the sign on each saloon. El Dorado. Mansion House. The Oriental. And then—she clutched Hiram's arm. "There on the left—The Gold Star Hotel & Saloon."

"I see it." Hiram tried to act his usual unruffled self, but the rasp of excitement in his voice gave him away. He pulled the wagon to a stop in an empty space not far from the wide-open double doors of the Gold Star. "You're sure you want to do this right now? Maybe we should find a place to camp first, and then—"

"Now!" Sarah scrambled from the wagon and hastened across the muddy street, Hiram close behind. A piano tinkled as she walked through the doorway. She stopped to adjust her eyes to the dim, early evening light. The saloon was already more than half-full. Men sat at round, wooden tables playing poker, drinking their whiskey or beer. Across the room, a long, dark mahogany bar stretched from one wall to nearly the other. Two bartenders worked behind it. Could Florrie be working here today? Her gaze swept the room. Waiters were carrying huge trays of pitchers of beer to the tables. All men. Not a waitress among them.

They walked to the bar. "What'll ya have?" asked the older of the bartenders, a heavyset man with a drooping mustache and a white apron covering his big belly.

"We don't want a drink. We're looking for someone." Hiram pulled the tattered sketch of Florrie from his pocket and handed it to the bartender. "We're looking for our sister. Have you seen her?"

The man behind the bar took his time examining the picture. "Hmmm." He scratched his chin. Finally he looked up. "Sorry, can't say that I have."

"Her name is Florrie," Sarah said. "We heard she was working here, that she was serving beer."

The bartender shook his head and slapped the picture on the bar. "Haven't seen her. She couldn't have worked at the Gold Star. They hire only waiters, always have. The only women who work here are—"

"Jess, let me take a look." The other bartender, a younger man with a fresh, clean-shaven face had been pouring beer into pitchers with an ear cocked to their conversation. He came over and picked up the picture. At first glance, his brows flickered. Sarah and Hiram exchanged anxious glances. Could it be he knew her?

The older bartender frowned. "We don't know her, never saw her, *right, Ed?*"

Ed, the younger one, got a stubborn set to his chin. "I don't see it that way, Jess. This here's her family. If they want to know where she is, then we ought to tell them."

Sarah's heart leaped. "Then you know her?"

Ed looked up from the picture. "Her name's Florrie?"

"Yes, Florrie!"

Jess, the older bartender, gave a careless shrug. "None of my business." He walked away.

Sarah hardly noticed. She waited with bated breath for Ed to speak again. "If her name's Florrie, I know her."

"Did she work here?" Hiram asked.

"She did, but only for a little while. She's gone now. I can tell you where she is, though."

"Please do." Blood pounded in her temples. How she managed to get a word out, she didn't know. She clutched Hiram's arm. He, too, looked as if he was trying to control his emotions.

Ed continued, "It's on the next street, a big, two story, wooden frame with a red door. She's there."

"Is she all right? She's not sick or anything?"

"Far as I know, she's fine."

"Is there an address?" Hiram asked.

Ed got a strange look on his face. "You don't need an address. Go one block over to Pacific Street. Turn right, look for the red door. That's all I can tell you." Abruptly, he turned and went back to pouring beer.

They made a quick exit from the Gold Star Saloon. With a springy bounce in her step, Sarah headed for the wagon. "I can't believe this," she called over her shoulder. "I never thought it would be this easy."

Hiram followed close behind. "Neither did I. Only…"

"Only what?"

"I've got a bad feeling, Sarah."

After she crossed the busy street, she turned to face him. "About what?"

Hiram's face was unreadable. "I don't know exactly, but brace yourself. You'd better be ready for anything."

They had reached the house on Pacific Street and were approaching the front door when it burst open and a drunken man in gentleman's clothing staggered out and down the steps. They stepped aside to let him pass and continued to the porch where a stern-faced, middle-aged woman met them at the door. She wore a fancy maid's costume—starched white cap, black dress, frilly apron tied in a big bow in the back. She smiled at Hiram, caught sight of Sarah, and frowned. "What do you want?"

Sarah spoke up. "We're looking for Florrie Bryan. Is she here?"

"No."

The maid started to shut the door, but before she could, Hiram stuck his foot over the threshold. "Florrie Bryan is our sister. We know she's here, and we want to see her."

The maid hesitated, gave a curt nod, and swung the door wide. "Wait in the hall. I'll tell Mrs. Northcutt you're here."

The heavy aroma of jasmine met Sarah's nostrils as she and Hiram stepped into a marble-tiled entrance hall that had a wide, carpeted staircase leading to the second floor. Soft piano music played from somewhere, accompanied by the murmur of voices and tinkling glasses. Lips pursed with annoyance, the maid disappeared up the staircase. "What is this place?" Sarah asked.

Hiram nervously looked around. "I hope it's not what I think it is."

The piano music came from a room off the hallway. Sarah had to take a peek. She stepped close and peered into what must be the parlor. *Oh, my.* This wasn't the modestly furnished room she expected. An expanse of plush red carpeting covered the floor. A large, crystal chandelier hung from the ornately carved ceiling. Gilded mirrors and gaudy paintings lined the walls, and rich, red velvet drapes covered the windows. A huge portrait hung behind a mahogany bar at one end of the room. In it, a beefy, completely nude woman lay in a languorous pose propped on one elbow, chin in hand, bemused smile playing on her ruby lips. Every man in the room was nicely dressed, no miner's scroungy attire among them. Most of the women wore gaudy gowns, so low cut it was a wonder their bosoms weren't totally exposed. A couple of women wore no gown at all, just a lacy chemise and ruffled garters. One was sitting on a gentleman's lap, ruffling his hair.

Hiram peered over her shoulder, took one look, and pulled her back from the door. "I knew it," he muttered. "Sarah, don't look."

She didn't argue. "What is this place?"

"We're in a brothel, a bordello, a house of ill repute, whatever you want to call it."

A brothel? Goose flesh rippled up her back. She wanted to turn and run, but would do no such thing. "But what is Florrie doing here?"

Before he could answer, a large, florid-faced woman somewhere in her fifties appeared. She looked as if she was going to a fancy ball, her white hair swept into an elaborate coiffure, her black velvet gown embroidered with glittering spangles. She gave them a tight-lipped smile. "Hello, I'm Mrs. Northcutt, and you are?"

Sarah introduced herself and Hiram. "Florrie is our sister. We want to see her." Why had this feeling of foreboding crept over her? She'd found Florrie, and that was wonderful, but who was this unfriendly woman, and what was going on?

"You want to see Florrie? Very well, I'll find out if she wants to see you." Mrs. Northcutt leveled a hostile gaze. "But I warn you, she may not. In which case, I shall ask you to leave." Shoulders rigid with displeasure, she disappeared up the staircase.

Wordlessly, they waited in the hallway. Sarah couldn't think what to say and neither could Hiram. Long minutes went by—five, ten—Sarah wasn't sure. Twice someone knocked on the front door. Twice the maid let in a gentleman who headed straight to the parlor. At last Mrs. Northcutt came down the staircase, a frown on her face. "She says she'll see you. Go up the stairs, two doors to the right. Don't take too long. We're going to be busy tonight."

Sarah mounted the staircase, Hiram close behind. She ought to be thrilled and excited. Instead, she couldn't shake the numb feeling in the pit of her stomach that something was wrong. At the second door to the right, they stopped and looked at each other. "I don't know what to expect," she whispered.

"That makes two of us. Here goes." Hiram knocked sharply.

"Come in!"

Florrie's voice. Hiram swung open the door. They stepped into a large, lavishly furnished bedroom that smelled of heavy jasmine perfume. Florrie stood in the center of the room dressed in a long, beautiful blue satin gown, hair flowing down her back. "Sarah, Hiram!" Before they could say a word, she flung herself into their arms, face wet with tears. "Oh, it's so good to see you!"

For Sarah, the first few minutes passed in a blur. Amid her tears, Florrie couldn't stop talking. She had missed them terribly, Ma and Pa, too. She'd feared she would never see them again, and how had they ever found her? Sarah had to wipe away her own tears. With Hiram's help, she described their heartbreaking search, and how an old miner named Ethan Cartwright gave them the clue that helped find her. When the first wild exhilaration of their reunion began to wane, Florrie rang for a maid and ordered tea. Now the three sat at a small, round table with a velvet, red-tasseled cloth, sipping from teacups of delicate china that must have been very expensive indeed.

In all the excitement, Sarah hadn't looked closely at her sister. Now, as she gazed at Florrie, she had to conceal her surprise. The old, thick-waisted Florrie with the pudgy figure was gone. Her fancy blue dress defined her now-slender waist and hips while its low-cut neckline revealed far more bosom than Ma would have approved. Her hair was different. The old Florrie never bothered much to fix it, just gathered it in a bun with no style at all. Now it cascaded in lovely dark waves down her back with little curls framing her face that... *Oh, my God. Florrie's wearing makeup.* Those rosy cheeks couldn't be natural. They had to be rouged. Those crimson lips couldn't be natural, either. Ma would faint if she discovered a daughter of hers using makeup like some brazen hussy. And yet, Florrie looked so much better than Sarah had ever seen her. Not only her face and figure had improved, so had her attitude. No more slumping shoulders. Head high, shoulders back, she brimmed with a confidence she'd never had before. She still wasn't beautiful and never would be, but the improvement was remarkable.

They spoke only in excited generalities until Hiram asked, "What happened, Florrie? Why did you disappear? Why did that Indian have your necklace? We got it back, you know."

"You have my necklace? That's wonderful. I'll tell you what happened." Florrie gazed toward the ceiling and sighed, as if she was dredging up bad memories. "It was the Indians who kidnapped me. That day, I'd gone for a walk in the woods. I'd gone farther than I thought when here came some Indians riding toward me. I tried to run, but it was too late. They grabbed me, bound my hands together, and made me ride behind one of them on his horse. I fought as best I could. I screamed and screamed but nobody heard. They were horribly rough. We rode for days—you can imagine how frightened I was—until finally one night I was able to escape. I was found by a man named Hannibal Palmer. You've heard of him? He owns this house and many others. He's the one who brought me here to Hangtown. At first I was staying at the Gold Star Hotel. That's where the old miner probably saw me. After a short time, I moved here, and I've been here ever since."

Hiram leveled a piercing gaze at his sister. "Florrie, this is a whorehouse."

She thrust out her chin. "I know that. I work here."

Sarah gasped. "You're admitting you work here as a...a...?"

"Sister of joy? Lady of the night? *Prostitute?* Yes, I admit it." Florrie shifted her gaze away from direct contact with their eyes. "I had no choice. They forced me into it."

Despite her shock, Sarah searched for words of comfort. She took her sister's hand and squeezed it tight. "We're here now, Florrie." Never had she spoken more from her heart than at this moment. "Thank God, we found you. I'm horrified at what you've had to endure, but you're safe now."

Hiram leaped to his feet. "Get your things. We're getting out of here, and that Mrs. Northcutt—she's the madam, isn't she?—had better not try to stop us."

Florrie remained seated. "It's not that easy."

"Why not?" Sarah asked. "You don't have to worry about Ma and Pa. They'll never know you worked in this awful place. Nobody will know. We'll make up a story. Maybe you didn't escape the Indians until just today. Maybe you got hit on the head and lost your memory. Maybe—"

"Stop." Florrie held up a restraining hand. "You don't understand."

"What don't I understand?"

Florrie heaved a resigned sigh. "What you don't understand is I don't want to go home. I like it here. I like doing what I do."

Sarah looked at Hiram. His mouth hung open in amazement. She stared at her sister until she could find words. "I can't believe this. Did I hear you right?"

"Yes, you did." Florrie flung her head back, a gesture of defiance Sarah well remembered from the old days when her stubborn sister insisted on having her way. "All my life I was the ugly sister." Sarah opened her mouth to protest, but Florrie continued on. "Don't argue, it's true. I lived in your shadow, Sarah. You were the one with the pretty face and figure. You were the one with all the beaux. I was the ugly one nobody paid any attention to. You think I didn't care?" Florrie arose from her chair, walked to the center of the room, and spread her arms. "That's all behind me now. Look at me!" She performed a pirouette, her satin skirt swirling about her in graceful folds. "I'm beautiful now. They give me stylish clothes. A maid does my hair. And yes, Sarah, I saw that look you gave me. I wear makeup now, and love it. Everyone loves me here. I dine on gourmet meals, drink the most expensive champagne. My steady customers are all fine gentlemen who pay a lot of money for the pleasure of my company."

"Oh, Florrie." Sarah pressed her hand to her mouth. She could think of nothing to say.

Hiram stared at his sister. "I can't believe I'm hearing this. You mean you actually like working in a brothel?"

Florrie flopped her hands out. "I'm here, aren't I? I will doubtless go straight to hell for saying the forbidden word, but I also enjoy the sex." She broke into a wicked little grin. "I've shocked you. Sorry, that's just the way it is." She came back to the table and sat down, her expression suddenly somber. "I know how you feel, and I'm sorry that you've come all this way for nothing. I'm sorry about Ma and Pa, too. You'll have to tell them—" Her voice caught, but she quickly went on, "But this is my life now. Please be happy for me. I wouldn't change it for the world."

Up to this moment, Sarah had blocked the truth from her mind. Now, as Florrie's words sunk in, a tide of anger swept through her. No getting around it, her sister had become a prostitute, had sunk to the lowest level a woman could sink, and that was an undeniable fact. She got up from the table. "You want me to be happy that my one and only sister works in a brothel? Her voice was shaking. She didn't care. "You have broken my heart, Florrie Bryan, and Ma and Pa's, too." She looked at Hiram. "I'm done. Come on, let's get out of here."

Chapter 14

They found a sprawling campground not far from town where round tents, square tents, plank hovels, and primitive log cabins dotted the wooded area in haphazard fashion. Their minds still benumbed by their encounter with Florrie, they hardly spoke. Hiram parked the wagon, fed the oxen, and pitched the tent. Sarah built a campfire, went for water, and cooked their dinner. Not until they had nearly finished eating did they touch upon the subject hanging over them like a black cloud.

Hiram took a bite of beans and slowly shook his head. "My sister's a whore. I'm saying the words, but I still can't believe it."

Sarah put her fork down. "I feel like I've been kicked in the stomach by a mule. What'll we tell Ma and Pa?"

"That's simple. We'll just say we couldn't find her." Hiram peered at her quizzically. "Do you believe Florrie's story?"

"What do you mean?"

"Remember those lies Florrie used to tell when she was little? I could always tell, and I still can. That story she told about getting kidnapped by the Indians is hogwash."

Sarah had been so shocked by her sister's announcement, she'd given it no further thought. "Now that I think about it…yes, I suspect she was lying."

Hiram cocked an eyebrow. "She's kidnapped by Indians and somehow escapes? Sounds fishy. It's like Florrie to lie because she's covering up something."

"But what? At this point why should we care?"

"You're right, why should we? We should be getting home. We'll leave tomorrow."

Of course they should go home. Florrie was a lost cause. No point in staying, yet Hiram's remarks had set her to thinking. If Florrie was lying, and she probably was, then she was hiding something. And if she was hiding something, Sarah wanted to know what it was. "I don't want to go home yet."

"Why not? What's left for us here? Florrie's not going to change her mind."

"The more I think about it, the more I'm realizing Florrie was lying. At the very least, I suspect she left a lot out. We need to find out the truth, if for no other reason than Ma and Pa deserve to know."

Hiram eyed her suspiciously. "Jack McCoy's in Hangtown. Is that why—?"

"Absolutely not. I hardly think of him anymore." Not true. She thought of Jack all the time, but Hiram needed to know her main reason for wanting to stay was Florrie. "There's something she's not telling. I'm going back to that…that *place* tomorrow. I'll talk to her again. You don't have to go. More likely she'll open up if it's just me."

"Fine with me." Hiram gave her the good-natured smile that always touched her heart. "But are you sure you want to go alone? It's a brothel, after all."

"I've been there once, and I can do it again. Don't worry." Poor Hiram, always so concerned, so helpful. He deserved something special, and she'd just thought what it would be. "Guess what I'm going to do tomorrow. I'm going to bake you an apple pie."

Hiram beamed. "Do you think you can find any apples in this town?"

"Real apples or dried apples, you're going to have your pie, my dear brother." Her spirits lifted, not by much, but at least she'd gone a bit beyond the shock and gloom of this terrible day. Tomorrow she'd see Florrie again and maybe, just maybe, come up with the truth. What it was, she didn't know, but how could it be worse than what she already knew?

The next morning, Sarah walked into town to shop at the general store. She would wait until afternoon to visit Florrie. As Hiram pointed out, they worked late at such places, and Florrie would still be sleeping. Bright sunshine and crisp mountain air with its hint of pine trees made this a perfect day, but she couldn't enjoy it. The full impact of her sister's fall from grace was still sinking in. *My sister is a prostitute. How awful. How unthinkable.* The general store was just ahead. She must concentrate on her grocery list and—

"Sarah?"

Jack's voice came from behind her. She froze in her tracks. For a brief moment, she closed her eyes as painful memories flooded her mind: his last words, *I've enjoyed knowing you and all your family,* so cold, so impersonal; those nights when she couldn't sleep for thinking of the times she'd been in his arms making a complete fool of herself; those endless days after they reached Mokelumne City when she waited for a letter that never came.

She turned to face him. There he stood in that same easy, self-assured pose, his casual smile telling her how much he didn't care, how much he'd never cared, and how stupid she'd been to have believed he ever would. She tipped her head, pasted a smile of nonchalance on her face. "Why, Jack McCoy! How lovely to see you again." She let sarcasm drip from her voice.

He drew in a shaking breath. "Sarah, my God, I... What are you doing here?"

"How could you possibly care?"

"Of course I care. I—"

"Don't bother." She made no attempt to hide the bristling anger in her voice. "Sorry, I'm busy. I don't have time to talk."

She started away, but he took her arm. "Sarah, listen, you don't understand."

She jerked her arm away. "I understand perfectly, Mr. McCoy, and I want you to understand I want nothing more to do with you, not now, not ever. Is that clear?"

Carrying the image of his stricken face, she turned away and headed for the general store.

Later in the morning, after she'd returned to the camp, Sarah built a fire outside their tent and started baking the apple pie she'd promised Hiram. By now she'd calmed down. Earlier, when she first entered the general store, she'd been a near-hysterical mess, heart pounding, mind seething with such an anger she could hardly think straight. What a shock to see Jack again. Coming on top of Florrie's devastating news, it was a wonder she'd managed to compose herself enough to shop, but thank goodness, she had. Jack McCoy was nothing but a bad memory. She wouldn't let him spoil her day.

Same as Gold Creek, she found sky-high prices, but by now she was used to them. At least she'd found flour, dried apples, sugar, cinnamon— everything she needed for the pie.

Hiram appeared just as she pulled the pie iron from the fire. After one sniff of the apple-cinnamon aroma wafting beneath his nose, he broke into a broad grin. Sarah cut them each a generous piece. They were still eating when Jake, their thin, gaunt-faced neighbor from the nearest tent appeared. Like many of the miners, he hadn't been eating right, probably nothing but beef jerky and beans. He cast a longing gaze at the remains of the pie. "Ma'am, I'd sell my soul for a piece of that."

How could she say no? She was reaching for the knife when Hiram spoke up. "We'll sell you a piece for a dollar."

As Jake hurriedly dug in his pocket, another neighbor arrived. Two more soon followed, and all practically salivated over Sarah's pie. "Let them have it," Hiram said. "A dollar each. You can always bake another."

The pie disappeared in no time, leaving them richer by several dollars. Hiram grinned. "Maybe you should go into the pie business."

"Maybe I should." Hiram might have been jesting, but he had a good idea. She'd think about it tomorrow. Right now she had other things to consider. It was time to visit that brothel and have another talk with her sister.

At two o'clock in the afternoon, all was quiet at the house with the red door on Pacific Street. Hiram was with her. "I'll wait right here in front," he said, "in case something goes wrong."

Despite the tensing nerves in her stomach, Sarah smiled with more confidence than she felt. "It's not every day I force my way into a brothel, but don't worry, I'll be back in no time." She went up the porch steps and knocked on the door. The same maid answered. "I've come to see my sister." She quickly stepped inside, brought her finger to her lips, and blew a quiet "Shhh" at the maid. "I'll only be a minute. No one needs to know." Not waiting for an answer, she headed for the staircase, walking fast, not looking back. If her luck held out, the maid wouldn't rush to Mrs. Northcutt and tattle.

Good. No one came after her. She reached Florrie's door and quietly knocked. When her sister opened it, she stepped inside. "Can we talk?" When Florrie nodded and closed the door, she breathed a huge sigh of relief.

Soon, they sat drinking tea, same as yesterday, only now Florrie was dressed in an elegant cream-colored silk wrapper embroidered with tiny pink flowers, matching silk slippers on her feet. She gave Sarah a curious gaze. "I'm surprised you came back."

Sarah took a leisurely sip of tea. Above all, she didn't want to appear intimidating. "First of all, I was hoping you might have changed your mind."

Florrie shook her head and giggled. "I wish you could have seen the lovely time I had last night. We had a party. We have lots of parties, and I'm always treated like a queen. So in answer to your question, no, I haven't changed my mind, and I'm not going to."

"I can see that." Sarah gave her a grudging nod. "We'll say no more on the subject. In case you're wondering, Hiram and I have decided we won't tell Ma and Pa we found you. Far as they're concerned, we made a useless trip to Hangtown, came all this way for nothing. They'll be disappointed, but not nearly as much as if they heard the truth."

Florrie's smile disappeared. "Don't think for a minute I don't miss them terribly, but it's too late. I can never go back."

"It's never too late, little sister," Sarah said in a gentle voice. "No matter what happens, you must always remember that." She sat back in her chair and looked her sister in the eye. "Just so we'll know, I want you to tell me what really happened."

"I don't know what you mean."

"Yes, you do. That story you gave us—getting kidnapped by the Indians. Hiram calls it hogwash, and I think so, too. I'd like the truth. You owe us that much, don't you think?"

Florrie opened her mouth to protest, but then seemed to change her mind. She picked up the teapot. "More tea?" When Sarah nodded, she refilled their cups with great deliberation, clearly giving herself time to think. "I was going easy on you. If you heard the real truth, you'd be beyond horrified."

"I want the truth. I deserve the truth."

"You're sure?"

Sarah nodded.

"Then brace yourself. I'll tell you everything." Florrie set the pot down. "You're not going to like it."

Sarah's heart jumped in her chest, but she managed a calm, "Try me."

Florrie tipped her head and looked at the ceiling, as if she was trying to get her thoughts in order. "It all goes way back before we left for California. Remember how shy I was? Shy, quiet, dull, boring, and not much to look at either. I had no beaux and claimed I didn't want any, but I did. I used to cry myself to sleep at night. I so wanted a man to love me, like you had, Sarah. I was so jealous of you and all those men who were after you. And then, do you remember Charlie, our handyman?"

"Of course I remember him. He had a cocky attitude, but he was a hard worker." *Charlie*? She would never have guessed. "What are you saying?"

"Remember he had that room back of the stable?" Florrie grinned mischievously. "This is going to shock you, but many's the time I sneaked out there. You never knew. No one knew. He wasn't much to look at, but he was awfully good in bed."

Sarah fought to conceal her astonishment and keep her face straight. "So go on."

"Charlie got me in a family way."

What! "You mean you...?"

Florrie nodded. "When we started for California, I was expecting a child, only I didn't know it. If I had, I'd probably be married to Charlie by now, so maybe it's better that I didn't know. We were well underway before I realized. When I did, I was horrified. It was awful. I couldn't tell Ma and Pa. You know how shocked and appalled they would have been. Time was going by, and I didn't know what to do."

"You could have told me. I would have helped."

"I thought of telling you, but what could you have done? I'd gotten myself into a fine mess, and no one, not even you, could have gotten me out. By the time we reached Fort Hall, I was beginning to show. Thank God for those stupid aprons we all wore, but even they couldn't conceal my condition forever. That day I disappeared, I really had gone for a walk in the woods, just as I said, only I was thinking I would kill myself. The trouble was I didn't know how to go about it. Besides, I really didn't want to die. That's when a man named Johnny Valentine came along, just as I left the woods and started walking back to the train. He was traveling alone—owned a small wagon and a couple of oxen, hell bent for the goldfields. We got to talking, and, well, he liked me, so he invited me to join him, and I did."

Sarah couldn't stay silent. "Didn't you give a thought to your family? We stayed behind because of you, let the train go on without us, so there we were stuck alone in the wilderness. Ma insisted. You have no idea how frantic she was. She got another of those horrible asthma attacks and would have died if it hadn't been for—" She must stop thinking about Jack McCoy and all the good things he'd done. "You caused us all kinds of grief. I see now it's not over yet."

Florrie lifted her chin. "Do you want to hear the rest or not?"

She'd better calm down or she'd never hear the whole story. "Go on. I won't interrupt again, I promise."

"Johnny Valentine took me to Gold Creek. At first he'd been nice to me, but then he started getting mean. Nothing I said or did could please him. He took to shouting at me, and worse. He stole from me, too. When we met those Indians, he took my beautiful necklace away from me and traded it for some beaver skins. Later he sold them and kept the money."

Sarah recalled Beatrice Butler's reaction when she saw Florrie's picture. "When you were in Gold Creek, did you ever eat at a restaurant called The Miners' Heaven?"

"I remember it well. We got into a big argument there. He almost hit me."

So that explained Beatrice's reluctance to say she'd seen Florrie. Obviously, she hadn't wanted to get involved. "Did he ever actually hit you?"

Florrie nodded and hung her head. "That's not all. He had his way with me any time he wanted, which was just about every day, and it was... well, just plain brutal. After a few days, we left Gold Creek and headed for Hangtown. By the time we got here, I wanted desperately to get away from him, but I couldn't. I had no money, no nothing. As it turned out, I needn't have worried. We were camped close to here. The day after we arrived, Johnny sent me to shop for groceries. When I got back, he was gone and so were the oxen and wagon. He'd sold them and took off for the goldfields."

"Nice fellow."

Florrie nodded grimly. "Wasn't he, though? So there I was, stuck in a strange town, not knowing a soul, nothing to eat, no money, and...and..."

"Expecting a baby," Sarah finished for her, voice brimming with sympathy. "I can't imagine how awful it must have been for you."

"It was pretty bad, all right. I'd never been hungry before. With the baby, it was even worse. I walked into town, pretty near starving. The first place I came to was the Gold Star. I went around to the back thinking I'd look for something to eat in the garbage. Someone must have seen me and told Mr. Palmer—Mr. Hannibal Palmer who owns the Gold Star and a lot more. What a wonderful man. He personally came out to get me, brought me inside, took me to the dining room, and ordered the most scrumptious meal I ever had in my life. Raw oysters, curried sausages, brandy peach pastry—anything I wanted. When I asked how I could repay him, he said I could work for him as a dancehall girl." Florrie's eyes went bright. She clapped her hands together. "Such fun! I got to dress real fancy, danced every dance. I loved it when the men crowded around, dying to pay a whole dollar for a three-minute dance. By then I was really showing, but it didn't matter. When a man's been out in the wilderness and hasn't seen a woman for months, he's not going to care how thick-waisted she is. I made good money, but when I saw how much the girls on the third floor were making—"

"The prostitutes you mean?"

"Better to call us 'ladies of easy virtue.' When I asked Mr. Palmer, he said he'd be glad to try me out. As you can see, I worked out fine."

"Wait!" Sarah raised a protesting hand. "This wonderful man, this Hannibal Palmer, he's the one who hired you to be a prostitute?"

"No, no, no." Florrie fervently shook her head. "It was my idea. He never pressured me at all. Like I told you, I love what I do. I'm good at what I do." A prideful smile touched her lips. "I started my career at the Gold Star where they cater to lowlifes—whoever walks through the door. It wasn't long before Mr. Palmer saw how good I was and sent me here." She made a sweeping gesture with her arm. "This is the crème-de-la-crème of brothels. Everyone's screened. Only the finest gentlemen are allowed in."

Sarah let out a groan and slumped back in her chair. "Oh, my God, Florrie. Don't you see...?" What was the use? Clearly, nothing she could say would change her sister's mind. With a despairing sigh, she asked, "What about the baby?"

"The last couple of months, I couldn't work. Mr. Palmer was very good about that. Finally I went into labor. It was awful. I've never had such pain in all my life."

"What did you have?"

"A little girl, but she was stillborn."

Just when she thought Florrie's story couldn't get any worse, it did. This last took her breath away. "I am so, so sorry. You must have been devastated."

"I couldn't have kept her. Even so, I felt terrible. I never saw her, but I did give her a name. I called her Adeline, Addy for short. Is that a nice name, do you think?"

"That's a lovely name."

Florrie leaned back, suppressing a sigh. "That's all behind me now. Sorry I lied to you. Now you've heard the truth, you can understand why I will never go back to my old life. I know you feel sorry for me, but quite frankly, it's I who feel sorry for you." She cocked her head and gave her sister a saucy grin. "If you get tired of your exciting life in Mokelumne City, let me know, and I'll get you a job."

Sarah broke into laughter. It was either that or break into useless tears. "I'll keep that in mind. You never know." She gave up. Any further persuasion would be useless. Florrie loved this life, and nothing would change her.

Sarah kept the rest of the conversation on a light note. When it came time to leave, Florrie begged her to please write when she got home and let her know how the family was doing. Sarah promised she would, even though her "lost" sister couldn't reciprocate. After one final, heartfelt hug, she left with a smile on her face, wishing her sister well.

Not until she was outside the door and headed for the staircase did she whisper a soft, "Oh, Florrie," and wipe away a tear. Nothing could be done about it, though. So sad about the baby. *Addy, my little niece, I'll never get to know you.* She paused at the top of the stairs and looked around. She'd rather not run into anyone, especially the dreadful Mrs. Northcutt. No one in sight. She was halfway down the stairs when a tiny maid scurried across the entry hall below, a pile of towels in her arms. Something familiar…where had she seen her before? She couldn't believe it! She stopped and called softly, "Anming?"

The maid looked up, her expression bewildered. When she saw who it was, a look of astonishment crossed her face, followed by a delighted smile. "Sarah!" she said in a loud whisper, "What are you doing here?"

Sarah hurried down the staircase and hugged Anming, towels and all. "It's a long story. What are *you* doing here?"

The little Chinese girl backed away and set the towels on the staircase. "I couldn't stand working in Fatt Cheng's laundry for practically no pay."

"But a brothel?"

Anming shrugged. "At least it's better than twelve hours a day of steam and hot irons. After what I've been through, nothing here can shock me." She frowned in puzzlement. "What are you doing here? You're not—?"

"Oh, no. My sister is here. Her name's Florrie."

Anming's eyes went wide. She slapped a hand over her mouth. "Florrie's your sister?"

Sarah nodded. "I tried to get her to leave, but she won't go. It breaks my heart."

"You know about the baby?"

"Little Addy was my niece. So sad she died."

Anming's brows drew together in a frown. "Are you sure? I heard Florrie's baby isn't dead. They took her away."

Sarah caught her breath. "Addy's alive?"

"Anming!" Here came Mrs. Northcutt stomping down the staircase. "Get back to work. You're not allowed to talk."

"Yes, ma'am." Anming cast an apologetic look at Sarah. She picked up the towels and hurried away.

Mrs. Northcutt huffed herself up. Her face got red. She glared at Sarah. "Get out. You have no business here. If you come here again, I guarantee you'll regret it."

Sarah didn't doubt her. She hadn't seen a guard yet, but doubtless they were around and no doubt armed. Anming had disappeared. Nothing to do now but leave with as much dignity as she could muster. She wished she could come up with some scathing remark that would put the madam in her place, but nothing came to mind. Head held high, she walked out the front door, not saying another word.

Hiram waited outside. He took one look at her face and asked, "My God, what happened?"

She had to get away from this horrible place. "Wait 'til we get back to camp, and I'll tell you."

Chapter 15

Sarah waited until they were sitting by their campfire before she related the astonishing news about Florrie. When she finished, Hiram frowned in bewilderment. "She had a baby? Then it died, but maybe it didn't? What are we supposed to believe?"

"I'm not sure, but I tend to believe Anming."

"So do I. Florrie's full of lies."

"Maybe she's not lying. In a place like that, they wouldn't have wanted Florrie to keep the baby. What would be easier than to tell her the baby died? Without her knowing, they could have taken it away and—"

"And what?" Hiram flashed a rare look of anger. "What kind of a world do we live in that people could steal a baby from its mother?"

Sarah nodded a silent agreement. "I've got to talk to Anming again, but how? Mrs. Northcutt warned me never to come back. She wouldn't let you in, either. Even if one of us did get in, how could we find Anming? By sheer luck, I saw her in the hallway, but that's not likely to happen again."

"Any chance Anming might come to us?"

"How can she? I never had the chance to tell her where we're staying."

Hiram grimaced. "We don't have much money left. Maybe we should just go home."

"Wait, I can hardly think straight." Sarah placed her fingers on her temples. So many things to consider. She had to get organized, think of a plan. "We can't leave yet. If Anming's right, we've got a little niece out there somewhere. Think of it, Hiram, Florrie's baby, our own flesh and blood. What would Ma think if we knew her very own granddaughter was out there somewhere, and we didn't try to find her?"

Hiram took a moment before he answered, "What was I thinking of? We should stay, at least until we talk to Anming and find out what she knows. Truth be told, I..." In a wistful voice he continued, "There are times when I wish I could stay here and never go home."

He had to be thinking of Becky. "I'm not surprised."

He shook his head. "You're thinking I'd like to stay away from that terrible wife of mine?"

"She's not terrible, but—"

"I know what the family thinks of Becky, and they're right. She's a nag, know-it-all, and selfish to boot. But the funny thing is I love her." Hiram's voice nearly broke with feeling. "The way I figure, she'd be a lot easier to live with if I could give her what she wants. A child, of course, but that's not happening. She wants nice clothes, a nice home—you know what I mean. But I can't give her those things because I'm a failure in life." Sarah opened her mouth to protest. He held up a hand and continued, "Just yesterday, a Frenchman came into town with seven thousand dollars in gold dust. Men are getting rich all around me, but what have I found?" He let out a bitter laugh. "My so-called big find in Gold Creek? Finding that nugget was a fluke. It'll never happen again. Other than that, I've found five ounces of gold dust—enough for a couple of beers in this town."

Sarah couldn't argue. Most of what her brother said was true. She would never agree he was a failure in life, but now was not the time to discuss it. She searched for the right words. "You never know what the future holds." Oh, no, what a platitude. Why had she said such a stupid thing?

"You never know what the future holds," Hiram repeated, mocking her words. Not like him at all. Face distorted with bitterness, he gazed down at his twisted leg. "I'll tell you what the future holds for me. I'll go home a failure, a cripple. I'll use the nugget I found to buy a beet farm. Becky will be happy, but me? I'll be digging up beets, hating every moment of it until the day I die."

What could she say? "You know I didn't mean it that way."

After a long pause, Hiram squared his shoulders. "All right. I'm finished feeling sorry for myself. Let's get back to Anming."

Thank goodness, her brother had gotten over his bad mood and was back to his normal easy-going self. She'd never seen him so bitter and upset. He'd never let on how much he was hurting. Like a typical man, he'd concealed his feelings well, and she'd never guessed his inner turmoil. She did now. She'd never take him for granted again.

For a long time, Hiram sat silent, looking up at the treetops. In a wistful voice, he finally continued, "We don't have much money, but let's stay at least until the money runs out. That should give us some time to look for Florrie's baby."

Until this moment, Sarah hadn't realized how much she wanted to stay. Now that Hiram agreed, a weight lifted from her shoulders. Now they could find out more about Florrie's baby, one way or the other. And then also... *Jack*. No, no. She was through with him. Through forever, and she had to stop allowing him to creep into her thoughts. "If we run low on money, I could start baking apple pies."

"You'd make a fortune." Hiram's eyes twinkled. "You should do it. You could be Hangtown's Queen of Pies."

They were back to light banter, thank goodness. "Seriously, I just might. I'll write to Ma and Pa tomorrow and let them know we plan to stay a while."

"What about Anming?"

"Somehow I'll find a way to talk to her." At the moment, she had no idea how.

Later that night, Hiram stomped out the campfire and went to bed in the wagon. Holding a lantern, Sarah was about to go to bed in their tent when the clip-clop of a horse's hooves made her turn her head. No doubt someone was just riding by, but no, whoever it was stopped at their campsite. She raised the lantern high. *Jack*. He was riding Bandit, the horse she loved most except Rosie. She set the lantern on the ground and hurried to the horse's side. "Bandit!" She threw her arms around his neck and buried her face in his thick mane. "I've missed you, old friend. How good to see you again."

"Hello, Sarah."

She looked up. Jack sat on his horse gazing down at her. "How did you know where I was?"

He swung from the saddle. "Now that you've said hello to my horse, do I rate a greeting?" His left brow raised in amusement.

She wanted to laugh but stopped herself. "I thought I told you—"

"You were easy to find." He stepped into the circle of light from the lantern, casual as ever, a disarming grin on his face. "Word gets around. There aren't that many good-looking women in this town."

"I clearly said I never wanted to see you again."

"We're going to start over." He walked to a seat by the campfire and sat down. "Come sit."

She ought to refuse, demand he leave, but his voice held such authority she'd rather not defy him, at least not yet. Besides, she was not only curious, his near-irresistible charm was getting through to her again. Taking her time, she walked to the remains of the campfire and sat across. "What do you mean, start over?"

"I mean exactly that. You recall our last meeting?"

How could she forget? "I remember."

"Your first words to me were, 'Why, Jack McCoy, how lovely to see you again.'"

"As I recall, yes."

"Would you care to rephrase that?"

"Why...why...I...uh..." What was he getting at?

"I'm asking because you weren't happy to see me, were you?"

"No, I was not."

"You were being sarcastic."

"Yes, I was."

He nodded as if she'd just confirmed what he already knew. "You were angry with me. You still are, and I don't blame you. When we parted in Gold Creek, I acted like I didn't care. After that, you never heard from me."

"You might have at least dropped me a line." She accompanied her remark with a careless shrug. No need to mention the ache in her heart each time the mail had arrived and no letter from him.

"I want you to know I..." Despite his casual manner, she could see he was struggling for words. "No matter how it looks, I have feelings for you, Sarah. I've missed you." He gave a self-deprecating laugh. "'Missed' is hardly the word, but we won't go into that. I don't know why you and your brother are in Hangtown, but whatever the reason, I'm here to help in any way I can. I wanted you to know that."

The old hurt still lingered. She should tell him goodbye, don't ever come back. But on the other hand... The light from the lantern flickered. It would soon go out, but it didn't matter. Every good-looking inch of him was etched in her memory. Oh, no, she couldn't turn him away, and yet she could never let him hurt her again. "All right, we'll be on speaking terms, but I want it clear we're just friends and nothing more."

"Of course."

"You know what I mean."

"Yes, I know what you mean, Sarah. I won't touch you." He laughed softly. "Unless you say otherwise."

"No chance of that." He'd better not mistake the firmness in her voice.

"That's settled then. Let's talk. We've got a lot of catching up to do. One thing I want to know right now."

"And what is that?"

"What the hell were you doing in a whorehouse?"

* * * *

Shirley Kennedy

Next morning, Ben Longren was standing behind the counter of Longren & McCoy's General Store when Jack walked in. Ben took one look and inquired, "What happened to you?"

Jack shrugged. "What do you mean?"

"You've been dragging around here like you lost your last friend. Now you look like you just discovered the world's biggest gold strike."

"Must be the weather." Leave it to his friend to catch his change of mood. He hadn't wanted to admit, even to himself, how Sarah's crushing words had knocked the wind out of him. She would never know his surge of relief last night when she'd said, *we're just friends and nothing more.* He'd wanted to swoop her into his arms, kiss her in a way she'd never been kissed before…

"Did you talk to Sarah?" Ben asked.

"I did." Ben was the one who worked in the store all day and picked up all the gossip. Not much stayed secret in a place like Hangtown. When rumor spread that a respectable lady named Sarah was seen visiting Hannibal Palmer's fancy whorehouse, he immediately knew who she was and told Jack. "It's a puzzlement. Why would a pretty little widow like Sarah visit such a place?"

A customer came to the counter and paid for a purchase. Jack waited until he left. "You were right, Ben. It was Sarah who paid two visits to Palmer's establishment. You would never guess why…"

He told Ben about Florrie, the baby, the Chinese servant girl named Anming. "Sarah wants to talk to her. The madam who runs the place won't let Sarah in again, but there's got to be a way to reach her."

Ben rubbed his white-bearded chin. "I dunno, Jack. You don't want to tangle with a man like Hannibal Palmer. He's got a lot of influence in this town."

"According to Sarah, her sister believes he's a kind-hearted philanthropist."

Ben hooted with laughter. "Hannibal Palmer is rich as Croesus and as evil as they come. He's one of the lucky ones—got to the diggings back in forty-nine when there really were nuggets lying all over the ground. He staked a claim on the American River that paid twelve thousand in gold in eleven days. Golden Hill, it's called."

"I've heard of it—one of the richest strikes in the gold country."

"Yep, the dang thing's still paying off. He didn't stop there, though. Hannibal Palmer's got his hand in all sorts of dirty dealings, from a string of brothels to jumping claims and running people off. Mostly foreigners. They say he's the one responsible for running a bunch of Chinamen off their claims, and worse. He'd just as soon murder them as not. He employs a bunch of men, all with guns, to do his dirty work for him."

"I don't care if he's the devil himself. How can we get to Anming?"

"It won't be easy. They keep a close eye on them who work there. You say the girl's Chinese?"

Jack nodded.

"Then she's probably more a slave than a servant. I doubt they ever let her out. There are those who think a Chinese person is less than human, and Hannibal Palmer is one of them. He's sure to have thugs with guns guarding his brothel."

"I'll think of something."

Jack was about to turn away when his friend got a gleam in his eye. "Wait! I've got an idea."

* * * *

The next few days, with Hiram's help, Sarah spent her time baking apple pies and selling slices to her neighbors in the camp. She became an immediate success with the first one she sold. Drawn by the aroma of apples and cinnamon, hungry miners lined up while the pies still baked over the campfire. They gladly paid a dollar a slice, grumbling only when they couldn't buy more. "If only I had a big oven," Sarah complained, "I'd make a fortune."

Despite how busy she was, her worry over Florrie and her baby hung heavy on her mind. As yet, she hadn't thought of a way she could talk to Anming. Jack said he'd try to help, but so far she hadn't heard from him. Since their talk the other night, her turmoil over his total neglect had vanished. She could trust him. They were friends now. She very much wanted to keep it that way, although…

No matter how it looks, I have feelings for you, Sarah. Her heart did a flip whenever she thought of what he'd said that night. She thought of it far more often than she wished, but she must be sensible. Never again would she risk the anguish he'd caused her.

Four days after she'd last seen Jack, she was cleaning up after the sale of her last pie when he rode up on Bandit. He dismounted and asked, "So you're selling pies?"

She grinned. "Yes, and making a small fortune. If I had a regular oven, I'd be rich."

"I've got news about Anming." At her quick, sharp breath, he raised his hand. "Don't get your hopes up. She may not know anything that would help you."

"I still want to talk to her."

He gave an understanding nod. "I've arranged for you to meet her tomorrow morning, early, back of the brothel. It's the best time. Everyone's asleep after their busy night."

Did she detect a note of bitterness in his voice just then? "How did you—?"

"That brothel's got a fancy French cook named Bastien. He comes in the store all the time. Ben has done him a lot of favors, so he figured maybe Bastien could do us a favor and get word to Anming that you want to see her. With a grin, he added, "I suspect some sort of promise concerning a load of lobsters from San Francisco was involved." He grew serious. "This is risky, Sarah. Anming will slip out to talk to you, but she can't stay long. I don't know if you realize, but she's practically a slave in that place and not treated well. The man who owns that brothel is evil as they come. "

"I hear what you're saying," she answered grimly. "How early should I be there?"

"I'll come get you as soon as the sun comes up."

"You don't have to—"

"You want to go alone?" He looked amused. "Didn't I just tell you how risky this is? You will not go alone. That's final."

"All right, I won't argue." Actually she didn't want to argue. Returning to that awful place was nothing she looked forward to. What a relief to know a man who knew no fear would be by her side.

Jack looked around the campsite, now cluttered with sacks of flour and sugar, bags of dried apple slices, all the ingredients needed to bake a pie. "If you want to go into the pie business, this isn't the right place. You need to be in town."

"You're right. I should be on Main Street, but I have no idea how to go about it and neither does Hiram."

"I'll see what I can do. See you tomorrow." He stuck out his hand. Taken aback, she simply stared. He laughed. "Did you forget we're friends now? Friends shake hands."

She caught on fast. "Right you are." She slipped her small hand into his large one. He gripped it tight. As they shook, the feel of his roughened palm spiked an unexpected warmth in the pit of her stomach. *Enough of that.* She withdrew her hand and said primly, "I truly appreciate what you've done, Mr. Mc Coy. I do so value your friendship."

He remained solemn and straight-faced. "And I enjoy yours, my dear Widow Gregg. See you in the morning."

He swung onto Bandit and rode away.

* * * *

Early the next morning, Sarah carefully picked her way through the trash-strewn backyard of the brothel on Pacific Street. It wasn't a pretty sight with its piles of garbage and countless empty whiskey bottles strewn around. Thank heavens, Jack was right behind her. It might be early morning, all quiet, no one in sight, but her heart raced just the same. She reached the back door. "I hope we don't have to wait long," she whispered to Jack. The door slowly opened. Anming peered out. Seeing Sarah, her little face beamed with joy. "You came!" She slipped out the door and hugged Sarah like a long lost friend.

Sarah hugged her back and looked around the cluttered backyard. "I hate to talk here. Can we go somewhere?"

"No, no!" Anming's eyes widened with fear. "I dare not go far. We must talk here, and I can't be long. I don't want them to catch me."

Sarah stepped back and examined the Chinese girl with a critical eye. She'd been thin before, but now she looked as if a slight breeze might blow her away. An ugly bruise covered her right cheekbone. "Good heavens, what are they doing to you in there?"

Anming hung her head. "It's not so bad."

"You're not getting enough to eat. What's that bruise on your face?"

"Please!" Desperation filled Anming's voice. She flicked a panicky glance at the door. "I can't talk long. If they find me out here, they'll be very angry. You wanted to know about Florrie's baby?"

Jack stepped forward. "We understand. We'll be quick as we can. Tell us what you know."

Anming gave him a grateful nod. "Here's what I found out. Florrie gave birth to a baby girl. They told her the child was stillborn, but they lied."

"So she's alive?" Sarah held her breath.

The Chinese girl spoke barely above a whisper. "Very much alive."

"If she's alive, what happened to her?" Jack asked.

Anming lowered her voice even further. "They took her away."

"Who took her away?"

A distant sound of voices from inside the house caused Anming to throw a panic-stricken glance at the door. "I must go."

"No! Anming, you don't have go back."

Jack's jaw tensed with anger. "Come with us. They have no right to keep you."

Anming took in a deep breath, seeming to calm herself, and gazed at Sarah with grateful eyes. "Thank you, but I must stay. I said some day I would repay you for all your kindnesses, and this is my chance. I will find out who took the child and where she is now. When I do, I'll get word to you." As silently as she'd slipped out, the little Chinese girl gave them a slight bow and slipped inside.

Jack's eyes narrowed in disgust as he looked around the trashed-out yard. "Let's get out of here. I need some fresh air."

Chapter 16

"We've got mail!" Hiram triumphantly held two letters high.

Sarah was about to roll out pastry for a pie. She dropped the rolling pin and hurriedly wiped her hands on her apron. "Are they from home?"

"Straight from Mokelumne City." Despite the excitement of living in a gold mining town, they both missed their family and longed to hear from them. Hiram had been going to the post office every day to look for mail that had never come until today. "One's from Ma and Pa addressed to both of us. The other's to me from Becky." A flash of remorse crossed his face. "I've been planning to write, but what with helping you with the pies, I just haven't gotten around to it."

Sarah read the letter from their parents. They were fine. The store was fine. Theodore Goetzmann was fine. Any word of Florrie? When were they coming home? Sarah breathed a guilty sigh. "I hate lying to them."

Hiram looked up from the letter he was reading. "You want to tell them Florrie's working in a whorehouse and loving it?"

Sarah winced but couldn't argue. "Maybe it's silly, but I have this dream that Anming will find out who has little Addy. Somehow we'll get her back. We'll take her to Florrie, and when she sees how sweet and adorable her baby is, she'll give up the life she's leading and go home to Ma and Pa."

She expected a laugh from Hiram. Instead, tears moistened his eyes. "I can only hope your dream comes true, Sarah. I think of Florrie all the time in that awful place." He held up his letter. "Becky wants me home. She says I'm being selfish and shirking my responsibilities. It's high time I stopped my drinking, gambling, and carousing around in this sinful town. She says it's time I sold that nugget I found and bought a beet farm, same as Theodore Goetzmann."

As usual, Sarah bristled at the mention of her sister-in-law. She must watch what she said, though. Nothing would change Hiram's mysterious devotion. "Becky doesn't understand. Maybe someday she will, although I wouldn't count on it. Why go rushing home? You know she's perfectly safe with Ma and Pa. Besides, you can't think of leaving yet. It's only been a day since we talked to Anming."

Hiram's shoulders slumped. "You're right. We can't go home yet. I just wish Becky thought more highly of me."

Words of protest rushed to Sarah's lips. *That awful woman has hurt you again. Why do you let her?* She kept her mouth shut. Anything she said would upset him even more.

She went back to making her pies. She baked them every day now, still selling every slice, making a modest profit. The trouble was she could bake only a limited number of pies over an open campfire. Hiram chopped the wood and kept the fire going, but still, by the end of the day, she was exhausted, her back aching from having to bend low countless times.

Wouldn't it be wonderful if I could bake my pies in a regular kitchen like Beatrice Butler's?

The thought struck with sudden clarity and wouldn't go away. As the afternoon went by, it produced a flood of exciting ideas. Why couldn't she run a restaurant, same as Beatrice was doing? Maybe not a restaurant, but if she served only pie and coffee, the miners would come in droves. *Sarah's Pie Shop.* She would put it right on Main Street in the heart of Hangtown. It wouldn't have to be fancy. Resembling most shops in town, it would have just a tarp roof, canvas sides, and a plank floor.

Ideas were still swirling in her head when Jack came visiting in the late afternoon while Hiram had gone to town. No, he had heard nothing yet from Anming. "But it's only been a day. How are the pie sales going?"

She invited him to sit by the campfire and gave him a cup of coffee. "I've just had this idea. Tell me what you think."

Jack listened attentively. When she finished, he raised his eyebrows and declared, "That's a great idea. I mentioned it once, remember? I'm all for it. Here's what I can do to help you…"

The more Jack talked, the more her enthusiasm grew. Jack and Ben had a lease on their general store and the empty space beside it. She was welcome to use that space. They could put up a canvas-sided building in no time. No doubt Hiram would help. When she said she would need a stove, an oven in particular, Jack said not to worry, no problem at all. They discussed what else she would need. Even for a simple pie shop, it was quite a list. Tables, benches, dishes, forks, pie pans, cups, and more. Again, not a problem. What they didn't have in the store, Jack would have shipped from San Francisco.

At mention of the costs, her high spirits sank. "I wasn't thinking… that'll cost money. We don't have that much."

"I'll make you a loan. I consider you a good investment."

"You do?" Was he joking? Maybe not. He sounded serious enough.

When they finished discussing their plans, Jack remarked, "So this means you'll be staying for a while."

Until that moment, she hadn't given a thought to what a serious commitment she'd be making. Her family expected her and Hiram to return to Mokelumne City soon. They couldn't keep making excuses much longer. Up until now, she'd simply assumed she would return home like a good daughter should. But she didn't have to go back if she didn't want to. To open a restaurant of her own—what a challenge. By God, she could do it! She threw her head back and looked Jack in the eye. "I'll be staying for while. I'm not tied to Mokelumne City."

Although Jack kept a straight face, she caught a fleeting gleam of gratitude deep in his eyes. "So we'll be business partners."

She recalled how Pa got a certain dead serious expression on his face whenever he talked business. She did the same. "I'll pay back your loan and also a percentage of my profits for the use of your land. I believe that's how it works."

"I'll take two percent."

She sniffed. "I don't know much about business, but that's not enough. Ten percent."

He laughed. "What a shrewd businesswoman you are, Widow Gregg. All right, ten percent it is." He reached to shake her hand. "It'll be a pleasure doing business with you."

She took his hand. Once again, its warmth sent a hungry, hot throb surging through her veins. An urge to lean into his arms took ahold of her. She caught herself just in time, stifling the gasp that trembled on her lips. Casually, she withdrew her hand. "Strictly business, of course."

"Strictly business." He raised his coffee cup. "Here's to Sarah's Pie Shop. Long may it prosper."

With a smile, she raised her own cup, even though she wondered, *what have I done?* Never in her life had she made such a momentous decision. What if she failed? No! She was not going to fail, and when she pictured herself running her very own restaurant—in charge!—making money!— she knew she was doing the right thing.

When Sarah told Hiram about the pie shop, he heartily approved. "I'll help in any way I can, but you'd better write the family, let them know we won't be home anytime soon."

Sarah wrote home that day. They were still looking for Florrie—still weren't sure when they could come home. She felt bad about lying but not bad enough she'd give up her pie shop. It went up fast. In what seemed no time at all, a new structure stood on the vacant space next to Longren & McCoy's General Store. Jack did most of the work with Ben's and Hiram's help. When Sarah came to look, Jack proudly showed her around. "The dining room's in front. We've ordered tables and chairs. We've screened off an area in the back for your kitchen where you can wash dishes, roll out your pies, and all that. We'll open soon as we have all the furnishings. It shouldn't take long. Ben's already ordered knives, forks, plates, everything you need, from San Francisco."

"That's wonderful. Now if I only had a stove."

Jack grinned. "Come back tomorrow."

In the morning, Jack accompanied Sarah and Hiram to the pie shop and told them to look out back. When they did, Sarah could hardly believe her eyes. A dome-shaped object, high as her head and made of bricks, stood just behind the back entrance of the building.

"What is it?" she asked.

"It's a beehive oven. Ben and I built it last night. It heats with kindling and wood. That means you'll have to get up early in the day to fire it up and keep it going, but it's big enough you can bake several pies at once, or anything else you'd like to, all day long."

Jack had done so much for her already, and now this. Seeing him standing there, his smile full of careless charm, she was hard put to remember why she wanted to be just friends. Oh, yes, she remembered. Jack McCoy was everything wonderful a man could be. He was also completely, forever unavailable, one of those men who wandered and would never settle down. She pulled her thoughts together and politely inquired, "How can I thank you?"

"Don't bother. Glad to do it." His answering tone was as polite as hers.

Good. She'd gotten past the momentary lapse in her otherwise strong control. In the future, she must concentrate on her new business and keep those lustful thoughts of Jack McCoy totally out of her head.

Later, while Jack, Sarah, and Hiram still stood talking, Ben came rushing over from the store. "Bastien, the French cook from the brothel, was just here. He's got a message from Anming. She wants to see you tomorrow, same as last time."

* * * *

Back of the brothel, the tiny Chinese girl slipped out the back door. "I'm glad you came," she whispered. She looked terrible. Even in the first light of dawn, Sarah could see she was thinner than ever. The old bruise on her cheek had faded, but now she had a new, bigger bruise on the other side.

"Did you find out anything?" Sarah held her breath.

Anming nodded. "Mr. Hannibal Palmer was there that night with some of his men. He's the one who took the baby away."

Sarah got a sudden knot in her stomach. "Do you know where he took her?"

"It wasn't easy finding out." Anming glanced uneasily at the back door. "Mr. Palmer and his wife have a fine house in Coloma. They say that's where he took the baby, but I'm not sure."

"And she's all right?"

"As far as I know. That's all I can tell you. I hope that helps, Sarah. I'm glad I was able to repay you." Anming looked even more frightened than last time. "I can't let them find me here. I must get back."

She started away, but Sarah clasped her arm. "Wait, you mustn't. I want you to come with me."

Anming bowed her head. "Mr. Palmer is a powerful man. If I leave, he'll find me. You'll get in trouble, too."

Jack had been silently listening. He stepped forward. "I'm familiar with Hannibal Palmer. He's not going to hurt you. Come with us. You don't have to stay here."

"But where would I go?"

Sarah didn't hesitate. "Don't worry, you can stay with me."

"With you?"

"Of course with me." During the following minutes, Sarah used her best powers of persuasion before, finally, the fear faded from Anming's eyes, and she firmly declared, "You're right. I'm not a slave."

"Go inside and get your things. We'll wait right here."

The faintest of smiles touched Anming's lips. "I have no 'things,' Sarah, just the clothes on my back."

The words touched Sarah deeply, but right now she couldn't spare time for sympathy. She looked at Jack. He gave her a quick let's-do-it nod. Sheltering the tiny Chinese girl between them, they departed the yard with considerable haste. Not until they reached Sarah's campsite did she breathe a sigh of relief. She put Anming in her tent where she couldn't be seen, then sat down outside with Jack. "She's exhausted, and I think she'll sleep—probably been working all night in that place. Do you think they'll come after her?"

Jack shook his head. "Now that she's gone, they won't try to find her. One small Chinese servant is nothing to them. They only care about the swarms of Chinese who've sailed over from China and staked claims in the goldfields. From what I've heard, men like Hannibal Palmer will stop at nothing, even violence and murder, to roust them out, even though their claims are legitimate."

"But that's not fair. The Chinese are as entitled as anyone else."

"The world is full of unfairness."

Sarah bit her lip in thought. "How fair is it that they've stolen my little niece away? Where is Coloma? How am I going to get her back?"

"This isn't the time for a history lesson, but Coloma's the site of Sutter's Mill where James Marshall discovered gold." A wry smile curved Jack's mouth. "Thereby turning this country—the world—upside down. It's on the American River about thirty miles from here. It's built up even more than Hangtown. Some nice homes, I hear."

"How soon can I get there?"

Jack thought carefully before answering. "I'll find out about Hannibal Palmer's home in Coloma, but it will take a while. Meanwhile, be patient. Do what you can to help Anming. Open your pie shop. If you need me, I stay in a room above the stables back of the store."

"It's almost hopeless, isn't it?" Sarah flung out her hands in frustration. "Even if we find where Palmer lives, what are our chances of getting the baby back? I mean, we can't just walk in and take her."

"I won't lie to you. Hannibal Palmer is a dangerous man. He's got a gang of cutthroats who consider themselves above the law—that is, what law there is around here. Even so, we'll give it a try." Tenderness filled Jack's eyes. "Take heart, Widow Gregg. You know I'll do my best for you."

* * * *

Anming slept through the day. When she awoke, Sarah gave her some nourishing stew, as much as she could eat, and sat with her by the fire. The girl still looked exhausted, yet she couldn't stop smiling. "I'm so grateful," she kept saying. Sarah assured her she could stay as long as she wanted. She could sleep in the tent. It was big enough for two. Sarah would find her some clothes. Anming frowned. "I can't take charity. I must earn my keep,"

Sarah had the perfect answer. "I'm opening a pie shop and need lots of help. If you agree, I'll hire you to work for me."

Nothing could have been more gratifying than Anming's beaming smile of acceptance.

* * * *

Sarah's Pie Shop opened on a bright sunny morning when Main Street teemed with miners. With its canvas walls and rough-hewn tables and benches, the shop was about as primitive as a shop could be, yet as soon as Sarah tacked the Open for Business sign on a wooden post in front, a line formed. Customers came in a steady stream, willing to wait patiently for a cup of coffee and piece of apple pie.

From the minute Anming arrived at the shop, she never sat down. Well before dawn, she was piling firewood into the huge beehive oven and starting it up. During the day, she was tending the oven, keeping it roaring hot, shoving the pies in, timing the baking and taking them out when done. In-between, she helped clear the tables, mopped the floor, and helped Sarah in the kitchen. Despite Sarah's urging, she never took a break.

Hiram appointed himself keeper of the money. He stood at the front entrance, taking either a dollar cash from each customer or an ounce of gold dust. So he could measure, he'd constructed a makeshift scale out of sardine cans with silver Mexican *reales* as counterweights. Sometimes scales weren't needed. A miner would simply open his bag of gold dust and Hiram would reach in and take a pinch. At the end of the first day, when he counted the receipts, he gleefully exclaimed, "Four hundred ninety-eight dollars in cash and sixty-five ounces of gold dust. At fourteen dollars an ounce, that's nearly a thousand dollars. We're rich, Sarah!"

After a strenuous day of baking pies while managing the shop, Sarah was almost too tired to celebrate. Even so, she was walking on clouds. The first day had gone far better than she ever expected. As in Gold Creek, she loved meeting the miners who came from all parts of the world. Their boisterous laughter and passionate talk concerning every aspect of mining for gold filled Sarah's Pie Shop with a constant aura of excitement. Every piece of pie readily sold. They could have sold twice as many, maybe more. "We're going to need more help," Sarah told Hiram. "Then we could bake different kinds of pies, and other things, too."

"There's a boarding house just opened up the street," Hiram said. "We can afford rooms now. What do you think?"

What a wonderful idea. The next day, they stored the wagon, arranged for the oxen to be fed, and rented rooms in Mrs. Keller's Boarding House. Sarah found herself in heaven with a room of her own and someone else preparing all the meals. The boarding house had refused to accept Anming, but she solved the problem by sleeping nights in the Pie Shop.

Finally, Sarah could indulge herself. In Mokelumne City, she'd replaced the two tattered dresses she'd worn from Indiana with two "serviceable" dresses that weren't the least fancy. Now she bought three bolts of the finest fabric at Jack and Ben's store, found a local seamstress, and ordered new dresses made. The day she entered Sarah's Pie Shop in her new, full skirted, cotton calico, she felt like a queen. She wished Jack would come in so she could twirl around, show him the pretty pattern of tiny roses, slightly scooped-out neckline, tiny buttons down the front and full sleeves, all of which made her look her best, and very pretty indeed, if she did say so.

A week after they opened, Sarah's Pie Shop had its first crisis. The usual crowd of miners, all of them white, was sitting at the tables when a small group of Chinese walked in. An immediate, angry stirring brought Sarah from the kitchen. At one of the tables, a husky young man with long, unkempt blond hair, dressed in grimy miner's clothes, leaped up and shouted, "Get them coolies out of here." A roar of approval arose from his fellow diners.

Sarah was dumbstruck. She looked toward Hiram who stood at the front door. He called, "They paid their dollar," and gave her a helpless shrug.

How strange these men from faraway China looked with pantaloons so wide they resembled petticoats, short, loose garments on top, stiff bamboo hats, and long braided queues hanging down their backs. All but one young man, taller than the rest, looked so frightened they were ready to bolt. The taller one stepped forward. Showing no fear, he bowed in her direction and said what sounded like, "Pay dollah, wantchee catchee pie."

Sarah could hardly hear him over the shouts and catcalls. She was about to ask him to repeat his words when Anming appeared, took one look at the young man, and began speaking in a tongue that had to be Chinese. When they finished, she turned to Sarah. "He says they won't leave. They paid their dollar, and they want their piece of pie."

From the door, Hiram called, "I'll give them their dollar back, Sarah. We don't want trouble."

The men at the table were still hurling insults at the Chinese, if anything louder and angrier. The Chinese appeared ready to flee, yet were hesitating because the taller one had folded his arms in a gesture of defiance and appeared to be standing his ground. Sarah had no idea what to do. If only Jack were here, but he wasn't. She could run next door and ask Ben to help, but no, she didn't dare leave now. Only one solution. She should take Hiram's advice—give the Chinese their money back and get them out of here. But what had the Chinese done? Why should she give in to a bunch of bullies?

She smoothed her apron, pulled her shoulders back, and strode to the noisiest table, the one where the blond-haired man still hurled his insults. She directed her remarks to him. "I'm afraid I must ask you to leave."

The man's jaw dropped in amazement. "Me leave? Ma'am, those coolies are less than human, and you expect me to go?"

Sarah softened her stern expression. She tipped her head and inquired, "What's the problem, sir? Are you afraid of them?"

The man's jaw dropped even farther, if that was possible. "I—I—hell no! I—"

"Here's the problem. These men"—she gestured toward the Chinese—"have all paid for their pie. That means they have every right to be here, same as you."

The man was still sputtering. Before he could reply, Sarah went on, "I'm going to clear a table just for them. They will eat their pie at their table, and you will eat your pie at your table. You will not speak to each other. You will not look at each other. They won't bother you, and you won't bother them. That's a reasonable solution, don't you agree, sir?"

The blond man's expression of high indignation faded fast. "Well...I suppose we—"

"Thank you, sir, it's settled then." Sarah gave him a brisk nod. Without another word, she turned and quickly cleared off one of the tables. Heading back to her kitchen, she waved at the Chinese. "You can sit down now!"

Not until she got behind the curtain of her makeshift kitchen did she press her hand to her pounding heart and breathe a huge sigh of relief. Her first crisis. She'd solved it, and without help from anyone. A very nice feeling indeed.

Chapter 17

Late the next day, after the last customer left, Jack came into the pie shop. He'd been on a buying trip to San Francisco and brought back a load of goods for the store. Not easy, considering they went by ship to the port of Stockton, then on to Hangtown by pack mule. "Come sit at a table," he told both Sarah and Hiram. "I've got a proposition for you."

What now? Sarah was more than curious. "I hope this has nothing to do with investing in a gold mine." She was only joking, although rumors abounded concerning gold mines being "salted" with gold nuggets and sold to the unwise.

"This is a different kind of gold mine." Jack addressed Hiram. "Along with everything else, I brought back two faro tables. I can easily sell them to one of the local saloons, but I thought maybe you'd be interested."

"In gambling tables?" Sarah asked in an incredulous voice.

Jack smiled amiably. "Hear me out. There's still space next to the store we leased and haven't used. We can build an extension to your pie shop— another big room walled off by canvas. Build a little bar. Install the faro tables and maybe another for monte. One for poker, too."

Sarah stared aghast at Jack. "You're seriously saying we should open a gambling establishment?"

Hiram had listened with rapt attention. "Let's hear him out."

Sarah struggled to find words. "You know what Ma and Pa would say about gambling."

"This may surprise you," said Hiram, "but in this part of the world, gambling's an honorable profession."

"He's absolutely right," Jack said with quiet emphasis. "There's no stigma attached to running a gaming table or two, as long as they're honest. Look around you. The streets are full of men who've found gold—maybe an ounce of gold dust, maybe enough wealth to last a lifetime. They come into town, all of them, and what are they looking for?"

"Whiskey, women, and a gaming table," Hiram replied.

"Absolutely right. They're hell-bent on gambling. If they don't go to your tables, they'll go someplace else, so why not you be the one to rake in the profits?"

Hiram broke into an elated smile. "I like your idea, Jack. I could do it, you know. I'm good at figures, and I've got a good head on my shoulders. I've been waiting for an opportunity such as this, just didn't quite know what it was. By God, I know I could do it." He turned to Sarah. "What do you say?"

Sarah laughed. "My brother, the owner of a gambling hall? Oh, Hiram, I don't believe this!"

Jack said softly, "He needs this, Sarah."

He was right. Like her, Jack knew how her brother badly needed something to boost his sagging confidence. How clever he'd thought of a gambling hall. She hadn't seen Hiram this enthusiastic since before that awful day he fell off the wagon and crippled himself. That settled it. If a couple of gaming tables could give him a new interest in life, make him feel more of a man again, especially in the eyes of his wife, she was all for it. They'd deal with Ma and Pa later. She addressed Hiram. "I would want more than just a canvas dividing the gambling tables from the pie shop. We can put a door in-between, but if you're going to install a bar, it must stay locked. I most certainly wouldn't want any drunks staggering into my pie shop. Is that clear?"

Any doubts she may have had were swept away by Hiram's whoop of delight.

After her brother left, Jack asked her to stay. "I've got more information about Hannibal Palmer."

There went that leap of her heart again. "You found out where he lives?"

"I did. Anming was right. He's built a new house in Coloma. Lives there with his wife, Isobel. I rode by. It's a big place, pretty fancy, and it's guarded."

"Do you know if the baby is there?"

"It's Hannibal Palmer's home. That's all I know. Maybe she's there, maybe not."

Florrie's baby—her own niece—living with strangers. She fought to control her rising anger. "What do we do now?"

"I don't know. Palmer outright stole that baby, but he likely can get away with it. California's a state now, but we don't yet have the laws to handle such matters. We're still pretty much living in a lawless land."

"I can't think what to do, other than walk up to their front door and ask for the baby back." She tried to smile. "Somehow I don't think that will work."

"Probably not, but it might be worth a try. At least you'll know what you're up against. There's no rush. Think about it. I'll take you to Coloma whenever you want to go."

"How long would it take?"

"For thirty miles? It's rough terrain, so I'd say a day and a night if we go by horseback."

Spend the night with Jack? Alone, in the wilderness? That would never, never work. Up until now, she'd managed to stick with her "just friends" declaration, but just barely. The thought of those times they'd made love still did strange things to her insides. Did he know what she was thinking? Her eyes locked with his, but his dark depths were unreadable. "We would be alone?"

"I suppose, unless you want to bring someone along to chaperone." His mouth curved into a barely discernable smile. "But that won't be necessary. I haven't forgotten we're just friends."

She ought to feel grateful. Instead, all she felt was an odd twinge of disappointment. But that was stupid. Once and for all, she'd better accept the fact that Jack would never get serious, never settle down. But if he was such a wanderer, why was he still here? She tipped her head and inquired, "I'm glad you remember we're just friends, but I'm curious. Up to now you've been a drifter. That's the way you like it, or so you say. You can't stay in one place more than a few months, yet here you are a respectable store owner in Hangtown. I don't see any signs you'll be leaving soon. Am I mistaken?"

Jack gazed at the ceiling, then down at the floor. "You ask a good question. I'm not sure of the answer. All I know is…" He stood abruptly. "Got to go." He leveled a long, hard gaze into her eyes. "Widow Gregg, I'm not sure if you're the best thing that ever happened to me or the worst."

Before she could answer, he was gone.

* * * *

After Jack left the pie shop, he walked next door to Longren & McCoy's General Store and found Ben working behind the counter. His partner took one look and inquired, "What's wrong? You look like you swallowed a bullfrog."

Jack ignored the humor. "Do I look like a respectable citizen of Hangtown to you?"

"Well, now, I suspect you want me to say you're not. You're a man who still goes his own way—picks his own battles and listens to no one—lives by his own rules, so to speak. Is that what you want to hear?"

"Could be."

Ben shook his head. "Trouble is you can't have it both ways. When we opened this store, we never talked about being responsible citizens, but that's what it amounts to, don't it? You're putting down roots whether you like it or not. I'd wager you didn't give it much thought. You figured you'd try it for a while and then be on your way to your next fine adventure, same as always."

"I suppose."

"Then here comes the widow. You didn't expect that, did you?"

Ben's shrewd perception stopped him cold. He wished he'd never asked. "I don't know what I expected." He turned and started for the door.

"Maybe you better figure it out," Ben called after him. "She's a pretty woman, and that ain't all. She'd have every man in town after her if she so much as crooked her little finger, but she don't because she likes you."

Jack paused at the door and threw his final remark over his shoulder. "I have no further interest in her."

Ben's whoops of laughter followed him out the door and down the street. Ben could go to hell. *Time for me to sell my half of the store and be on my way.* He'd thought about it often enough but had been dragging his feet. He'd done enough dithering. Maybe he didn't know where he was going, but the one thing he knew for sure was he must get out of Sarah's life, even though he loved her so much he'd lay down his life for her. He could never make her happy, would be doing her a favor if he left and never came back. Yes, time for Jack McCoy to move on. Not quite yet, though. He'd promised Sarah he'd help get Florrie's baby back. He'd do his best to help her. Soon as he did, he'd be on his way.

* * * *

The next few days were so busy Sarah hardly had time to think. Jack and Ben installed another beehive oven in the back. She could now bake at least twice the number of pies but only if she had more help. She was lucky to find Cedric Purvis, a down-and-out Englishman who'd lost his claim, but didn't say how. A feisty little cockney from London's East Side, Cedric was working in a bakery when he heard the astonishing news about the land of gold. He spent his last farthing on a ticket, sailed halfway around the world, and ended up in Hangtown. Now, half starved and broke, he was happy to accept a job in Sarah's Pie Shop. From the start, he proved so competent in the kitchen that Sarah now had time to spend on other things besides paring apples and rolling out pie crusts. Her menu expanded. Customers now had a choice of three kinds of pie, plus milk or coffee for a beverage.

Anming had turned into Sarah's invaluable assistant. No longer did she slave in the back feeding wood to the ovens. Sarah hired another down-and-out miner for that onerous chore. Instead, with her unending energy and complete devotion to duties, Anming pretty much managed the dining room by herself. At first, Sarah expected some of the miners might object being waited upon by a "celestial," as they were called, just as they had with the group of Chinese miners. No one said a word, perhaps because they saw Anming as a servant, not a threat.

Only one of the Chinese miners returned. The tall one, whose full name was Yi Ling, came to the back door every day. Sarah informed him he had every right to come in the front, but in his strange pidgin English he made her understand he would never cause any further trouble. At first, either Sarah or Anming brought his slice of pie to the back door, but Sarah soon realized only Anming could bring that instant beam of pleasure to his gentle eyes. Often they would carry on long conversations in what Anming told her was their native Mandarin. "Ling is from Hunan Province, same as I. Before he came to California, he worked twelve hours a day in a coal mine. He's lucky to be here. I very much admire him."

When Sarah teasingly accused Anming of having a romance, the Chinese girl broke into a rare fit of laughter. "Me have a romance? What man would have me with this horrible scar on my face? Ling takes pity on me, and that is all."

"If you say so." Sarah wasn't at all convinced.

Hiram named his new establishment The Bella Union. To Sarah's relief, he'd found enough wood to construct a solid wall between his saloon and the pie shop with no door between the two. A quick lesson from Jack taught him how to act as banker at the faro tables. He soon found more dealers and a bartender from Hangtown's many down-on-their-luck miners. The walls were bare. The bar consisted of a few wooden planks resting on sawhorses, yet from the beginning, miners crowded the tables and bar at the Bella Union Saloon. "I can't believe it!" In a high state of excitement, Hiram celebrated at the end of a highly successful opening night. "This is only the beginning. With enough space, I could add a hotel. Who knows how big we'll grow?"

Sarah wasn't sure. There was still that little matter concerning Becky and what she would say when she found out her husband was now the wicked owner of a gambling saloon and bar. So far, he'd chosen not to operate a brothel out back, like most saloons did, but she wasn't sure how far he'd go. Would he have the courage to stand up to his wife? No time to think of that now. All that mattered was seeing her brother standing tall and proud, despite his crippled leg, with a triumphant gleam in his eye.

Her dilemma over Florrie's baby stayed on her mind, but the bustling business in the pie shop kept her so busy she had no time for deciding what to do. Jack had gone on another pack trip. Whatever she planned would have to wait until he returned.

One afternoon, on a peaceful, pleasant day in the shop, Sarah and Cedric Purvis were working in the kitchen when Anming burst in and cried, "I must hide!" When Sarah asked what was wrong, she continued, "Hannibal Palmer just came in." Her little face was distorted with fright. "Oh, Sarah, he knows who I am. What if he tries to take me back?"

Hannibal Palmer. The name struck both anger and fear in Sarah's heart, but she wouldn't let it show. "You're not his slave. He has no right to take you back. Stay in the kitchen. I'll wait on him myself." She was about to meet the man who'd ruined Florrie's life, stolen Florrie's baby—*my niece*! Never mind all that, she'd stay calm if it killed her. She smoothed her apron, pushed back a strand of hair, and walked into the dining room.

Three gentlemen sat at a table, their formal attire a sharp contrast to the scruffy clothing of her other customers. When one of the men addressed the tallest of the men as "Mr. Palmer," he confirmed what she'd already guessed. Of the three, Hannibal Palmer was the one who wore the self-assured look of success. Full head of white hair, piercing blue eyes, finely trimmed mustache. Dressed in a frock coat, matching trousers, and vest, he had a look of authority about him. If she didn't know better, she'd take him for a judge or some sort of government official—certainly not an owner of brothels, leader of a gang responsible for countless vicious murders.

They ignored her almost completely while she took their orders, not even a friendly nod, as if acknowledging her presence wasn't worth their time. Involved in an intense conversation, they were using phrases like "damned celestials," "that claim up Sandy Gulch," "midnight raid," "wipe them out." As she listened, the meaning of their words sunk in. These men were planning to raid a Chinese-owned mining claim in Sandy gulch. There would be no survivors.

When she returned to the kitchen, she reassured Anming that Palmer and his men had no idea she was there. "Nor would they care. All they care about is planning some sort of raid on a Chinese mining claim up Sandy Gulch."

Anming gasped. "Ling left this morning to join his friends at Sandy Gulch. They'd found a good claim. He was so excited. Oh, you don't suppose…oh, no!"

Sarah did her best to back off her words, trying to convince Anming otherwise. Maybe she hadn't heard right. Even if she had heard right, Sandy Gulch, an area known for many rich gold strikes, was staked with hundreds of claims. Most likely Palmer and his gang were after someone else. Anming listened with her usual stoic expression, but it was easy to see she wasn't convinced Ling would be all right. Obviously, she had feelings for the man with the gentle eyes from Hunan Province.

Cedric Purvis had been listening. When Anming left the kitchen, he dolefully shook his head. "Anming ought to be concerned, what with the way crime's out of control around 'ere. I came to 'angtown during the first year of the Gold Rush. It's 'ard to believe now, but back then, there wasn't any crime. People minded their own business. You could leave a thousand dollars in gold dust in your tent and not worry."

"But those days are gone now," Sarah replied.

"Bloody right! Dishonest men started to arrive, from back East, Mexico, Peru, the British penal colonies, all over the world. Now you've got theft, swindling, shootings, lynching, and all kinds of violence. You've got claim jumpers who'd just as soon slit your throat as not." Cedric sniffed in disgust. "That's what 'appened to me. I 'ad a good claim going, at least fifty dollars in gold dust every day. Then I got jumped by a gang of no-good thieves who took my gold and drove me off my claim. They wanted to kill me. I was lucky to escape with my life."

Sarah had never heard Cedric's full story before. "That's terrible. Couldn't you have called the sheriff?"

"We 'ad a sheriff, but the coward was more interested in saving 'is neck than getting justice for me." Cedric frowned with concern. "When I see the likes of 'annibal Palmer in 'ere, my blood runs cold. That man is the worst of the worst. Mean, vicious, and ruthless. Now Palmer's building 'imself a mansion in San Francisco—up on Nob 'ill with the rest of the snobs. It's all with blood money. That scoundrel 'as built 'is fortune off the claims 'e's committed murder for, and some of it off those poor women 'e exploits in 'is brothels. Oops, pardon, ma'am. I shouldn't be talking about such subjects with a lady."

If he only knew. "I heard he lives in Coloma."

"'E does, with that 'igh and mighty wife of 'is, but only till 'e gets 'is fancy mansion in San Francisco built. Did you 'ear about the babies?"

"No, I didn't."

"Those poor women 'e keeps in 'is brothels 'ave babies. Rumor 'as it when they do, 'e takes them away and either kills them outright or keeps them, some say for servants, but I dunno. It could be for a reason far worse than that. Poor little creatures never 'ave a chance."

Sarah felt the blood drain from her face. Her knees went weak. "I...I had better go sit down."

"Sorry!" Cedric helped her to the nearest chair. "I should 'ave realized a lady like you is too delicate to 'ear such things, even though those women are only 'ores."

"Just leave me alone a moment. I'll be fine." The room started spinning around. She bent forward and put her head between her knees. She almost lost consciousness but not quite, and soon the light-headedness passed. Cedric hovered over her. "Are you all right, Mrs. Gregg? Did I say something wrong?"

"Of course not, Cedric. I'm fine, really. Get back to work. I'll just sit here a minute."

For a long time she sat quietly, alone, recovering from the shock of the little cockney's words. *Either kills them outright or keeps them, some say for servants....* Why had she waited so long? Why had she cared more for her own concerns than her sister's child? But wait, Hannibal Palmer was here. She could talk to him right now. She leaped to her feet and rushed into the dining room. "Oh, no," she muttered. The table was empty.

One of the customers overheard. "They're gone, ma'am. I heard them say something about heading back to Coloma."

That settled it. Come tomorrow, Jack or no Jack, she was going to Coloma, and when she got there, she'd rescue her sister's child.

Chapter 18

In deepening twilight, Jack unpacked the last of the mules and led the animals to the stables behind the store.

"Jack?"

He looked around. She was picking her way toward him, carefully lifting her skirt, a wise precaution in a stable yard. "Sarah? What are you doing out here?"

"I've got to talk to you." She came close. She wasn't smiling. "I've got to go to Coloma, and I want you to come along."

"What about Hiram?"

"He's much too busy running his saloon."

"When do you want to go?"

"Tomorrow, early. Here's what's happened…"

When she finished relating Cedric's horror story about the babies, she asked, "So, can you go with me? If you can't, I'll go alone."

Was she crazy? The trail to Coloma was far from safe. No trail was safe these days, what with bandits, thieves, wild animals and God-knew-what-else lurking along the way. *My God, woman, did you honestly think I'd let you go by yourself?* "He gave a casual shrug. I've got nothing better to do. Sure, I'll go. I'll get you a horse."

She smiled with relief. "If we ride hard, maybe we can get there in a day."

"Maybe." Or maybe not. What a shame the now-virtuous Widow Gregg might be forced to spend a night alone in the wilderness with Jack McCoy, notorious gambler, ne'er-do-well drifter and man who loved her so much he'd be hard put to remember they were just friends.

* * * *

Thoughts of confronting Hannibal Palmer and his wife lay heavy on Sarah's mind as they took to the trail the next morning. Even so, she couldn't help but enjoy the bright sunshine, crisp, pine-scented air, and a trail that took them through thick growths of Ponderosa pines, past blooming mock orange bushes ten feet high covered with pretty white blossoms, past fields of wildflowers the colors of the rainbow. Jack rode Bandit. She rode a mare named Star, not as good a horse as Rosie, but perfectly fine. Aside from a just-in-case bedroll, she'd brought what she considered her best outfit for visiting. Her new, rose-sprigged calico dress was carefully packed in her saddlebag. She adored the bonnet she'd just bought at the General Store. Made of straw braid, trimmed with green and white moiré ribbon, it suited her perfectly and sat in its place of honor, carefully attached to the saddle behind her. Jack had specially ordered food for at least two meals from the El Dorado Hotel and packed it in his saddlebags.

Once they got underway, Jack had remarked, "I can't guarantee we'll see Palmer. What if he isn't home? Chances are he won't be."

"Chances are his wife will be home, don't you think?"

"No guarantee."

"That doesn't discourage me in the least. If the wife isn't home, I'll wait." Nothing was going to stop her. She would *not* be discouraged, no matter what. "Actually, I haven't worked out a plan yet. I have no idea what I'll say."

From Bandit's back, Jack raised an eyebrow. "Maybe it's time you gave it some thought."

"It will all work out." Because it had to. She'd figure the details later.

At noon, they stopped and ate fried chicken and potato salad in the middle of a field of wildflowers. Jack produced a flask filled with brandy and poured a small amount into two tin cups. "To get us through the afternoon."

Sarah sighed with contentment. This was like a picnic back home, only better. What could be more enjoyable than sitting in a beautiful meadow, stomach comfortably full, spot of brandy sliding deliciously warm down her throat, her companion the man she dreamed of at night, never mind the rest. She could almost wish it wasn't going to end soon. "Will we get there by nightfall?"

"I don't think so. With this rough terrain, the horses won't make more than twenty miles."

"Then I guess we'll be sleeping under the stars tonight."

"Looks that way."

Oh, my God.

They stopped for the night in thick forest by a cold, fast running-stream. Enough food remained that they didn't bother with a fire. They washed it down with brandy and sat facing each other on soft grass by the stream, watching the sun disappear behind the mountains to the west.

The anxiety that earlier had tied Sarah's stomach in knots had disappeared. "Nothing like riding a horse all day to make you forget your troubles."

Jack smiled back. "I'm glad, considering tomorrow you'll be taking on a madman."

"Do you think I'm crazy?"

"I think you're a brave woman who's willing to sacrifice her own safety for the sake of a child she doesn't even know."

She didn't answer right away, basking in the glow of his flattering words. She enjoyed looking at him as he leaned casually on one elbow, that charming smile on his face, his long, tough body stretched out across from her. Throughout the day, he couldn't have been more patient and helpful. Just now, when they stopped for the night, he unsaddled the horses, got them watered, fed, and hobbled for the night while making it all seem effortless. If she hadn't insisted on laying out their dinner on the hotel's small linen tablecloth, she wouldn't have lifted a finger. Not like when she was married to Joseph.

"What are you thinking?" he asked.

"Did I make a face? I was thinking of my late husband. Not a pleasant memory."

"Sorry."

"Oh, but I have many pleasant memories, not of Joseph, but my childhood."

"So tell me."

It seemed a perfect night for reminiscing. As the full moon rose and a million stars started twinkling, she told him about her happy childhood in Fort Wayne, Indiana, how close her family was, how they hardly ever argued. Then came Pa's earth-shattering decision to pack up and head west, followed by the awful shock when her sister disappeared. "Florrie wasn't lovable. She was an awkward and difficult child, and that's why I think I loved her all the more—just because no one else did. When I saw her in that brothel…" Sarah closed her eyes. "What's to become of her? She thinks it's all a party and it's…it's…"

"I know," Jack answered softly. He'd listened attentively to her every word.

"You told me once you were raised in a brothel." Oh, no! She'd spoken without thinking. He was always so secretive about his past, and she didn't mean to pry.

Jack sat straight, poured the remnants of the brandy into his cup, and drank it down. He looked up at the moon, as if seeking a decision from above. He looked back at Sarah and began in a calm, almost deadly quiet voice, "I told you my mother was a prostitute, and that is true. She worked in a brothel on Rum Alley in Five Points." His lips twisted into a sour grin. "Not the finest neighborhood in New York. It was an old, rotted building, dark and dank, full of rats and cockroaches."

"You actually lived there?"

"Since I was five or six. Before that, we lived in a classier brothel, but my mother... That's another story. When I was little, the whores used to make over me—put me on their laps and give me candy. When I got older, after we moved to the Rum Alley brothel, my mother put me to work. I carried towels, cleaned up messes, washed dishes. I spent a lot of time standing in the hallway while she conducted her business in her room. Sometimes I'd cover my ears because I hated hearing the sounds. She warned me not to come in while she was 'working,' no matter what I heard. I disobeyed her only once, when she was screaming for help and I couldn't stand it. I burst in and threw myself on the swine who was pounding on her with his fists. He brushed me off like I was a bug." His mouth twisted wryly. "Guess who got beat up the worst?"

"You did?"

He nodded grimly. "My mother had no time for sympathy. If it hadn't been for—" He stopped to control a tremor in his voice.

She waited. If he didn't continue, she wouldn't press him. "Shall we change the subject?"

"Do I shock you?"

"No. I have the feeling you've never told anyone what you just told me."

"Good guess."

"You don't have to say anymore."

His shoulders relaxed, as if he'd just made a decision he was fine with. "Her name was Jenny. She was a whore, just like my mother, but that's where the resemblance ends. My mother was a hard, brittle woman. Life had been cruel to her. Her bitterness showed in her face and the way she treated me. I can never remember her smiling. I can never remember her once saying a kind word. But Jenny..." He smiled, remembering. "Soft blue eyes, long, blond hair, and she always smelled of lavender. She wore those silk robes with the flowers, the ones the Chinese wear. Sometimes she'd bend over a bit and the robe would open. I was only a boy, but I'll never forget those tantalizing glimpses. Of all the women in that place, she was the only one who cared about a little boy whose home was a brothel. I never went to school. She's the one who taught me how to read and write, and just about everything else I know. I never asked, but she must have come from a good family. How she ended up in a brothel in Five Points, I'll never know."

"Couldn't that be said of all women who end up in such places?"

"They each have their story. Sadly, it's always a story with a bad ending."

"What happened to Jenny?"

"She—" He bit his lip and breathed deep, as if he could no longer face an agonizing memory. "The sun's gone. It disappears fast in these mountains."

She got the hint. "It certainly does."

"We'd best get some sleep. You sleep here. I'll sleep over there."

How gallant he was, how gentlemanly, how respectful. But she didn't want respectful. Desire clawed at her, hot and sharp. She put her hand on her hip and tipped her head. "Do you really want to sleep apart?"

The next moments were all a blur. His cry of gladness, his strong arms encircling her, his breath hot and heavy in the hollow of her neck as he lowered her to the ground, his hands at the buttons of her dress. "No, I did not want to sleep apart," he murmured as the sweet pull of desire ended all rational thought, and she gave herself up to the delights of making love under the stars with Jack McCoy.

* * * *

When Sarah awoke in the morning, Jack was already up saddling the horses. "Two hours more and we should be there," he called. "We'll have breakfast at one of the hotels."

"Sounds good." No mention of last night, and that was for the best. She must concentrate on other things today. From the saddlebag, she pulled her carefully packed cotton calico. "I'm heading for the creek. Be right with you."

Today would be difficult, to say the least. Up to now, she hadn't thought beyond her resolve to get Florrie's baby back, never mind how. She'd figure that out later. But "later" had arrived. Dressed in her best, she was going to walk right up to the front door of Hannibal Palmer's mansion, ring the bell, and ask to see the owner of the house. She would be asked in, ushered into the presence of the supposed great man himself, and say what?

"You took my sister's baby, and I want her back."

No, too confrontational.

"Sorry to bother you, but I was hoping you'd return my sister's baby."

Absolutely no. She would not grovel.

No use planning ahead. When the moment came, she would know what to say. She washed in the creek, slipped into the cotton calico dress, combed her hair and set the straw braid bonnet with the green and white ribbons on her head. When she returned to camp, she held out her arms and did a slow turn. "What do you think? Will Hannibal Palmer be properly impressed?"

Jack's gaze was soft as a caress. "I don't know about Palmer, but you've got me properly impressed and then some."

Her heart just about melted. How easy it would be to fall into his arms again, relive the heated passion of last night. But no, Florrie's baby came first.

* * * *

Hannibal Palmer's imposing new mansion sat on a hill overlooking the booming mining town of Coloma. At least four stories high, it looked as if it had been put together without a plan with its different sized windows, cupolas both round and square, fancy cornices, and several porches edged with intricate latticework.

Sarah had decided she'd have better luck if she faced Hannibal Palmer alone, a non-threatening female. Leaving Jack waiting in the curved driveway, she mounted the ten stone steps that led to the carved, double front doors. She reached to touch her hat. Yes, it sat squarely atop her head in all its glory. She looked down at her rose sprigged dress. Not a wrinkle. Fighting the urge to turn and bolt, she rang the bell. The door soon opened and a maid peered out. "Yes?"

Sarah had to clear her throat. "I am here to see Mr. Hannibal Palmer." Thank goodness, her voice came out firm and steady.

"Mr. Palmer is not at home."

"Mrs. Palmer then."

The maid peered suspiciously. "Mrs. Palmer wasn't expecting anyone. May I have your name?"

Sarah drew her shoulders back. "Mrs. Joseph Gregg from Hangtown." She spoke in a positive voice, with a touch of arrogance thrown in, as if her name alone should gain her immediate entrance.

"One moment."

The maid soon returned. "What was it concerning?"

She thought fast. "It's concerning a charitable matter." She tilted her nose as if to imply, how dare this mere servant not allow her in?

The maid left, but returned shortly. She swung the door wide. "Mrs. Palmer will see you."

Concealing her relief, Sarah swept in, head high. The maid led her through a circular entry hall into an elegantly furnished salon. A woman somewhere in her thirties arose from a blue and cream silk upholstered sofa. She looked the height of fashion in a green, paisley patterned dress with a full, bell-shaped skirt supported by crinoline petticoats underneath. Her dark hair was piled in elaborate curls atop her head. She had a full-bosomed, slim-waisted figure and a beautiful, doll-like face with smooth, white skin, full red lips, and heavily fringed, deep set blue eyes. Her illusion of beauty shattered the moment she opened her mouth. "You are Mrs. Joseph Gregg?" she asked in an annoyingly shrill voice.

The maid disappeared. Sarah stepped farther into the room. "Yes, I am. You are Mrs. Hannibal Palmer?"

"I am Isobel Palmer." She sat back down. "You're here concerning some charity?" Her voice was awful, not only shrill and nasal but edged with a thinly veiled arrogance, as if whoever Sarah was, she had to be of a lower class.

Sarah nodded toward a giltwood chair with an arched back and down-swept arms. "May I sit down?" This was going to take time, and she wasn't going to stand here like some beggar.

Sitting stiff-backed on the sofa, Isobel gave a reluctant wave toward the chair. "Do sit."

Sarah carefully seated herself, tucking her reticule beside her. Small talk should come first. "You have a lovely home here."

"In Coloma?" One corner of Isobel's mouth rose in a sneer. "My husband is building a home for us on Nob Hill in San Francisco. That's where anyone who's anybody lives. Meanwhile, here I am, stuck in the middle of nowhere." She leveled a piercing gaze. "Why are you here?"

So much for small talk. Now what? She had expected to talk to Hannibal Palmer. Dealing with his wife was an entirely different matter. She might know about the baby, but how much did she know about her husband's sources of income? Was she aware her husband owned a string of brothels located in practically every gold mining town in the Sierra Nevada Mountains? If she did know, did she care? If she didn't know, she was about to receive a shock. A multitude of questions cut through Sarah's mind. Should she talk to Isobel? Should she leave? Should she wait till she could talk to Palmer himself? But when would that be? An opportunity like this might not come again. She braced herself and plunged ahead. "I'm here on behalf of Florrie, my sister. I won't bore you with details, but through a set of unfortunate circumstances, Florrie became a prostitute in one of your husband's brothels." She stopped and waited for Isobel's reaction. Far as she could tell, there was none. The woman remained stone faced, her eyes flat and hard.

"Do go on." Isobel's ice-filled voice held neither interest nor compassion.

Everything to gain—nothing to lose. "While working in your husband's brothel in Hangtown, my sister gave birth to a baby girl. She was told the baby was dead, but I have reason to believe she's alive. I also have reason to believe the baby is here, with you." There, the words were out of her mouth. She leaned back in her chair. Maybe she'd get thrown out, but too late now. Like Lady Macbeth said, *what's done cannot be undone.*

Isobel's mouth twitched. Her forehead furrowed in the slightest of frowns. "Just what do you want, Mrs. Gregg?"

"That baby is my flesh and blood, Mrs. Palmer. She was taken unlawfully, and I want her back."

Isobel's expression couldn't have been more unmoved as she rose from the sofa and walked to a velvet pull rope hanging from the ceiling. She gave it a tug and turned back to Sarah. "My husband is a legitimate businessman, both honorable and respected. You're saying he owns a string of brothels? The very idea! How dare you?"

The last thing Sarah wanted was to make this woman angry. She would try a softer approach. "I don't mean to upset you. It's just, you have my sister's baby, and I want her back. I can understand how you would have feelings for the child, especially if you were planning to adopt her, but—"

"Are you joking?" Isobel fairly screeched. "Do you think I'd have anything to do with the child of a whore?" She paused to calm herself. "For your information, a business friend of my husband owns the brothels. Out of the kindness of his heart, Hannibal has found homes for several of those children unfortunate enough to be born through the wickedness of the mother. It's an ideal arrangement. They're given adequate care. As soon as they're old enough, they start earning their keep." She smiled. "Rest assured your sister's child is in good hands."

Never had Sarah seen such a chilling, nasty smile. "Is she here?"

"Never mind, Isobel. I'll handle this." A male voice, coming from behind her.

Sarah turned toward the door. *Hannibal Palmer.* A tall man, he was splendidly dressed as before in frock coat, striped trousers, and vest with a gold chain looped across the front. Taking his time, he let his gaze sweep over her. She didn't miss the lethal calmness in his eyes. Finally he spoke. "And you are…?"

She mustn't let him know her knees had suddenly gone weak. "I'm Mrs. Joseph Gregg. I am here because—"

"I know why you're here." He spoke in a velvet-edged voice, not bothering to disguise the menace underneath. "How dare you upset my wife?"

She took a deep breath against the panic surging through her. "I only want my sister's baby back, Mr. Palmer."

"Absolutely not."

"Is she here?"

"What if she is? You'll never see her."

When a maid appeared, Palmer instructed her, "Get Nick. I want this lady escorted out in a fashion she'll understand." He turned back to Sarah, jaw clenched, eyes hard as granite. "You will leave immediately. You will never come back to this house or approach me or my wife in any way, is that clear? If you do, I can assure you, you'll not like the consequences. Now get out!"

A tall, burly man appeared. He cradled a rifle in his arms. Sarah clutched her reticule and stood. "I don't need an escort."

Isobel stepped forward, lifting her chin triumphantly. "You're going to get one all the same, Mrs. Gregg. For your own sake, I do hope you heard what my husband said. I'd hate to think something bad might happen to you."

Afraid she might collapse the way her knees were shaking, Sarah headed for the door. With each step, she forced herself on. She would not show fear in front of Isobel Palmer. She would reach that door with her head held high. She would keep her dignity if it killed her.

She made it to the door, swung it open, and managed to stroll through in a leisurely fashion.

Damned if she'd close it behind her.

Jack was waiting on the wide, circular driveway, holding both their horses' reins. "Well?" he asked as Sarah came down the steps. "How did it go?"

She could hardly talk over the hot, humiliating lump growing at the back of her throat. "Not so very well. Let's just go home."

* * * *

Sarah had immensely enjoyed the ride to Coloma when she'd been full of hope and had that passionate night with Jack. What a contrast to her dispirited ride back to Hangtown. She'd never thought her visit to Hannibal Palmer's home would end the way it did. The scene played over and over in her head: how she'd been threatened by Hannibal Palmer himself, insulted by that arrogant snob, Isobel, ushered out by an armed guard. Such a humiliation! Worse, she'd lost her last shred of optimism.

"How can I possibly get the baby back?" she asked Jack. "I was a fool to think they'd simply hand her over to me."

Jack didn't say much except, "There might be a way."

His reply only deepened her gloomy mood. "There is no way. It's over." He was only trying to be kind. As if that wasn't enough, her heart ached just thinking about last night under the stars when she'd willingly gone into his arms. How different things looked in the harsh light of day. Her pulse throbbed when she thought of their passionate night together, but to what end? He'd made no promises, nor would he. *It doesn't matter.* She'd dredged the admission from somewhere deep within herself, a place beyond logic and reason. If she had any sense, she'd say goodbye forever and put him out of her mind, but she couldn't and wouldn't. Never again would she deny herself his touch, no matter what the future held. She loved Jack McCoy with all her heart, and that would never change until the day she died.

They rode the thirty miles back to Hangtown all in one day, arriving after nightfall. Jack accompanied her to the boarding house, dismounted, and kissed her lightly on the forehead. "You'll be all right?"

"I'll be fine." She meant what she said. Her confidence was back, thanks, she suspected, to her finally making her mind up about Jack. In her room, she cleaned up and changed. She dreaded giving the news to Hiram, but no sense putting it off.

In her next-to-best dress, a blue calico, and a plain, gray bonnet on her head, Sarah approached the Bella Union Saloon. Amidst excited shouts from gamblers and a rousing piano rendition of "Sacramento," she stepped inside. She hoped no one would notice her, but no such luck. "A woman!" someone shouted. She immediately became the center of attention. Some of these men hadn't seen a female for months. The way they gazed at her, she could be an attraction in P.T. Barnum's freak show along with General Tom Thumb.

Hiram came limping to her rescue. "Sarah! Let's get you out of here." He took her arm, guided her through the crowd and out back where the noise wasn't nearly as bad. "Did you have any luck?"

She told him all of it: the fancy mansion, snooty Isobel, imperious Hannibal, her mortifying ejection from the premises. "The baby's there, Hiram, I know she is, and that awful woman wouldn't even let me see her."

"I should have gone with you."

"You couldn't have helped. As things stand now, we have no rights. There aren't any laws to help us"

"There must be a way."

"That's what Jack said, but the only 'way' I can think of is to break into that fancy house of his and take the child."

"Not a practical idea, I'm afraid."

"No, it's not." For a time they stood without speaking, wrapped in their own dejected thoughts. The piano started playing "Clementine."

"Do you hear the piano?" Hiram asked.

"When did you get it?"

"Just yesterday, along with two new faro tables. The place is packed every night, Sarah." As Hiram spoke, his enthusiasm grew. "You should see the way these miners throw their money around. Just last night, we had a miner saunter over to the tables and bet a big bag of gold on the turn of a single card. He lost."

"That's wonderful. I'm truly happy for you." Sarah put her sad thoughts aside. Nothing to be gained by staying in a bad mood. "We have lots to be grateful for, Hiram. Me with my pie shop, you with your saloon."

Even in pale moonlight, she saw her brother's beaming smile. "I'm a success, Sarah. Did you ever think I'd own my own saloon?"

She had to laugh. "Heavens no! I pictured you on that beet farm Becky was always talking about."

He joined her laughter. "Times have changed, haven't they? I could never go back to Mokelumne City now."

"What *are* you going to do about Becky?" Sarah asked. "You're the owner of a gambling establishment on Main Street. Do you honestly think you can keep it a secret?"

"Not for long, I suppose. Do you think she might possibly change her mind?"

Poor Hiram. "Not likely. You know how dead set she is about gambling. Drinking, too, which makes you twice a sinner."

They went back inside. Hiram said he'd escort her home. As they pushed their way through the crowded saloon, the piano played a lively tune; rowdy men, whooping and hollering, pressed around every gambling table and stood two-deep at the bar. Halfway through the saloon, Sarah saw a man and a woman come through the entrance, hesitate, and stop. *Oh, my God.*

Grim faces reflecting utter bewilderment, Pa and Becky stood in the entrance of the Bella Union Saloon.

Chapter 19

"Pa! Becky!" Sarah called as she and Hiram hastened to the entryway.

Pa saw them and waved. Becky glared. She couldn't have looked more out of place with her stiff, brown taffeta bonnet, her corseted figure encased in a bell-shaped, high-necked gown of brown bombazine.

When they got to the door, Hiram eagerly reached for his wife. "What a wonderful surprise. Give me a hug." He could hardly be heard over the noise.

Becky avoided his arms and backed away. She pursed her lips, like she'd been sucking a lemon. "What is this place?"

"It's a saloon."

"Do you work here?"

Hiram smiled proudly. "I own it."

Becky's eyes went wide. Her palm slammed her heart. She looked at Pa. "I'm going to faint."

Pa took her elbow. "Let's get her out of here."

The four made their way to the wooden sidewalk, away from the rowdy noises coming from inside. Sarah managed to find her voice. "I can't believe this, Pa. You and Becky actually came all the way from Mokelumne City?"

"We just arrived. I wasn't sure where to find you, so I got us rooms at the El Dorado Hotel. They told us where we'd find Hiram."

"But why are you here? You never mentioned you were coming in your last letter."

Pa looked tired, thinner and more stoop-shouldered than ever. "Your mother and I were worried. We knew something wasn't right. We suspected you were keeping something from us." He regarded Hiram with disbelief. "You own a saloon? Is that possible?"

"Yes, it is, Pa." Hiram puffed his chest out. "I had a little financial help from Jack and Ben, but the Bella Union Saloon is all mine." He patted Sarah's shoulder. "That's not all. Sarah owns a pie shop!"

"And you never told us?"

Sarah tried to collect her thoughts. Her father's unexpected appearance changed everything. She'd known sooner or later she must tell her parents the truth about Florrie, but she'd put off the inevitable. Now that Pa was here, she wouldn't hold back. She'd tell him everything. A group of boisterous miners walked by, one jostling Sarah's shoulder. They mustn't stand here on the sidewalk, not in this wild town. "Let's get back to your hotel. We'll talk there."

Finally away from the hustle and bustle of Main Street, the four members of the Bryan family sat facing each other in the lobby of the El Dorado Hotel. Becky sat stiffly, tapping her foot. She was dying to speak, but she'd have to wait. Sarah took a deep breath. "I'll tell you what happened, all of it. And then perhaps you'll see why we wanted to stay."

Pa and Becky sat transfixed as Sarah, with Hiram's help, unfolded the astonishing story of how they'd found Florrie. She didn't mince words. "I know how hard this is to believe, but she was working in a brothel—and still is."

Pa kept shaking his head. "But why didn't she want to leave when you and Hiram found her?"

"Because she thinks it's all a party and she likes it there."

"Unbelievable!" Pa was truly stunned and horrified.

When Sarah told them about the baby, her father got tears in his eyes. "I have a grandchild?"

"Yes, you do, a little granddaughter, only she's gone now." She told them about Hannibal Palmer and how he'd stolen Florrie's baby. "I tried—oh, how I tried! But it's impossible. We have no rights. I can't see any way to get her back."

Hiram added, "Hannibal Palmer is one of the most powerful men in the region, and one of the most dangerous. It would be folly to go against him."

Pa sadly nodded. "Now I understand. You were right, not wanting us to know about Florrie. For me, it's bad enough, but you know how frail you mother's health is. I doubt she…" He paused to collect himself. "She must never find out her daughter is a prostitute. If she does, it will kill her."

Sarah could tell from the rapid tapping of Becky's foot that her patience was almost at an end. "You had something to say, Becky?"

Becky's foot stopped tapping. "I'm not surprised about Florrie. I always thought that girl was—"

"That's enough." Sarah swallowed the instant rage in her throat. Ordinarily, she could tolerate her sister-in-law's narrow-minded, snide remarks, but not tonight. After all the heartbreak and aggravation she'd been through, the last of her patience had fled. "Have you anything else to say?"

Becky drew herself up, full of righteous indignation. She glared daggers at Hiram, who sat quietly listening. "I cannot believe what you've done. Never in my wildest dreams did I think you, my own husband, would own a saloon."

Hiram shrugged his shoulders, looking as if he'd like to flee. "It seemed a good opportunity, so I took it."

"Gambling is a sin." Warming to her task, Becky arose from her chair and pointed an accusing finger at her husband. "I saw that bar—all those drunken men under the influence of the demon rum."

"It's not a very big bar."

Not again! Stand up to her, Hiram. Sarah hated the sight of her poor brother shrinking back in his chair, his weak voice wavering.

Becky crossed her arms and glared at her husband. "Here's what you're going to do, Hiram. You will get rid of that—that—house of wickedness immediately. You will return with me to Mokelumne City. You will buy a beet farm and become a respectable farmer, just as God intended you to do. Is that clear?"

Sarah opened her mouth to defend her brother, but why waste her breath? Apparently he'd forgotten how he'd stood up to Becky when he decided to come to Hangtown. Poor Hiram, he was going to give in as he usually did. What a shame. For a time, with his newfound confidence, Hiram had walked tall and proud, despite his crippled leg. Now, thanks to his overbearing wife, he'd lost his backbone again.

Frowning, Hiram bent forward and clasped his hands between his knees. He appeared to be in deep thought. He looked up, the frown gone. Tilting his head back, he looked directly into his wife's eyes. "No."

Becky flinched. "What do you mean no?"

Hiram rose to face her. "I mean, no, I'm not going back to Mokelumne City. Matter of fact, I will never go back to Mokelumne City. Jack McCoy helped me see what I could do if I put my mind to it. He was right. I'm a success here. God didn't intend for me to own a beet farm. He intended for me to own a saloon. You want me to give that up? Sorry, it's not going to happen."

"But—but—" Becky sputtered, "A gambling saloon? A bar? Do you want to disgrace me? I can just imagine what the Temperance Union will say."

"Frankly, I don't give a damn what they say." Becky gasped, but Hiram seemed not to care. "You have a choice. Go home, spend the rest of your life marching in step with the ladies of the Temperance Union. Or stay here in Hangtown with me. I love you. I can make you happy if you'll let me. If you'd just stop getting your bloomers in a twist over every little thing, we'll have a great life together."

Becky's face turned red. She looked as if she'd been struck by a thunderbolt. "Here in Hangtown? Never! Mark my words, Hiram Bryan, keep up with this wickedness, and you will come to a sad end." She spun around and marched to the entrance of the lobby, turned and marched back to Hiram again. "You have twenty-four hours in which to change your mind."

"Really?" He stifled a laugh. "Let me make this clear, Becky. I will never go back to Mokelumne City. I will never be a beet farmer. You'd best just go on home because I'm staying here."

"Well!"

After Becky's gasp of surprise and quick departure, Pa broke the shocked silence. "Are you sure, son? I know she can be difficult sometimes, but she's your wife, after all."

Hiram's brows drew together in an agonized expression. "I love Becky. That was hard."

Sarah beamed at her brother. "I'm so proud of you I could burst."

"Even though I've lost my wife?"

"But you haven't. You don't understand women. Becky will change her mind."

"How do you know?" Hiram looked skeptical.

"Because you stood up to her."

"I don't understand."

"Don't worry about it, Hiram. Just mark my words."

"Jack!" Pa cried and rose from his chair.

Jack McCoy walked into the lobby, smiling widely when he caught sight of Pa. "Mr. Bryan! Nice to see you. Don't tell me you came all the way from Mokelumne City." He and Pa embraced, clapping each other on the shoulders in the rough manner men had. Sarah's heart ached at the sight of him, but when he nodded a greeting in her direction, she returned a casual nod. Never let it be said Sarah Gregg wore her heart on her sleeve. "Do please join us, Jack. I've told Pa what happened."

With Jack's help, Sarah filled in Pa on the details of her ill-fated visit to the residence of Hannibal Palmer. Pa looked more stricken by the minute. "There's no way?"

"No way."

"I want to see her."

"See who?"

"Florrie."

"But you can't. She lives in a brothel." In her mind's eye, Sarah pictured her straitlaced father hob-knobbing with the skimpily dressed ladies of the night in Hannibal Palmer's house of ill repute. "You absolutely can't."

Pa got his stubborn look. "I can and I will."

"Could you please hold off? The reason I'm asking is…" She had no idea what the reason was. She only knew her father's heart would break if he saw Florrie the way she was now. She cast a warning glance at Jack. "We haven't given up. We're coming up with a plan to get the baby back. Until then, it's best you don't interfere in any way."

"Well, I suppose…" Pa frowned with suspicion. "Does your plan involve violence? Because if it does, I don't think—"

"No violence involved. We'd be fools if we thought we could outgun Hannibal Palmer and his gang." Her mind had gone totally blank. She could hardly think of her name, let alone an elaborate plan to outwit the likes of Hannibal Palmer. She cast desperate eyes at Jack. "We have lots of ideas, haven't we?"

Without hesitation, Jack nodded decisively. "Sarah's right. It's only a matter of which plan we should chose. I think you should wait, Mr. Bryan. It won't take long before you're reunited with your daughter."

For a moment, Pa deliberated. "All right, you've convinced me. I have every confidence in you, Jack. I'll wait, but whatever you're going to do, it had better be soon. Luzena is waiting to hear from me."

Sarah breathed a sigh of relief. But what now? How could she come up with a plan to rescue Florrie's baby when the whole thing was impossible?

They continued chatting until Pa excused himself and went up to bed. The moment he left, Sarah turned to Jack. "Thanks for saving me."

Jack gave a low chuckle. "What was that all about? Last I heard you were sure there was no way to get the baby back. Have you thought of something?"

"Not exactly…no, I haven't. Oh, Jack, what have I done? I have no plan. I just didn't want Pa seeing my sister in that awful place. Now what do I do?"

"What do you do?" Jack twisted his lips and looked toward the ceiling. "I'd say we'd better come up with a plan to get that baby back, Hannibal Palmer be damned."

* * * *

What to do? What to do? Next morning, Sarah's head was spinning as she went to work in the pie shop. After spending a near sleepless night discarding one useless plan after another, she'd come up with nothing. At least the pie shop was running smoothly. Between Cedric and Anming, they'd done a fine job. "We sold more pie than ever," said Anming. "I just hope Ling returns today."

Sarah had been so wrapped up in her own problems she'd forgotten how the young Chinese and his friends were working their claim in Sandy gulch and the possible threat from Hannibal Palmer's gang. "You haven't heard anything?"

Anming regarded her with troubled eyes. "I worry. He should be back by now."

Sarah couldn't find any reassuring words. She'd overheard enough to know that throughout the gold diggings, foreigners were resented and treated poorly, the Chinese most of all.

In the early afternoon, Sarah was serving customers when Anming rushed in from the back and got her aside. "It's Ling! He's hurt."

Sarah slipped outside and found the young Chinese man sitting huddled against the Beehive oven, clothing torn and bloodied, face scratched and bruised. Anming knelt beside him and started talking in Mandarin. At Ling's first response, a horrified expression crossed her face. It deepened with each of his answers. Finally Anming looked up to Sarah. "Ling says the stream that ran through their claim all of a sudden dried up. They didn't know what to do because you must have water to work your claim. They were about to pack up and leave when at least fifteen, maybe twenty, men, all with guns, swooped down out of nowhere. These men took all the gold Ling and his friends had collected. They shot up their camp and left." She spoke to Ling who answered briefly. "Four of his friends are dead. He pretended to be dead or they would have killed him, too."

"Ask if it was Hannibal Palmer's men," Sarah said, a cold fury building inside her.

Anming spoke in Mandarin and got a quick answer. "Ling says yes, it was Palmer's men. He recognized some of them. They didn't bother to disguise themselves."

They helped Ling inside to the kitchen. He appeared to be all right except for cuts and bruises. With Cedric's help, they got him fed, cleaned up, and a few cuts bandaged. Sarah told Anming to see that he got back to his camp. She was not to come back the rest of the day. After they left, the little cockney went livid with rage, waving a rolling pin as he spoke. "Ruthless men like 'annibal Palmer should be wiped off the face of this earth. That villain thinks 'e's above the law—gets away with murder, anything 'e pleases, and we're 'elpless to stop 'im."

"I couldn't agree more." *So frustrating.* More than ever, Sarah wanted to settle the score with Hannibal Palmer. She'd racked her brain, but any semblance of a plan still eluded her.

Cedric calmed himself down. "Did Ling say the water dried up?"

"Yes, but I don't know why."

The little cockney snorted with contempt. "You can thank Palmer for that. 'E's got two claims that made 'im wealthy. There's the first one, Golden Hill. It sat on a little stream. You've got to 'ave water to work your claim, so when Palmer decided 'e didn't 'ave enough, guess what 'e did?"

"I have no idea."

"'E went upstream, over to the American River, built a dam, and diverted the river so it would flow 'is way down to 'is claim. What did that thief care about the 'undreds of claims along the riverbed that dried up and were useless?"

"What about his other claim?"

"Looks like 'e did it again. Mad Mule, the second claim, lies to the north of Sandy Gulch. It's not as rich as the first—what could be?—but it pays off well. Like as not, what 'e's done is build another dam that diverts the water running through Sandy Gulch. I wouldn't put it past the low-down skunk."

A glimmer of an idea flitted through Sarah's mind. "These dams they built. What would happen if they were destroyed?"

"I'd say Palmer would get mighty mad because 'is claims below the dams would be flooded out and ruined. 'E's got millions tied up in those claims. Nobody would 'ave the guts to do it, though."

"Certainly not." She chose her words carefully. "But what if, just for instance, you wanted to destroy that dam? How would you go about it?"

"That's easy. I'd blow 'er sky 'igh."

"And how would you do that?"

"That's easy, too. I'd ask Ling. Anming says 'e worked in the coal mines in China, so 'e knows all about gunpowder. That's what they use in the mines to blow out rocks and the like." Cedric frowned, as if he'd just had a revelation. "Say, Mrs. Gregg, I 'ope you're not thinking of—"

"Of course not. What a silly idea."

The Englishman looked relieved and started to laugh. "What was I thinking? A nice lady like you is going to blow up 'annibal Palmer's dam and ruin 'is priceless mining claim? That's a good one!"

"Indeed it is, Cedric. A good one."

As soon as she could, Sarah left the pie shop in search of Jack McCoy. She found him brushing Bandit in the stables back of the general store. She appreciated the way his eyes brightened when he saw her, but that wasn't why she was here. "Hello, Jack."

After a greeting, he looked apologetic. "I haven't come up with a plan to get Florrie's baby back. I'm still looking."

"You can stop looking. What would you say if we blew up that dam Hannibal Palmer built over his Sandy Gulch claim and flooded it out?"

Jack threw down the brush. "What?"

"You heard me." She gave Bandit an affectionate pat on the nose. "Do you want to hear the rest?"

A corner of Jack's mouth twisted into a wry grin. "You are something else, Widow Gregg. Yes, I'd like to hear your plan." He led Bandit back to his stall. "Let's take a walk. I suspect it's best you not be overheard."

By the time Sarah finished, they had walked the length of Main Street and were practically out of town. "What do you think?" she asked.

"I think you're crazy." She was about to protest, when Jack continued on. "But it just might work."

"You mean you'll help me?"

"It'll be tricky, but if Ling agrees to come along, I can do it."

She hastened to correct him. "Not I, we."

He laughed. "You can't mean you're coming with us."

"Why not? I've heard of women working in the goldfields."

"But they're few and far between." Jack stopped smiling, as if he suddenly realized she meant what she said. "It's a different world up in the diggings, brutal and harsh. Why would you even think of going?"

"Because it's my plan, and I feel responsible. But also…" She struggled to put her thoughts in order. "There was a time when I wouldn't have done anything more daring than try a new brand of tea. That's before I got a taste of life in a mining town. The excitement, the adventure—it's contagious. I know this sounds crazy, but maybe I've caught the gold fever, too. I don't expect to find a twenty-pound nugget or anything. I just want to see with my own eyes what's up there, and why shouldn't I? Am I forbidden just because I'm a woman?"

"I give up." Jack's face split into a wide grin. "But you won't be wearing that dress. I'll get you a pair of trousers, a shirt, and hat."

"You mean I must look like a man?"

"Don't worry, I'll know the difference."

"Fine, then. Let's get back to town. I'll talk to Ling. We'll head for the diggings as soon as we can."

Chapter 20

Early morning the next day, Sarah, Jack, and Ling set out for the diggings above Hangtown. Pa and Becky were still at the hotel, but Sarah had told them she'd be "very busy" for the next couple of days and likely wouldn't see them. She carried a bedroll on her back, as did the two men, along with loads of gunpowder and long fuses. "You're sure you want to do this?" Jack asked her.

"More than ever." She'd dressed in men's clothing as Jack suggested. How strange not to feel a skirt swirling around her ankles, but how much easier it was to walk. No wonder men wore pants. She might actually pass for a boy in her wide-brimmed men's hat and loose cotton shirt—that is, if no one looked too closely at her not-so-flat chest.

So these were the diggings! Traveling ever upward, they passed deep riverbeds and ravines, many of them swarming with men wielding picks and shovels, wrestling with boulders, packing dirt to make dams. Others were hammering together the long, wooden flumes that carried water to their claims. At one point, Sarah stood in a spot where she could see hundreds of flumes zig-zagging their way downhill, along with countless waterwheels.

Tents and cabins of rough logs dotted the hillsides. Everywhere men toiled in the streams—all kinds of men like the Mexicans with their huge uncombed beards, Colt revolvers in their belts, and knives stuck into the legs of their pantaloons.

They came across a black man who said he was an ex-slave. He had to work by himself. No white man would associate with him, but he didn't care. With a broad smile on his face, he told them, "I'm just glad they made California a free state. Could have gone either way." He was saving his money to buy his wife and family, still slaves in Georgia.

A grizzled, old miner took a moment from his labors to talk. "Look at them," he said, sweeping his hand over the swarm of miners. "All of them crazy, me included. Either we're standing in ice-cold water for hours or we dig, dig, dig. When we're not working, we're getting sick with scurvy or downright starving. Look at that man." He pointed to a nearby miner with a pale, cadaverous face. "He uses mercury because it binds to the gold. Trouble is it's poisonous. He'll be dead soon, and what will all his gold do for him then?" He grimaced and put his hand on his hip. "My back is lame. I'm a wreck. Don't know if I can hold on much longer."

"So why do you do it?" Jack asked.

The miner looked surprised he would ask. "Why do any of us do it? We're killing ourselves out here, and all for the same reason. I've got the same dream as everyone else. There's a twenty-five pound pure gold nugget lying in a stream out there, just waiting for me to find it. That's what keeps me going."

They climbed higher. The terrain got rougher. Ling seemed tireless, climbing with the ease of a mountain goat. Much as Sarah wanted to show she could hold her own, she welcomed Jack's help when she stumbled or had a hard time hauling herself up a steep hill. By now they'd left all the miners behind. They got so high Sarah could see the timberline in the distance above them. They followed as Jack veered to the left. After a short hike, they looked down on the Mad Mule diggings. When she saw the crew of men toiling in the stream and working the sluice boxes, she had a moment of doubt. "Wait! I don't want to drown anyone."

"You won't." Jack pointed to the scattering of tents and lean-tos high on the hillside. "We'll wait for dark when they'll be safe in their beds."

They climbed higher till they came upon a dirt dam with a lake behind. Several long, wooden flumes led into it. Others lead downhill. Jack pointed. "There it is, Hannibal Palmer's dam. See those flumes? That's where he diverted the stream that ran through Sandy Gulch. Those other flumes lead down to his Mad Mule claim." He looked at Ling. "Are you ready?" Using exaggerated gestures, he pointed to the dam, then to the packs on their backs. "Time to plant some gunpowder."

Ling eagerly nodded.

"I want to come, too," Sarah said.

"Not on your life."

She was going to insist, but the sternness in Jack's voice told her further discussion was useless. "It's dangerous?"

"I'd hate see that beautiful figure of yours blown to kingdom come."

End of discussion. Only after Jack and Ling left did she realize that hauling gunpowder on their backs and planting it with fuses might be dangerous. Up to now, she hadn't given it a thought, but Jack's *blown to kingdom come* remark caused a tightness in her chest. She waited with growing dread, expecting to hear an explosion at any moment. After two anxious hours, a cry of relief broke her lips when they returned. "You're back! Did it go all right?"

Jack wearily sat on the ground, laying his backpack aside. "It's done. We've set enough gunpowder and fuses to blow half the Sierra Nevada away." He grinned. "You weren't worried, were you?"

She grinned back. "What was there to worry about?"

"We'll wait till after dark before we set off the charges. Palmer's men will be out of the valley and up on the hillsides by then. Not that they'll thank me for saving their lives."

"So we wait some more?"

"We wait."

* * * *

Under a quarter moon that barely lit the sky, Jack and Ling left again. It wouldn't take long for them to light the fuses. Sarah stood breathlessly waiting until a tremendous blast shook the ground. She heard, more than saw, the dam crumble and the wall of water crash through and head down the valley below. Jack and Ling returned shortly, and the three stood peering into the near darkness. Sarah clasped Jack's arm. "You did it!"

Jack gave a nod of satisfaction. "Blowing up the dam was the easy part. You've got the hard part."

"Are you sure Palmer will come?"

"We've just wrecked his pride and joy, his second best moneymaker. You think he won't come running? I give him two days, three at the most, before he arrives in Hangtown steaming mad." He punched Ling on the shoulder. "Good job!"

The young Chinese smiled as if he understood, and maybe he did. Together they stood and listened as the last vestiges of water drained from the remains of Hannibal Palmer's dam.

* * * *

A day later, after a quick, uneventful hike down the mountain, Sarah returned to the pie shop and found the air abuzz with only one topic of conversation, the destruction of the Mad Mule diggings. From what Sarah could glean, speculation over who blew up the dam ran rife. Maybe Joaquin Murrieta, the notorious bandit, blew it up. Maybe one of Palmer's millionaire rivals was seeking revenge. Back in the kitchen, Cedric greeted her with a twinkle in his eye. "'Ave you 'eard the news? Someone 'ad the nerve to blow up the dam above Mad Mule. There's ten feet of silt over the diggings. It'll take months for Palmer to clean it up and get it going again, if 'e ever does." He made an exaggerated clucking sound. "What a shame. I'd wager Palmer will show up in town any minute now."

"Do you think so, Cedric?" Sarah asked sweetly. "Poor Mr. Palmer. Who would do such a terrible thing?"

Late that afternoon, Jack brought her the word. "Palmer's just arrived. He checked into the El Dorado Hotel. Early tomorrow he'll travel up the mountain to see the remains of Mad Mule."

"Then I'd better see him tonight." Sarah looked around to make sure she wasn't overheard. "Is everything in place?"

"We just got back," Jack said softly. "It's ready to go."

The big moment had arrived. Her stomach filled with fluttering butterflies. *Florrie. Little Addy.* The thought of them steadied her. She must do what she had to do and not let fear get in the way.

* * * *

Dressed in a high-necked, dark grey calico, a plain grey bonnet on her head, Sarah entered the lobby of the El Dorado Hotel and asked for Mr. Hannibal Palmer's room number. Upon receiving it, she climbed the stairs to the second floor and knocked on his door. Palmer opened it himself. He stared at her blankly. "Yes?"

"Don't you remember me, Mr. Palmer? Not so long ago you had me escorted from your home."

He frowned in recognition. "Ah, yes, Mrs. Gregg, is it not? What could you possibly want?"

The last of the butterflies disappeared from her stomach. Where her newfound courage came from, she wasn't sure. Maybe it was simply the knowledge that justice and decency dwelt on her side, not on the side of this evil man standing before her. "There's a certain matter we must discuss."

Palmer gave her a cold stare. "I have nothing to say." He started to close the door.

She stopped it with the palm of her hand. "But I have lots to say to you."

"See here," he began, "I don't have to—"

"Oh, but you do." Her voice rang with confidence. "I assure you, you'll face dire consequences if you don't hear me out."

Palmer frowned in thought. Easy to guess he'd love to shut the door in her face, but he didn't quite dare. He swung the door open. "All right, come in, but make it brief."

"Gladly." She wasn't the least bit glad to step into the room of a ruthless killer. Even worse, what she was about to say would make him angry. She'd come this far, though, and wouldn't back out now. She swept into the room and turned to face him. "I won't ask to sit down because this won't take long."

"Then speak up. I don't have all night." He was annoyed, yet curious, too.

The words came readily to her mouth. She didn't even have to clear her throat. "As you know, the Mad Mule is in ruins."

Palmer's face suffused with anger. "What has that got to do with you, Mrs. Gregg?"

"I'm the one who blew up your dam."

If the situation hadn't been so serious, she would have enjoyed seeing his expression change from annoyance to a mixture of astonishment, suspicion, and just plain disbelief. "What do you mean? You couldn't possibly have—"

"I assure you, I did. Would you care to know why?"

"Go on."

"As you may recall, I asked for my sister's child back, and you refused. I still want her back, so I have a proposition for you."

"And what might that be?" A thread of skepticism ran in his voice, as if he were talking to someone not quite bright.

"It's like this, Mr. Palmer. I'd venture to say that as much as you might regret the destruction of Mad Mule, it would be nothing compared to losing Golden Hill. Wasn't that the claim that made you rich? Twenty-pound nuggets lying on the ground and all that? I understand it's still paying handsomely. Am I right?"

As she talked, a growing suspicion filled Palmer's eyes. "What do you mean? What are you talking about?"

This time she had to take a deep breath. *Stay calm. This is now or never.* "Do you recall how you diverted the American river and built a dam above your Golden Hill claim?"

"What are you getting at?" His superior expression was starting to fade.

"That dam has been planted with enough explosives to blow half the Sierra Nevada Mountains away. I have only to send the signal and pouf!"— she flipped her hand—"Golden Hill will be lying under tons of silt."

A small vein near Palmer's left eye bulged as his face grew red. Fingers curled, he reached toward her throat. She stepped back and held up her hand. "Stop! Hear me out. Did you think I'm alone? You'll pay a huge price if I'm not outside this hotel in twenty minutes. I have people waiting. When they get the word, one touch of a match to a fuse, and your dam is gone. There's no way you can stop them, even if you and your men race up there at top speed. That's because the dam will be long gone before you got there and Golden Hill washed away."

Palmer's face blanched. "You didn't plan this yourself. Who's behind this?"

"That's not important. What's important is you can easily save Golden Hill. All you have to do is return my sister's baby." Her heart started hammering in her chest. She was getting slightly dizzy. *Don't ruin it all and faint.*

"That's blackmail." His lips curled with scorn. "I don't believe you."

She turned toward the door. "I shall wait in the lobby." She hadn't intended to leave, but the man was way bigger than she was, and she'd started to wither under the force of his hateful glare. She was getting dizzier. Her knees had gone weak. She very much wanted to sit down. In her boldest voice, she declared, "You have fifteen minutes to decide."

When she reached the lobby, she sank into an upholstered chair and checked the clock behind the registration desk. *Fifteen minutes, and not a second more.*

Five minutes later, Hannibal Palmer came down the stairs and confronted her. "How do I know you're telling the truth?"

She rose and gave him a smile. "Think about it, Mr. Palmer. We took the trouble to blow the dam above Mad Mule because we were either after revenge or we wanted something. If it was revenge, wouldn't we have blown the dam in the middle of the day when your men were working? We waited until dark because our purpose was to send you a message, not kill everyone." She gave the clock a purposeful glance. "Your time's almost up." She softened her voice. "I'm not asking for a penny of your money. I just want my sister's baby back."

A nerve twitched in Palmer's jaw. He was breathing short, tight little breaths. Easy to see he'd love to strangle her if they weren't in the busy lobby of the El Dorado Hotel. Through gritted teeth, he finally spoke. "I'll send for the child. Meantime, you'd better make sure Golden Hill is safe."

She'd won! She wanted to clap her hands, do a little jig. Not a good idea, though, with Palmer close to exploding. She remained straight-faced and dignified. "I prefer to get the child myself. Is she still in Coloma?"

Palmer smirked. "Do you think I'd allow the child of a whore in my home? She was never in Coloma. She's not far from Hangtown. She's called Mary. If you wish to get her yourself, I'll send my carriage. You give me your word—?"

"I give you my word." She boldly met his eyes. "But don't forget Golden Hill will be in danger until I hold that baby safe in my arms."

Minutes later, Ruben, one of Palmer's men, picked her up in a two-seater carriage in front of the hotel. His bushy black beard and gun strapped to his side made him look ferocious, but when she asked where they were going, he gave her a friendly smile. "Moose City is where we're going. About ten miles. The road's bad in spots, but we'll make it." He flicked the reins and frowned. "Don't know why you'd want to go to that hellhole."

"Why is that?"

Ruben shook his head and spat a chaw of tobacco over the side. "Hangtown's a paradise compared to Moose City. It grew up practically overnight when some lucky fool found a fifteen-pound gold nugget in a ravine close by. Just about the whole town's thrown together with canvas and spit. Not the brothel, though. It's about the only wooden building in town, but that ain't saying much."

A horrible thought occurred to her. It couldn't be, but she'd better ask. "This place you're taking me to, it's not the brothel, is it?"

Ruben glanced at her in surprise. "You don't know? Yep, that's where we're going." He dug in his pocket and pulled out a letter. "You're supposed to give this to Mrs. Dawson. She's the madam who runs the place."

By now, Sarah was familiar with mining towns. She'd traveled the main streets of Gold Creek, Hangtown, and Coloma, but never had she seen anything so ugly as the main street of Moose City. Nearly every foot of the muddy street was covered with trash of all sorts—old boots, sardine cans, empty bottles, broken picks, and shovels—everything imaginable. With few exceptions, the buildings were constructed of canvas, all with sagging roofs. At the far end, a two-story, unpainted, rickety-looking wooden structure stood out like a sore thumb. The Hangtown brothel was a palace compared to this place. Ruben stopped the carriage in front. "We're here."

Sarah didn't hesitate. Her heart knocking in her chest, she stepped from the carriage, carefully made her way through the muddy yard, up the steps, and knocked on the door. A slovenly woman in a flowered silk wrapper, hair uncombed, swung it open. "You're too early. We're not—" She stopped when she saw who it was. "What do you want?"

Sarah introduced herself. "I'm to speak to Mrs. Dawson."

"That's me. I don't like being bothered at this hour."

Without apology, Sarah handed Mrs. Dawson the letter. "Here, read it. It's from Mr. Palmer."

The madam practically snatched the letter from her hand. When she finished reading, she asked, "You want just the one?"

What did she mean? Sarah had to think fast. "I've come for the little girl you call Mary. She'd be around six months old."

"Oh, that one," Mrs. Dawson muttered. "Well, come on in." She led Sarah through the house, out the back door, down wobbly steps to a sea-of-mud backyard. She pointed to a tent pitched at the back. "She's in there with the other two. Watch your step."

A trail of carelessly laid wooden planks led across the mud to the tent. Mrs. Dawson followed as Sarah stepped across them, cautiously lifting her skirt, her thoughts shifting between joy and dread. At last she was about to see Addy! But what was the poor child doing in this wretched place, and who were the "other two"?

They reached the tent, entered, and were greeted by an Indian woman in a buckskin dress with long, white braids down her back. "This is White Flower," the madam said. "She takes care of the children."

Children? Sarah looked around the dim room. It contained two makeshift cribs, a couple of beds, stove, rough-hewn table, and chairs. A few brightly colored toys lay on the rough plank floor. A blond, curly-headed little boy of around two toddled toward her, smiling and holding out his arms, but she had to ignore him. She looked toward the cribs. In one, a little girl with big brown eyes stood holding the railing. She appeared to be around a year old. *Not Addy.* Sarah stepped to the other crib where a baby about six months old, neatly dressed in a long, white, embroidered gown, sat playing. With her chubby cheeks and happy gurgles, she appeared to be well cared for. As Sarah approached, the baby looked up at her with bright gray eyes. *Florrie's eyes.* She didn't have much hair, but the few wispy curls on her head were blond, exactly the color of Hiram's hair when he was a young boy. The baby lifted her arms, squealed, and smiled. Sarah couldn't hold back her burst of joy. "Addy, Addy, I found you!" She scooped the baby into her arms. "This is my sister's child. I'd know her anywhere." Tears welled in her eyes. She couldn't help it. White Flower, seeming to understand, started crying, too, bobbing her head up and down, a happy smile on her face. Sarah turned triumphantly to Mrs. Dawson. "This isn't Mary. This is Addy, my niece."

The madam's annoyed expression softened. "Notice she's been well cared for. They're all well cared for. Mr. Palmer wants it that way."

Sarah cradled the baby tight in her arms. "I can't see why he's going to all this trouble just to turn them into servants."

The madam frowned. "Where did you hear that?"

"From his wife, Isobel."

"Isobel!" A burst of harsh, derisive laughter broke from Mrs. Dawson's mouth. "That old whore? Since she married Palmer, butter won't melt in her mouth."

"I don't understand."

"Mr. Palmer plucked her right out of his brothel in Downieville. Now she puts on airs like she's better than the rest of us. Well, she can try all she wants, but she'll always be a whore."

Isobel Palmer a prostitute! If Sarah hadn't been so caught up in the joy of finding Addy, she would have had a good laugh at the uppity woman who'd treated her to shabbily.

Ms. Dawson wasn't finished. She gave Sarah what amounted to a look of scorn. "Servants, indeed. How naïve you are."

"What do you mean?"

In an angry gesture, the slovenly woman drew her wrapper closer around her. "I may be the madam of a whorehouse, but I don't hold with depravity."

Again, Sarah was baffled. "Depravity?"

"Not in this house, but lord knows where he plans to take these children, or what he plans to do. Just take the baby and go. Wait a minute." She signaled to the Indian woman. "White Flower will get her clothes and diapers together."

Sarah waited, not saying another word. She'd get nothing more from the madam, so she didn't ask again about depravity. When Addy's pitifully small bundle of clothes was ready, she clasped her tight and headed for the entrance, catching one last glimpse of the little girl with dark eyes staring at her from her crib. The little boy with the golden curls reached his arms out. Why were these children here? Why did she have a sick feeling that they weren't safe and that the reason they weren't safe was so unspeakably ugly that a woman like herself, brought up sheltered from a harsh, cruel world, couldn't possibly understand?

At the curb, she handed the baby up to Ruben and climbed into the carriage. To her surprise, Palmer's gruff henchman broke into a wide grin. "A baby! I ain't seen one of these since I left Tennessee." He cooed at little Addy, chucked her under her chin before, with reluctance, he handed her back. "She's lucky to get out of that place," he said as he picked up the reins.

Again, Sarah got a bad feeling. She set it aside. Nothing was going to mar this joyful day.

Chapter 21

When they got back to Hangtown, Ruben let Sarah off at the El Dorado Hotel. Jack was outside waiting. His eyes lit when he saw she held a baby in her arms. "By God, you did it! So we won't be blowing the Golden Hill dam after all. What a woman you are."

She had no time for compliments. "Is my father—?"

"He and Becky are in the dining room. I've got to send a message to Ling—you know what that's about. Go on in and see your father."

Sarah couldn't remember a prouder moment in her life than when she walked to the table where Pa and Becky were dining, Florrie's baby in her arms. "Here she is, Pa. I got her back."

Pa rose from the table and eagerly stretched out his arms. "My granddaughter! Let me hold her."

As if the baby knew she was in safe hands, she smiled and thrust a tiny fist toward her grandfather. For a long moment, he held the baby tight and couldn't speak. His eyes got damp. What a teary afternoon this was! Finally he looked at Sarah. "Just wait till your mother sees this beautiful child."

Thinking of her mother, Sarah wanted to cry all over again but managed to choke back her tears. She sat at the table and told them how she got the baby back—not the whole story, especially the part where they blew up the dam—but enough that they knew it hadn't been easy. Pa nodded his enthusiastic approval. "I can't thank you enough, Sarah. I couldn't ask for a better daughter than you."

A knot of emotion still lodged in her throat, but she got past it and spoke again. "Thanks, Pa, but I'm not done yet."

"Ah yes, there's Florrie, isn't there?"

"I've got to see her."

"I'll go with you. I'd wager when she sees this baby, she'll come to her senses and leave that evil place."

"Let's hope you're right, Pa. It would be better if I spoke to her alone, though, and I'm not taking the baby to such a place." Sarah looked over at Becky who was getting all fidgety. Obviously she was dying to hold the baby. "Becky, will you—?"

"Of course I will." Becky's arms shot out. She took little Addy and cradled her close. "I trust you brought some diapers. She's bound to need a change by now."

Becky's caring attitude toward the baby reminded Sarah how much Becky and Hiram had yearned for a child of their own. What a shame. Becky would be a different woman if she had children. And that reminded her of something. "I thought you were leaving. You said—"

"I've decided to stay."

"Really?" Her patience with Becky had just come to an abrupt end. "Why would you want to stay with such a sinner as my brother?"

A flush crept over Becky's cheeks. "I was wrong. When Hiram told me he wasn't leaving Hangtown, and I should just go home, I realized how much I loved him and—" Her voice broke. In a tremulous whisper she continued, "I didn't want to lose him."

Sarah welcomed the opportunity to at long last speak her mind. "I'm glad to hear you're staying, but only if you respect my brother for the wonderful man he is and stop your constant nagging and belittling."

Becky nodded eagerly. "Never again. I know I've been horrid. That's going to change. "

"I'm happy to hear it. I hope you mean it."

Pa gave his daughter-in-law a pleased smile before he turned to Sarah. "I'm concerned. Is it wise to go alone to see Florrie?"

No, it wasn't wise. Sneaking into a brothel owned by Hannibal Palmer would be dangerous, indeed, and perhaps the most stupid thing she'd ever done. "Nothing to it, Pa. Just keep your fingers crossed that our Florrie will want to come home."

Jack met her outside. "Everything's fine. I've sent word to Ling. Palmer can relax, but not too much. We'll clear most of the explosives away, but not all." He grinned. "Just in case he decides to change his mind."

She told him she was on her way to see her sister.

"I'll come along."

"So far today, my luck is holding, so thanks, but I'm going in alone."

At four o'clock in the afternoon, not much was stirring at the house with the red door on Pacific Street. Jack accompanied her to the back where they'd met with Anming. The rear door was open. Sarah said a quick, "Wait here" and slipped inside. Nobody around. With stealthy steps, she crept down a hallway, past the kitchen, and up the back stairs. She knocked on Florrie's door.

"Sarah!" Florrie couldn't hide her surprise when she opened the door. She looked none too pleased. "I thought we—"

Sarah stepped inside. "Sit down, I want to talk to you."

"What is it now?"

After they were seated, Sarah continued, "This will come as a shock, but there's no other way than to tell you straight out." She took a deep breath. "Florrie, they lied. Your baby didn't die."

Florrie gasped and grabbed the pearls at her throat. "Addy's alive?"

"Very much so."

Sarah proceeded to tell her how Palmer's people had lied on the night Addy was born. Without going into the harrowing details, she simply said she'd persuaded Hannibal Palmer to give her back. "Isn't it wonderful, Florrie? She's a darling baby, perfect in every way. You should have seen the look on Pa's face when I put her in his arms."

"Wonderful, indeed." Florrie looked truly grateful.

"Pa wants you home. We'll make up some excuse so Ma never need find out about…well, you know, everything." With a wave of her hand, Sarah indicated the lavishly furnished room. "Haven't you had enough of this? Now that you know your baby's alive, I know you'll want to come home."

Florrie got a pout on her face. "No."

Her answer practically blew Sarah back in her chair. "Did I hear you right?"

"You did." Florrie reach out with pleading hands. "How can I make you understand? As I said before, I love it here. For the first time in my life, men want me. I see the admiration in their eyes. Tonight we're having another wonderful party. I'll have my choice of men. They'll all be after me, and I can take my pick. They shower me with presents. See this?" She held up a wrist circled by a bracelet of sparkling diamonds. "Sorry, Sarah, but I can't give up this life. Let Becky raise the baby. She'd love to do it. You know how she's always wanted a child. As for me…" She nearly choked up but carried on. "Can't you understand how much this all means to me?"

"No, I don't understand. I'll never understand."

Florrie threw up her hands. "Then there's nothing more to say, now is there?"

Florrie was right, nothing more to be said. Sarah got to her feet, out of words, out of patience, out of hope. She headed for the door.

"Aren't you going to say goodbye?" Florrie called.

"Why? You're dead to me now. I don't have a sister anymore."

With a bitter heart, Sarah left Florrie's room and walked down the main staircase. No one around. Not that she cared. The mood she was in, she wouldn't mind tangling with the awful Mrs. Northcutt or anybody else who got in her way.

She didn't slow down when she saw Jack waiting outside. He caught up with her and fell in step. "What happened?"

"She won't come. She's happy her baby didn't die, but she doesn't want to give up her so-called wonderful life. I can't believe it!" She made no effort to stifle the hysterical edge in her voice. She must calm down, but how could she get past her rage at her idiotic sister and her crushing disappointment?

Jack stopped in the street and cupped her elbow. "Stop. Calm down." He turned her toward him and clasped both her arms. "Tell me exactly what happened."

They stood on Main Street, people passing by, but she hardly noticed. She related her ill-fated meeting with Florrie in choppy little sentences with shaky gasps of breath in between. "She just won't come," she ended. "I feel sick. What am I going to tell Pa?"

Jack closed his eyes a moment. When he opened them, he nodded, as if he'd come to a decision. "Come on, we're going back."

"Back where?"

"Back to see Florrie."

"But I just told you—"

"I know what you told me. Florrie talked to you, but she hasn't talked to me. Let's go. I have a lot to say to that foolish sister of yours. She won't like to hear it, but, by God, she's going to listen."

When they returned to the house with the red door, they didn't go around to the back. "We'll go in the front," Jack said. "You have every right to see your sister. God help anyone who gets in our way."

Jack's clenched jaw and the sheen of determination in his eyes told Sarah not to argue. "Of course, that's fine." What on earth was he going to say to Florrie? The question hammered at her, but she said nothing more.

Jack didn't bother to knock. They walked in and were halfway up the staircase when Mrs. Northcutt appeared in the entryway and called up to them. "You can't—"

He hardly bothered to turn his head. "We can and we will."

The gritty resolve in Jack's voice made the desired impression. Mrs. Northcutt shrugged, spun on her heel, and left. They continued up the stairs. Sarah knocked on Florrie's door again. This time, when her sister opened it, she was dressed for the evening in a red satin, low-cut gown, a jeweled comb in her hair. "You're back?" Florrie frowned. "What more is there to say?"

Sarah introduced Jack. "He's my friend and wants to talk to you. I met him right after you disappeared. He saved Ma when she had an asthma attack. He's helped us a lot."

Florrie nodded reluctantly and swung the door wide. When they were seated at the table, Florrie asked, "Well? Really, I don't have much time."

Jack gave her a long, hard stare. "You will take the time to listen to me. I'm about to tell you things I've never told anyone before. Why do I bother?" He threw a glance at Sarah. "This woman means a lot to me. So does her family—your family, Florrie. They're kind, loving people, and they want you home. You have no idea how lucky you are to have such a family. Let me tell you about mine." His brows drew downward in a frown, as if he hated dredging up long buried memories. "My mother was a prostitute. I never knew who my father was. I doubt she did either. My first memories are of a room like this." He waved his hand. "Fine carpeting, velvet drapes, everything plush. She was beautiful then. She wore stylish clothes and laughed a lot. I remember I had a little room off hers. She'd lock me in nearly every night while she 'entertained' her clients. I couldn't call her 'Mother.' That would have spoiled her youthful image. She made me call her Stella. At the time, I didn't understand. I was only five or six, so I didn't know I was living in a brothel. But the good times didn't last. I was maybe six or seven when I saw my mother throw herself on the bed and sob like I'd never heard her before. She'd been tossed out of her fancy brothel. I didn't know why, but I do now. She'd started to lose her looks. By then, she was past thirty, getting those little wrinkles around her eyes. She was drinking heavily—a bottle of whiskey every day, and it showed, especially along with the opium she was smoking."

Florrie was listening with rapt attention. She drew herself up and exclaimed, "I would never do such a thing."

"Yes, you would. As time goes by, you'll do anything to ease the pain of the life you're leading. We moved to another brothel, far worse than the first. Stella's clients weren't well dressed, upper-class gentlemen anymore. They were uncouth working class louts with dirt under their fingernails. Not only had her looks coarsened, so had her soul. I couldn't please her, nobody could. While she worked, I had to wait in the hallway. It was either that or play outside in the dirty gutters where the street gangs might get me." A melancholy smile crossed his face. "I was a skinny kid, small for my age, so I didn't spend a whole lot of time outside. The trouble was, inside wasn't much better. Life in a brothel isn't pretty. There's nothing, no degradation, no cruelty I haven't seen. I never got a kind word from my mother. She would just as soon haul off and belt me one as look at me. By the time I was twelve, between the whiskey, opium, and the sordid life she led, my mother was pretty far gone, her cheeks all sunken in like she was dead already. They were going to throw her out, but she saved them the trouble and committed suicide. She took strychnine, the prostitutes' poison of choice."

Florrie gasped. "How awful."

"You go into convulsions. It's not a good way to die. If it hadn't been for—" Jack stopped, as if he'd gotten a catch in his throat.

"Jenny?" Sarah asked softly. "You've mentioned her before, the one with the soft blue eyes and long, blond hair who taught you how to read and write."

"Jenny." Jack looked toward the ceiling, as if giving himself an extra moment before he must carry on. "Her room was down the hall. She used to read to me, give me lessons. I was a lost, lonely kid, and she gave me the only love I ever knew. After Stella died, they were going to throw me out, but Jenny said she'd watch over me and see I earned my keep. So I stayed. The hardest part—" His jaw clenched. Sarah could tell each word was a struggle. "The hardest part was seeing how she suffered. She was sick. I never knew what was wrong exactly, but she was slowly wasting away. She had asthma attacks, too, really bad. She coughed a lot, sometimes couldn't stop. That's how I learned how to help her. But worse than the sickness was her despair. She was still in her twenties, but she was doomed. There was no way out of the horrible life she was living. You're new to this life, Florrie. All you see is the fun, the good times. Believe me, they won't last. Right now you can't imagine what it's like for a prostitute in one of those hellholes, but I guarantee you'll find out. They're forced to perform every sort of debased perversion imaginable and some you can't imagine. They suffer beatings at the hands of brutal, drunk men, and there's no one to defend them. That's what happened to Jenny. Like my mother, she told me never to enter her room when she was entertaining, no matter what I heard. One night I was out in the hall. A nasty, brute of a man was in there with her. He started beating on her—I can still hear the sickening thuds of his fists on her body. She didn't scream, but I could hear her pleading for him to stop."

"How terrible," Sarah cried. She'd listened to Jack's heart-wrenching story with growing distress. "I can see how painful this is. You don't have to—"

"I'll finish what I started." Jack breathed a shuddering sigh. A tear slid down his cheek. He made no effort to wipe it away. "I stood in the hallway, too scared to help. I should have gone in there, but like a coward, I waited in the hallway till he was gone. By the time I went in, Jenny was a bloody mess. You couldn't even recognize her face. She was coughing blood. She knew she was dying. With practically her last breath, she gave me the money she'd saved—three hundred dollars, all she had to show for a lifetime of misery. 'Leave New York,' she said. 'Go west, as far away from here as you possibly can.' Those were the last words she spoke before she died. No funeral. They dumped her body in the river."

Jack paused and ran a hand over his face. All these years, he'd hidden his unbearable pain. At last he'd allowed it to surface. Sarah wanted to throw her arms around him, comfort him, but she knew better. He must finish what he started. He wanted it that way.

When Jack could speak again, he continued, "So I did what Jenny told me to do. Took the money and headed west. Since then I've been on my own and lived with the guilt. If I hadn't been a coward, I might have saved her."

Florrie slammed her hand on the table. "That's not so! How can you blame yourself? You were just a child."

Sarah nodded vigorously. "She's right. What if you'd gone in the room and tried to help? You, too, could have been killed by that monster."

Jack took a long pause before he said, "Let me finish." His eyes drilled into Florrie's. "The worst of it is nobody gives a damn. You think it won't happen to you? You think your beauty won't fade? It will, sooner than you think, and when it does, you'll have nowhere to turn. By then you'll be so estranged from your family you'll be too humiliated and degraded to ask for help. So you'll die alone, like my mother and Jenny did, with no one to care."

Florrie pressed her hand to her mouth. "I never thought about it that way. It's been so much fun, the parties and all."

Jack nodded with understanding. "I know, but it's not the life for you. You're made of finer stuff than you think. Give up this life. Go home to your baby and your loving family. Only there will you find happiness and self-respect, the only things that truly matter in this world." He reached beneath his shirt, found the chain around his neck, and gave it a jerk. He pulled the chain out, slipped off the gold ring, and laid it in front of

Florrie. "This belonged to Jenny. She gave it to me when she died, and I've carried it ever since. If you walk out of here right now, she'd want you to have it and wear it in her honor. She'd be proud to think she'd played a part in bringing you home."

The door swung open, no warning knock. Mrs. Northcutt swept in looking highly annoyed. "You're wanted downstairs, Florrie. Your guests must go."

Florrie sat silent for a long moment, biting her lip as if in deep thought. At last she sighed and stood to face Mrs. Northcutt. "I won't be entertaining tonight." She picked up Jenny's ring and slipped it on her finger. "Nor ever again." She smiled at Jack. "I shall be honored to wear Jenny's ring. Now, let's get out of here."

Chapter 22

As Jack, Florrie, and Sarah descended the front steps of the brothel, Sarah drew in a fresh breath. How wonderful to get the last vestiges of heavy-scented air from her lungs. How wonderful to have her sister by her side. The bundle Florrie carried wasn't that big. She'd left the fancy dresses and gaudy jewelry behind. Jack walked beside her. That she'd been overwhelmed by his words to Florrie was an understatement. Never had she seen a man dig so deep inside himself, lay his emotions so bare despite the obvious pain. She clasped his arm. "Jack, I don't know what to—"

"Don't say anything." He was back to normal now. The one tear that had slid down his cheek was long gone. He was smiling. "You're taking her to the hotel?"

She nodded eagerly. "I can hardly wait to see the look on Pa's face when he sees Florrie and the look on Florrie's face when she sees her baby."

"I'll walk you to the hotel and be on my way."

"You don't want to come with us?"

"It's a family thing. You don't need me."

They had much to discuss—at least, she had much to discuss—and she wasn't going to let him get away that easily. "I won't be long. Where will you be?"

He lifted one dark brow and grinned at her. "Visiting my horse. When you're done, come see me."

* * * *

When Pa opened the door to his hotel room and laid eyes on Florrie, his reaction was beyond even what Sarah had imagined. "My daughter!" He pulled her inside and wrapped his arms around her.

Florrie buried her head on his shoulder and started to cry. "Oh, Pa, I'm so, so sorry—"

"Don't you be sorry for anything. That's all behind you now."

Pa understood. Thank God, he wasn't going to give Florrie a lecture or shower her with guilt. Sarah's heart filled with gratitude. "We'll make up a story. Ma need never know."

Pa gazed at Sarah over Florrie's shoulder. "There will be no stories. When Luzena sees her daughter and granddaughter, whatever the truth is, it won't matter. Did you think she'd turn them away?"

He was right. She could see that now. No one in the world had a more understanding heart than Ma. No need to make up some elaborate lie.

Becky appeared, holding little Addy in her arms. "Florrie! Well, it's time you showed up. Here's your baby." Her gruff voice belied the tear in her eye when she extended her arms and handed little Addy to her sister-in-law.

Florrie took the baby in her arms. It was easy to see from the warmth in her eyes it was love at first sight. "Oh, how adorable!" She touched Addy's cheek. "What soft skin she has. Look at her eyes. They're just like mine. And her hair! I love how it curls in those little blond ringlets." Eyes glowing, she looked at Sarah. "Thanks so much for getting her back. I hope it wasn't too much trouble."

Sarah couldn't keep the grin off her face. "Don't give it a thought. It was no trouble at all."

* * * *

When Sarah entered the stable back of the store, she found Jack standing beside Bandit, concentrating on running a brush over the horse's already shiny coat. "Hello," she said softly.

He looked up. "So Florrie's back with her family?"

"Yes, and it went beautifully. Already she loves her baby. I can't imagine she'd ever want to get into that life again, and it's all thanks to you."

In silence, Jack continued brushing Bandit. At last, he threw the brush aside and turned to face her. He placed the flat of his hand on his chest. "It's strange having the ring gone."

Words flew to her mouth, but she didn't say them. She must be careful, even though she longed to point out what to her was so obvious—that all those years the gold ring was a constant reminder of the guilt he felt over Jenny's death; that tonight, by opening his heart to Florrie, he finally realized Jenny's death wasn't his fault. He was only a boy of twelve. He couldn't possibly have saved her. So he didn't have to wander anymore, spend a lifetime running from his supposed guilt. That's what she wanted to say, but she wouldn't. If he couldn't figure it out for himself, she wasn't going to throw her pride away and try to make him understand. Maybe he'd never understand. Maybe he was born to wander, and nothing she nor anyone could do would change him. "Thanks so much, Jack. Florrie loves the gold ring. She'll wear it always." Now what would he say? Her stomach clenched tight as she waited for his answer.

"What happened tonight—it's a lot to take in." He threw back his head and let out a great peal of laughter. "My God! Suddenly I feel like a burden's been lifted off my shoulders. I don't know…maybe my talk with Florrie had something to do with it, do you suppose?" He clasped her arms. "Will you please tell me why I haven't asked you to marry me?"

"I really don't know." She kept her voice cool. "Does this mean you'd like to?"

His arms went around her. "I'd very much like to."

"Then I will."

She hardly got the words out before his arms encircled her and pulled her so close she could feel the beat of his heart. He asked, "Did I mention that I love you?"

Her arms slid around his neck. "Yes, but you can tell me again."

Epilogue

Placerville (Formerly Hangtown), California, July 4, 1865

Here came the parade!

With her husband and three children, Sarah McCoy stood amidst the crowd on a corner of Main Street waiting for the Fourth of July parade to start. What a glorious day this was. What fun to see all of Main Street decorated with bunting, flags, and garlands. She looked up at the new bell tower, a twenty-five-foot wooden structure with a big bell on top, used to summon volunteer firemen. It brought back a moment of sadness when she remembered the terrible fires of 1856 that swept through Main Street, destroying everything in their path. That included the pie shop and Hiram's hotel. They'd rebuilt, bigger and better. Faithful Cedric was her partner now. With his help, she'd turned her simple pie shop into Sarah's Bakery, the biggest in town.

"Mom, Dad, look, it's Anming!" Elizabeth, Sarah's ten-year-old daughter, pointed to the first float of the parade. A big sign on the side read Xiang Wei Lou Restaurant. With its bright colors and big, papier–mâché dragon, it was unmistakably Chinese. Anming and her husband, Ling, stood at the front of the float waving to the crowd.

They all waved back, Jack remarking, "They've come a long way, haven't they?"

Sarah glanced up at her husband. Fourteen years had past since she married him, but even now she loved being near him. He hadn't changed much—maybe a bit of gray in his hair, but that was all. He'd remained as kind and caring as ever, and now was wealthy, too, what with his and Ben's prospering businesses. "Yes, Anming and Ling have come a long way." Who would have thought the lowly coal miner and the slave girl with the awful scar would end up happily married, with five children and prosperous restaurant owners besides. Xiang Wei Lou, the first Chinese restaurant on Main Street, was famous for its Liuyang Lobster Sauce and hot, savory Hunan cuisine. The fires of 1856 destroyed it, but the undaunted couple quickly rebuilt. Now their restaurant was known far and wide, more popular than ever.

Sarah's older son, Nicholas, stood on her other side. At thirteen, he was already taller than she and looked just like his father. He pointed to a float that was coming. A big sign on the side read, The Bella Union Hotel & Casino. "There's Uncle Hiram and Aunt Becky, and look, there's Louise and Gregory."

Sarah waved. They looked so happy. Hiram, the successful hotel owner—how many did he own now? Becky, the social leader of Placerville—my, how she'd changed. She became a different woman when she and Hiram adopted Louise, a one-year-old little girl with big brown eyes, and Gregory, a two-year-old boy with blond curls. Not that Becky didn't still have a sharp tongue at times, but she was pleasant to live with now that motherhood had erased her bitter discontent. Sarah dimly remembered how she had often wished her sister-in-law would someday get her comeuppance. Whatever that meant, it never happened and was no longer necessary.

Once again, as she had many times over the years, Sarah recalled her part in the story of Louise and Gregory. It was a story Becky and the rest of the world would never hear. It began the night Sarah brought little Addy home from Moose City when she'd described to Jack the awful scene she'd encountered: the brothel, the muddy yard, the tent in back where Addy and two other children were being kept by an Indian woman named White Feather.

"What happened to the other two children?" Jack had asked.

"They're still there."

After that, Jack remained strangely quiet with a grim, thoughtful look on his face. He said nothing more but had a long, private talk with Hiram the very next day. Neither confided what was said. Shortly after, the shocking death of Hannibal Palmer was all anyone could talk about. Word had it he'd been checking on the Golden Hill dam when he accidentally tripped an explosive device someone had planted there, and that was the end of the notorious millionaire. No one mourned his loss, probably not even his wife, Isobel, who moved to their Nob Hill mansion in San Francisco shortly thereafter.

The day after Hannibal's death, Jack and Hiram went off someplace, they didn't say where. Hiram soon showed up with a little brown-eyed girl and a blond, curly-headed boy. As Becky told the story, all he ever said was, "I've got two children here who need a mother. Would you mind—?"

"Gladly," she'd cried, and that was the end of the discussion. Now the two rescued children were the light of Hiram's and Becky's lives. Sarah would never know what Hannibal's plans were, but later, when she heard horror stories about children sold to brothels, she was endlessly grateful to Jack and Hiram for their rescue. Both Gregory and Louise had turned out wonderfully well. At sixteen, tall, blond Gregory possessed an engaging personality, as well as a sharp mind. Already he was showing a keen interest in his father's hotel business. At fifteen, bubbly Louise was turning heads with her charm and pretty, dark looks.

The last float rolled by. The crowd dispersed. This afternoon there'd be picnics, games, and speeches. As Sarah and her family walked home, Timothy, her younger son, asked, "When will Aunt Florrie and Uncle Theodore be here?"

"By this evening, I hope," Sarah replied. "Don't forget, they're coming clear from Mokelumne City." *Florrie, what a miracle.* After all these years, Sarah still marveled at her sister's extraordinary luck. After her brief life of sin, she could have been disgraced for life. Instead, the day after she arrived in Mokelumne City from Hangtown, she met Theodore Goetzmann, whom Ma had wisely invited for dinner, and they fell in love practically at first sight. Sarah still had to chuckle. She'd found the beet farmer dull, ponderous, and boring, whereas her sister found him bright, witty, and a wonderful catch. Actually, he was a wonderful catch for Florrie, considering he'd become a loving father to little Addy. Now, in addition to his four children and Addy, they had three more of their own, and Florrie couldn't be happier. She never mentioned her brief life as a Sister of Joy, and most certainly no one ever brought it up.

"Looks as if the whole family will be at dinner tonight," Jack remarked as they strolled along.

"Yes, everyone." *Not quite true.* Even now, Sarah got a catch in her throat when she thought of Ma and Pa, both gone now. At least they'd lived long enough to know their grueling journey to California had been worthwhile. *I'm doing fine, Ma and Pa. Wish you were here.*

Jack took her arm as they strolled along. "It's not the same Main Street, is it?"

How true. The rough-and ready days when miners swarmed the streets were long gone, but the town had gained new life from the Comstock silver strike in Nevada. It had grown into a thriving trade center where well-built stores and business buildings lined the street, no more structures made of canvas.

"I'm so glad we're not called Hangtown anymore," Sarah remarked.

"Thanks to you."

"I suppose I helped." In 1854, Sarah worked on a committee that demanded a more dignified name instead of one that was a constant reminder of the town's not-so-glorious past. Now they were the City of Placerville, which was much more fitting.

"What would I do without you?" Jack stopped in the street and planted a tender kiss on her forehead.

As they continued their stroll along Main Street, hand in hand, a tiny smile played on Sarah's lips as she counted her blessings. Not every woman had three beautiful children and a husband who continued to be the love of her life. How lucky she was to have everything she'd ever wished for. She'd come *such* a long way from Fort Wayne, Indiana, in more ways than one.

Be sure to read the first book in the series, Wagon Train Cinderella. Each heartfelt tale is chock-full of history and adventure and is a standalone novel.

Wagon Train Cinderella

Can an oppressed young woman find love, confidence, and courage on a wagon train to California?

As a baby, Callie Whitaker was left on the doorstep of an isolated farmhouse in Tennessee. The Whitaker family took her in but treated her more like a servant than a daughter. Forced to work long hours each day and restricted from an education, Callie is scorned and ridiculed by her two older stepsisters.

A new world opens when the Whitakers sell the farm and join a wagon train to California. Rugged Indian guide, Luke McGraw, helps Callie realize how poorly she's been treated. With Luke's family teaching her to read and to see her own worth, Callie's confidence begins to flourish…and with each mile they cross, her love for Luke grows. Despite the dangerous trek and the terrible way her family treats her, Callie emerges the strongest of them all. Amidst deprivation, heartache, hardship, and death, her love for Luke remains steadfast. When disaster befalls Luke, only Callie's new-found courage and determination can pull them through.

Chapter 1

Along the Overland Trail, 1851

Walking through the woods, Callie Whitaker was drawn to the sound of a waterfall. When a snake slithered across her path, she dropped her bucket and stopped in her tracks. It disappeared into the dense undergrowth. *What brought me here? I cannot believe this is happening to me.* Only a month ago, she was leading a dull but safe existence in the Tennessee farmhouse where she'd lived her entire life and rarely left. Now here she was in the middle of a wilderness she never knew existed, heading to California, a place she'd never heard of. Bone-tired from the endless work, she was sleeping on the ground under a wagon instead of her tiny bed under the eaves. The farm wasn't much, but she'd give anything if she could return to Tennessee where she didn't have to worry about Indians, snakes, and who-knew-what-would-happen-next?

A lump formed in her throat. *Silly girl, you have no time for feeling sorry for yourself.* Darkness was about to fall. She must get to the stream, scoop a bucketful of water, and hurry back to the wagon where everyone expected their supper. She picked up her bucket and trudged on. Through tall trees, the flowing water came into view. Ah, there it was. She drew close. How beautiful. Cascading water falling over moss-covered boulders, gorgeous ferns in every shade of green, clumps of tiny violets growing around the pool beneath and standing in the pool, the water up to his knees… *Oh, my stars.* She froze in her tracks, backed a few steps away, and peered over the top of a red hawthorn bush. It was a man—tall, lean, sinewy, with long, dark hair—and completely naked. He appeared to be bathing, bending to scoop water into his palms, then bringing it up over his head with a giant splash. The water cascaded over a powerful set of shoulders, down over the rippling muscles of his stomach to his sturdy thighs, to his…

Why was she gawking like a schoolgirl? Shameful. She'd seen her little stepbrother's thing many a time. She'd never forget when crazy Grandpa Pearson from the next farm escaped and ran naked down the road. So, of course, she knew what a man looked like, but still…*oh, my*. Neither her brother's tiny thing, nor that of Grandpa Pearson's, all shriveled, looked anything like this…so big, so very, very…

He looked up. She ought to run before he spied her, but she couldn't move a muscle. His gaze caught hers and his eyebrows lifted ever so slightly. He'd spied her! Oh, she should run, but her feet refused to move, and her eyes refused to turn away from the fascinating sight before her. Taking his time, he casually looked to the left, then the right, as if he might find some kind of cover, which, of course, he could not. He shrugged, as if admitting defeat. With a mischievous smile, he spread his arms wide and bowed toward her. "Good afternoon, madam. Taking in the sights?"

Oh, Lord. His laughter brought her back to her senses. Her cheeks heating, she clutched her pail and started to back away from the hawthorn bush, intent on running off as fast as she could. But wait a minute. Why should she make a fool of herself and bolt and skitter off like a panicky calf? *He* was the one at fault, the one who should have done his bathing farther upstream. She didn't back off. Instead, gripping her faded skirt, she held it out and dipped a deep curtsey, boldly returning his grin as she did. Only after she'd risen, forcing herself to take her time, did she turn and head downstream at a dignified pace.

She hadn't recognized him. He must be from the large wagon train that had camped close by. In the morning, it would be gone, thank goodness, and she need never lay eyes on him again.

* * * *

"Callie!" Hester Whitaker glared at her stepdaughter. "It's about time you got back. Where were you? Did you expect me to fix supper by myself?"

"Sorry, ma'am." Callie stepped to the campfire and set down the heavy pail of water. She didn't attempt any excuses. Ma wouldn't listen anyway. Nor would it do any good to point out that never in Callie's memory had her stepmother fixed supper by herself. "I boiled a mess of beans this morning and baked some bread. It'll be ready in no time."

Lydia, Callie's older stepsister, tossed her blond curls and pouted. "I'm getting awfully tired of beans."

"So am I." Nellie, her other stepsister, loved to complain.

"Sorry, girls. We'll just have to bear it until we reach California." Ma settled herself on a log next to their wagon and frowned at her stepdaughter. "Did you bake a pie today, or anything?"

"No, ma'am, I did not." Long ago Callie had given up making excuses that always fell on deaf ears. Nor did she question why Nellie and Lydia, both older than she, were required to do only the lightest of chores. According to Ma, they were both much too frail and delicate for heavy work. Ma often said so, whereas she, the lowly stepsister, was as strong as an ox and should labor to pay for her keep and be grateful she had a roof over her head. That was the way of it, all she could remember since she was born. Not that she minded, or ever questioned her fate. Ma often pointed out how lucky she was the Whitakers had found her abandoned on their doorstep all those many years ago and, out of the kindness of their hearts, taken her in.

A ripple of laughter floated across their campsite. Pa, who'd been working on one of the wagon wheels, rose up and cast a look of disgust at the source of the sound, a large company of wagons, at least fifty, that had camped in a circle on the other side of the meadow. "We were here first," he muttered. "The damn fools should find their own place." He addressed his wife and daughters. "You're to stay away from them. Is that understood?"

"Yes, Pa," came quick answers. Caleb Whitaker ruled with an iron hand.

Ma gazed across the meadow. "Do you think I'd have anything to do with that trash? A while ago I saw one of the women wearing the most outlandish outfits I ever saw."

Lydia giggled. "Those are bloomers, Ma. They're like a man's pants only baggier and gathered on the bottom."

"Disgraceful." Ma's face took on its usual look of disapproval. "It'll be a cold day in hell before I, or any of my family, are caught in such an outfit." She addressed Callie. "Are you going to just stand there?"

"No, ma'am."

Callie went about fixing hot biscuits with fresh butter, salted meat, beans, and green peas gathered from vines along the trail. When supper was ready, she banged the bottom of a pan with a spoon. Tommy, the baby of the family at seven, came running. He was the only young'un left. Ma had birthed eight children altogether. The two older boys were grown and gone on their own. On the day the family left for California, Callie had paid her last sorrowful visit to the three tiny graves under the big oak tree. Far as Callie knew, Ma never went there. She had never mentioned the babies she'd lost at birth or soon after. As it was, she paid little attention to Tommy, whom she considered, "not right in the head." No one knew exactly what was the matter with the boy, except he seemed to live in a world of his own, never played with other children, and didn't like to be touched or held. Sometimes Callie wondered what would happen to Tommy if she weren't around to take care of him. The rest of the family had long since given up and considered him nothing but a burden.

Their two hired men joined them for supper around the cook fire. Andy and Len, both in their early twenties, helped drive the family's two wagons and cared for the hundred head of cattle they'd brought along. They were working their way west so they could get to the gold fields and make their fortune. Callie didn't much like Len, who had a sly way about him. She didn't trust him, either. Andy, the tall, awkward one, was "dumb as a stump," she'd heard Pa say, but at least he was always pleasant and did his work well. Lately, he'd been casting longing glances at Lydia. It was clear he was smitten. Sensing his feelings, Lydia had begun to make fun of him behind his back, calling him her little puppy dog, laughing at his "moonstruck gazes."

Callie felt sorry for Andy. He might not be very bright, but at least he gave Callie a sincere "thank you" after every meal, which was more than anyone else did. Tonight was no exception.

"Those beans was mighty good, Miss Callie," he remarked in his shy way.

"Why, thank you, Andy."

He was just being kind. They had been on the road for two weeks, eating beans every day. There was nothing special about them.

After supper, when Ma and her two stepsisters sat around the cook fire, and Callie had just finished washing up the dishes, someone approached from the wagon train across the meadow. Lydia pointed. "Looks like we've got company."

Ma looked toward the lone figure and frowned. "I do believe it's one of those women wearing pants."

"Bloomers, Ma," said Lydia.

Ma's lips tightened. "I don't want to talk to such a woman. I'm going in the wagon."

She half rose, but before she could retreat, the woman waved and cried a friendly, "Woo-hoo, everyone!" from halfway across the field. "Are you going or coming?"

"Too late now," said Lydia. "We're going to California," she yelled back.

"Now you've done it." Ma sat back down, brow furrowed in a frown.

The visitor approached. She appeared to be in her thirties, a big, full-bosomed woman with a round, smiling face, wearing a small white cap. Two young children clung to her short, full skirt that fell to her knees.

Below the skirt, a pair of bloomers extended to her ankles. How strange. Never had Callie seen such an outfit.

The woman reached their campfire. "We're going to California too. Hello, I'm Florida Sawyer, and these here are two of my young'uns, Augie and Isaac. There's more where they came from." Without waiting for an invitation, she seated herself on a log by the campfire and thrust her pantalooned legs before her. "Lordy me, it feels good to get the load off." She turned to Ma. "And who might you be?"

Ma's lips pursed, as if she'd bit into a persimmon. Would she be nice? Callie held her breath. Ma could be the soul of politeness when she wanted. She could also get downright nasty with someone she even faintly disliked.

"We are the Whitaker family, Mrs. Sawyer. As my daughter said, we're traveling west to California."

Callie let out her breath. Ma's reply was decidedly cool but at least civil.

If Florida Sawyer noticed Ma's less-than-friendly attitude, she didn't let on. Seeing Ma's gaze travel to her bloomers, she laughed. "I know they look strange, but they're the perfect thing for a woman to wear when she's got to walk clear across the country. You'd be surprised how comfortable they are compared to a long, heavy skirt. You ought to try them sometime."

"That's not likely to happen, Mrs. Sawyer."

Undaunted, Florida continued. "I'm a widow traveling with my brother, two hired hands, and my seven children. My husband, God rest his soul, passed on a short time ago—mind you, after we'd already sold the farm and bought the wagons. He was dead set on moving to Oregon. Then, all of a sudden, he was gone. His heart. One minute we were nearly ready to leave, and the next, there was Henry slumped over the milk pail, stone cold dead. Can you imagine? Left me and the young'uns to fend for ourselves. I didn't know what I was going to do until Luke, that's my brother, stepped in and saved the day. He's a trapper and mountain man, the perfect guide for our wagon train. I don't know what we would have done without him, bless his heart."

"How fortunate for you."

Callie inwardly winced over Ma's abrupt answer to their friendly visitor. How could she be so rude? To cause a distraction, she got to her feet and indicated a pot of coffee next to the campfire. "I believe the coffee's still hot, Mrs. Sawyer. Would you like a cup?"

"Well, I don't mind if I do."

Callie had scarcely picked up the pot when a horseman approached. A man on a horse was one of the most common sights imaginable, yet the graceful, easy manner in which he sat in the saddle held her spellbound. He drew close. He was casually dressed in buckskin. Closer still, he was somewhere in his early thirties with long, dark hair and… *Oh, no, the naked man in the river. It's him.*

He reined to a stop.

"Here's my brother now." Florida's voice filled with pride. "Luke McGraw. Ain't he something? Luke, say hello to the Whitaker family. They're traveling by themselves."

In acknowledgement, Luke briefly touched a finger to the brim of his hat and returned the briefest of smiles. He addressed his sister, "Better come along. Hetty needs you."

Florida threw back her head and laughed. "Hetty always needs me. Luke, you come down here and be nice to these people. Hetty can wait."

Luke gave her a reluctant nod and swung from his horse, performing a graceful dismount that revealed his lean and sinewy body, muscular legs, and broad shoulders.

Lydia stepped forward, cocked her head, fluttered her eyelashes, and thrust out her ample bosom. "So, you're going west, Mister McGraw? Are you going to hunt for gold or go into farming?"

"Don't I wish!" Florida gave her brother a rueful glance. "Luke's a trapper. His idea of a wonderful winter is to live in a lonely log cabin high in the mountains by himself. Can you imagine? Nobody to talk to for months and months, which I'll never understand. Now, out of the kindness of his heart, he's guiding the Ferguson wagon train west. I keep hoping when we get there he'll decide to stay, but he says no, he'd rather be fighting Indians and chasing grizzly bears."

Luke flashed a wry glance at Florida and seated himself beside her. "My sister exaggerates. She's right, though. I've got wandering feet. I wasn't meant to be a farmer or a gold seeker either." One corner of his mouth pulled into a faint smile. "I do better when I'm off by myself."

Lydia came up with her best, most flirty giggle. "Perhaps you should try it. Don't you want to settle down someday and raise a family?"

Don't be so obvious, Lydia. Callie hid her amusement with her stepsister, a silly girl to begin with, vain and rather shallow. Actually, she had every reason to be conceited, with her curly blond locks, blue eyes with long, fringed lashes, and tiny waist.

Luke, apparently realizing he couldn't make a quick getaway, turned his attention to Lydia. "The day I settle down is the day I'm dead."

The arrival of a handsome young man had dispelled Ma's hostile mood. She gave Luke a friendly smile. "This is my oldest daughter, Lydia, Mister McGraw." She nodded toward her second oldest. "This is my second daughter, Nellie."

Nellie remained seated and managed a barely acceptable greeting. A sullen girl, she contrasted with her flighty sister in temperament as well as looks. She tended to sulk a lot when she didn't get her way.

Luke gave the barest of nods to the sisters. His gaze shifted to Callie as she stood by the fire, coffeepot still in hand. She froze. If he said anything about their meeting by the stream, she'd die of embarrassment.

He didn't. Instead, with an interested nod of his head, he asked, "And you are...?"

Callie opened her mouth to speak, but before she could, Ma replied in an offhand way, "That's Callie. She's my stepdaughter."

If Luke noticed the contrast in introductions, he didn't let on. Solemn-faced, with only the slightest hint of a twinkle in his eyes, he looked at Callie. "Haven't we met before?"

"I don't believe so." Warmth crept over her cheeks and she wanted nothing more than to run and hide.

"Callie, if you're going to pour the coffee, then pour it. And offer Mister McGraw a cup."

Grateful for the diversion, Callie busied herself serving coffee to their guests. She hardly noticed Ma's pointed reference to her being a stepdaughter, not a daughter. Long ago she'd learned her place in the Whitaker household, which was somewhere between unwanted stepchild and lowly servant. She should be grateful just to have a roof over her head and three meals a day. Grateful forever, she supposed, although every once in a while she gave some thought to the fact she was now twenty-two, old enough to have a family of her own. Not often, though. Working from dawn to dusk on the Whitaker farm hadn't left much time for contemplation.

Night had fallen. Florida pointed across the meadow where the glow from a large campfire cut through the darkness. "See our campfire? We have one every night when the day has gone well and the weather's good. We sing, dance, play games, tell jokes and stories. Oh, we have grand time! One of the reasons I came over here was to invite you over to join us."

Lydia clapped her hands. "We'd love to come!"

Callie was about to echo her words when Pa, quiet until now, stepped forward.

A tall man with big square hands and massive shoulders, he gave the appearance of strength and rigidity, a man not likely to change his opinion. Like most older men in the train, he wore a bushy beard, which he seldom trimmed, wool pants held up by suspenders, a cotton shirt, and a wide-brimmed, round-crowned hat. The stiff way he held himself said it all. "This family doesn't hold with such frivolities, Mrs. Sawyer."

Ma nodded. "My husband's absolutely right. We keep to ourselves, so thank you, but we can't accept your invitation."

Callie wasn't surprised Lydia made no attempt to appeal her father's decision. She knew better. In the Whitaker family, Pa's word was law. None of them would dare disobey, although Callie was tempted to speak up. For once, it would have been nice to sit with people who were laughing and having a good time. The farmhouse where they'd lived in Tennessee had been isolated with only a few neighbors, none of them close by. She suspected Pa had wanted it that way. Aside from a monthly shopping trip, they had gone into town only on Sunday to attend church. Afterward, they had returned straight home, never joining any of the social activities. No picnics or parties, and certainly not the dances.

Another ripple of laughter filtered from across the field, causing Callie an odd twinge of disappointment. Yes, it would have been very nice indeed.

Soon after, Florida and her brother Luke bid them good-bye. The jovial woman left with a friendly wave of her hand. "If you folks change your minds, come on over."

Luke mounted his horse and followed, touching his hand to the brim of his hat. His eyes didn't seek Callie's. Why should they when Lydia was around? She was the beauty of the family. Nellie's dark looks weren't nearly as attractive, marred by a figure like Ma's, short-waisted and on the heavy side. Callie had no way to compare herself to her stepsisters. Pa didn't believe in the vanity of a full-length mirror, so she'd never seen her whole self reflected. Judging from Lydia's tiny, hidden scrap of a mirror, she had brown hair, maybe with a touch of red, which she pulled straight back into a bun and paid little attention to. Her face didn't seem remarkable in any way with its straight little nose and brown, wide-set eyes. Maybe not so bad—a face neither startlingly beautiful nor horribly ugly. *I wish Luke had at least glanced at me again.* She pictured how he had looked, standing in the creek in the altogether, an image that sent an unfamiliar tingle down her spine. *Am I crazy?* No man would look at her once, let alone twice. She wasn't much better than a servant girl and should be grateful for her keep. It wouldn't be fitting for her to forget her place and start getting grand ideas.

Meet the Author

Shirley Kennedy was born and raised in Fresno, California. In her early career as an author, Shirley wrote traditional Regency romances, one for Ballantine, the rest for Signet. Later on, she branched into other genres. She lives in Las Vegas, Nevada, with her older daughter, Dianne, and Brutus and Sparky, her two editorial assistants who love to nap in the sunshine next to her computer while she works on her next book. Please visit Shirley at www.shirleykennedy.com, or follow her Twitter account @ladyk360, or on Facebook at https://www.facebook.com/shirley.kennedy.52.